D0891547

AUG   / 2021

SCARRED

SCARRED

Nick Oldham

**SEVERN
HOUSE**

First world edition published in Great Britain and the USA in 2021
by Severn House, an imprint of Canongate Books Ltd,
14 High Street, Edinburgh EH1 1TE.

Trade paperback edition first published in Great Britain and the USA in 2022
by Severn House, an imprint of Canongate Books Ltd.

severnhouse.com

British Library Cataloguing-in-Publication Data
A CIP catalogue record for this title is available from the British Library.

ISBN-13: 978-0-7278-5014-0 (cased)
ISBN-13: 978-1-78029-800-9 (trade paper)
ISBN-13: 978-1-4483-0539-1 (e-book)

This is a work of fiction. Names, characters, places and incidents
are either the product of the author's imagination or are used fictitiously.
Except where actual historical events and characters are being described
for the storyline of this novel, all situations in this publication are
fictitious and any resemblance to actual persons, living or dead,
business establishments, events or locales is purely coincidental.

All Severn House titles are printed on acid-free paper.

Typeset by Palimpsest Book Production Ltd.,
Falkirk, Stirlingshire, Scotland.
Printed and bound in Great Britain by
TJ Books, Padstow, Cornwall.

For Belinda

ONE

1985

P C Henry Christie ducked behind a rack of skimpy ladies' underwear and, through a gap between see-through lacy bras and thongs, tried to keep his eye on the twelfth person he was going to arrest that day: a young lad, maybe twelve years old, no more than fourteen.

Henry – dressed in plain clothes – had been on the central staircase of the department store on his way up to the first floor, where he intended finishing the day with a browse through the record department, when he'd spotted the lad out of the corner of his eye, entering the store from Bank Hey Street. Because he'd already locked up eleven other shoplifters over the course of the day, he almost didn't bother – except he just couldn't let it go. His adrenaline had been pumping and he was on a high, and his cop instinct, still being honed after just seven years in the job, told him this lad was a slam-dunk certainty to make his arrest tally a round dozen. It also helped his competitive streak that it would nudge him ahead of his closest rival on the Support Unit team that day, who was also at eleven arrests and who, Henry knew, was currently floundering under a sea of paperwork at Blackpool nick. This was too good an opportunity to miss.

Even so, just for a fleeting moment, Henry almost turned a blind eye but found he couldn't. It wasn't in his nature to miss collaring even a kid-villain.

He stopped on the second step, backed slowly down and ducked into the weird jungle of the lingerie display, from where he hoped he could keep low in among the lace and observe the lad, who, Henry could sense, was definitely up for it.

All he hoped was that he would be able to catch him as soon as he stepped out of the front door after the lad had stolen whatever it was he'd come to steal.

Henry wanted to be on him quick because, as much as he wanted another arrest, he didn't really feel inclined to leg it after the lad around the streets of Blackpool. Two of his earlier arrests that day had ended up in silent-movie-like cop chases and he wasn't sure if he was bothered enough to make it a hat-trick. Not that he wasn't fit enough: now in his mid-twenties, he was probably as healthy and ripped as he would ever be in his life. Squash twice a week, five-a-side football once, rugby in season, running and weights every day saw to that. He was lithe, lean and fast . . . it was just that tonight was 'date night' with his newish wife, Kate, and she would probably want the best out of him. There had certainly been a sparkle of promise in her eyes when he'd kissed her goodbye that morning.

So this arrest had to be timed to perfection.

He manoeuvred stealthily through the underwear, head down, using the displays to keep hidden, stalking his unsuspecting prey.

The lad had stopped briefly on entering the store, and it was his body language in these few moments that signalled to Henry he was here to steal: that pause, the furtive glance around to get his bearings and to check for any obvious store detectives; then the pinpointing of his target . . . and by the time Henry managed to secrete himself in among the knickers and bras, the lad had begun his mission, was moving swiftly across the shop floor in the direction of the perfume counters, flipping open a supermarket carrier bag as he went for his swag. By this time, the lad was so locked in on his goal that he'd didn't spot Henry, who had clumsily stepped backwards into a mobile display of bras, lost his footing and grabbed one of the garments to steady himself. It was only by some fancy footwork, expert balancing and a silent pirouette that he managed to stay upright and not bring down the whole rack of underwear.

The lad made it to the perfume counter.

He moved quickly, precisely and with purpose. The carrier bag was now fully open, and he went directly to one of the locked glass cabinets, produced a spark plug – one of the favoured methods of breaking car windows in particular – and threw it hard against the glass door of the cabinet, which shattered instantly in a pretty crystalline shower. He was straight in the display, scooping boxes containing fragrances – all by Chanel – into the bag. Within a matter of seconds, three shelves had been completely emptied, maybe thirty boxes in total, easily over two grand's worth of high-quality perfume.

Then, before any of the nearby staff had even reacted, he turned and fled like a greyhound.

Henry disentangled himself from the spider's web of sexy underwear, chucking a large D-cup bra into the air behind him, and gave chase, knowing it would be much better to stop this one before he managed to get through the door.

Henry weaved between several counters, keeping the lad in view as he nimbly sidestepped various displays on his route to the exit. At that moment, Henry had the slight advantage, simply because the lad hadn't spotted him coming up behind him at a diagonal; Henry gritted his teeth, knowing if he timed it right, he'd flatten him just before he reached the door.

Normally in shoplifting cases, it helped to support the evidence if the offender had actually left the premises with the booty, so that any defence of 'Oh, I was going to put it back on a shelf' was negated.

However, when chasing someone who had blatantly entered a shop equipped to steal – in this case with a bag and a spark plug – it wasn't quite so pressing. To prove this youngster's intention to steal would be easy.

It was catching him that could be difficult.

Henry skidded around two naked mannequins, sending one toppling to the floor where it split into five distinct body parts, then he was in a race across a bare piece of floor to apprehend the lad who had, by now, seen Henry and upped a gear.

He reached the door ten feet ahead of Henry and flung himself out on to Bank Hey Street, which even at six p.m. was throbbing with shoppers, tourists and workers on their way home. The lad hurled himself into this hubbub of mankind and vanished from Henry's sight as soon as the young cop emerged from the store.

Henry kept going in the direction he assumed the little thief had gone, pulling a hard left on to the street, with Blackpool Tower rising high on his left-hand side, and for twenty yards Henry ran in hope rather than reality, at the same time using his personal radio to transmit details of the incident and pursuit to any other cops who might be out there.

It was a bad time of day, though.

Half of the local two-to-ten shift were in for refreshments and the Support Unit team he'd come into town with were all at the station, just about ready to roll back to headquarters as they'd been in the resort since eight a.m. on this special operation targeting shoplifters. Henry didn't get much in the way of an enthusiastic response: he wasn't under any physical threat of violence, it was just another shoplifter (he and his colleagues had arrested thirty-nine that day, like shelling peas) and not many could be bothered. So after a shout out for patrols to attend, the comms operator apologized and said the nearest unit was ten minutes away, minimum, although a town-centre foot patrol was making her way.

Henry slowed to a walk, frustrated but understanding. Cops couldn't just be magicked out of thin air, and maybe he'd have to take this one on the chin. The SU team had been deployed into town at the behest of the divisional commander because shoplifting seemed to have got out of hand, and at their briefing they'd been given a simple task – to arrest as many as possible, and then, released to harass an unsuspecting criminal world, they'd easily grabbed a bucketload and almost overwhelmed the custody officer, so losing one wasn't really a problem.

The annoyance for Henry was the value of the goods this lad had taken within about a minute of entering the shop, probably more than all his arrests that day combined.

He shrugged, kept walking.

The least he could do was check down a few alleyways before returning to the store, getting details of what had been stolen and submitting a crime report. He began to saunter, reaching the end of the street, and he paused here before spinning on his heels and heading back to the shop – but then turned into a narrow street that cut right down to the seafront and which he also knew had an alleyway running off it that ran parallel to Bank Hey Street, behind the shops.

He stopped at the alley and spotted two people about fifty yards along it, huddled together between two large industrial wheelie bins crammed with overflowing cardboard waste.

Two young lads.

Henry allowed himself a grim grin of satisfaction because he recognized the one with his back to him as the perfume thief – same jacket and jeans, he was certain – and both lads were peering into the carrier bag full of boxes containing bottles of expensive perfume.

They were concentrating on the contents as Henry dropped into a stealthy crouch and began to approach silently – like a panther, he liked to think.

He made it to ten yards away.

Still they hadn't clocked him.

Five yards.

He felt increasingly confident about grabbing the actual thief, even if it meant letting the other lad get away. Both were pretty scrawny kids, although the other one was quite a bit older, maybe twenty, and actually Henry felt that if he timed it right, he might be able to grab them both before they fled.

Four yards.

Henry was hardly breathing now. He flexed his fingers, worked out his moves: take the thief from behind by simply grabbing his collar, then barge him roughly into his mate and pin them against the wall between the bins before shouting for assistance.

His left hand slid around to the waistband of his jeans at the small of his back, curling his fingers around his handcuffs.

One more step taken. Three yards to go.

Almost in reach.

And still they hadn't seen him.

Two yards.

Then he moved – fast.

Or at least that was his intention.

He never made it.

The lads looked sharply up and saw him, then looked over his shoulder. Henry knew there was someone behind him even in the second before the blow that crashed on to the back of his head and poleaxed him. It felt as though his skull had been cracked open as a combination of a lightning flash and burning pain seared across his brain, cutting off every function and pitching him forwards between the two lads who had been divvying up their stash.

The filthy ground of the alley raced up to his face, and although he knew he should have brought up his hands to break the fall, they would not respond to that simple request from his mind.

His face slammed into the ground, hard.

It wasn't complete blackness.

That came a few seconds later when the first of the boots kicked him in the head – and then there was definitely nothing, not even pain, and certainly not understanding.

He didn't know he'd had a very sound kicking as it all took place when he was unconscious on the ground between the wheelie bins. They might as well have been kicking a Guy Fawkes or a tailor's dummy. He gave no resistance, just lay there flipping on the ground as he was assaulted and stomped on.

It was only when nothing more had been heard from him over the radio and he didn't respond to calls that the comms room and his Support Unit colleagues began to worry something had befallen him. Although the SU team were all ready to head off back to their office at headquarters, they piled into their personnel carrier, drove into the town centre and spilled out to search the streets.

But it wasn't one of their number who found him.

A young policewoman on town centre foot patrol was the first to discover him.

Her name was WPC Julie Clarke. Only months into her service, the discovery of Henry's battered, unmoving body was a huge shock for her. When she called it in, requesting an ambulance, her voice was shaky. Henry's colleagues raced to the scene to find Julie resting his head on her lap with a terrified expression on her face.

He felt the touch before anything else. That was the first thing. His hand being stroked gently, and through the haze of both numbness and agony, it felt good.

His lips were cracked and dry, splitting despite the balm, and it hurt to move them, even for a tiny bit.

So instead of doing anything else, he merely moved his fingertips to say he was back and then heard the voice he recognized and loved say, very quietly, 'Henry?'

He moved his fingers again: a response.

'Henry? Are you awake?'

More fingertip movement, then he said dryly in a croaky whisper, through his battered lips, 'After a fashion.'

He heard Kate begin to sob.

'Yep, one hell of a kicking,' the voice reiterated.

It was two days after Henry had finally come round, now four days after the actual assault, and Henry was sitting up in the hospital bed. He could now more or less open his left eye, the dirty swelling around it having deflated slightly, but his right eye remained clamped shut, encased in a bag of pus that a doctor had tried to drain away, but which had immediately refilled, matching the side of his head which was distended to the shape of a rugby ball with a gnarled ear.

He could talk now, thanks to plenty of liquid, honey and lip balm, but his voice was still hesitant and cracked, his throat still sore because, apparently, his attackers had attempted to throttle him, too.

'I agree,' Henry said with a groan. He shifted slightly and winced as pain shot through him. What might have been imaginary was how his mind's eye visualized his three cracked ribs grating together; what wasn't imaginary was the pain that caused.

With his one working eye, he looked at the source of the voice.

Detective Chief Inspector Robert Fanshaw-Bayley was sitting on a plastic chair pulled up to the side of the bed, his large, ever-spreading bottom spilling over each side. Fanshaw-Bayley, or FB as he was more commonly known to friends and foe alike, had been one of Henry's first detective inspectors and was now, following promotion, the DCI at Blackpool. 'FB' stood for many things: 'Friendly Bear', 'Father Bob' or 'Fat Bastard.' Mainly, though, the letters stood for 'Fucking Bastard', although no one ever dared say it to his face.

FB had been the DI in Rossendale when Henry worked there and had been promoted to Blackpool, seeming to follow Henry's foot-steps – although Henry hadn't actually been transferred to the resort and had instead joined the HQ Support Unit based at police head-quarters at Hutton Hall near Preston, though he did now live in Blackpool itself.

'A few more well-placed kicks and this could've been a murder enquiry,' FB informed Henry gleefully.

'They missed all the vital organs,' Henry said, 'although it doesn't feel like it.'

'So, come on,' FB said. 'This is about as close to the murder of a cop as you could get without an actual dead body in uniform. Got detectives working on it, and your uniformed mates, and this is about the first time you've been able to talk coherently . . . so what *do* you remember?'

Henry managed a shrug. Even his shoulders hurt. 'Not much to be honest.'

'You chased the lad out of the department store,' FB prompted him.

'Which lad?'

FB rolled his eyeballs in their sockets and tried to jog Henry's memory with a list of bullet points: 'Teenager . . . nicked a load of perfume, plastic bag, spark plug, did a runner, you behind him.'

'Oh, right, that lad.'

'Yes, that lad. It's on CCTV.'

This was the first Henry had heard of this development. 'Oh, OK. So can you ID him?'

FB made a doubtful noise. 'Clever little sod kept his face turned away from the cameras; obviously knew exactly where they were positioned.'

'So, no face?'

'No, but you saw it.'

'Don't recall,' Henry said.

FB tutted with irritation.

'I did get my head kicked in,' Henry said defensively.

'And this lad was one of the two you encountered in the alley, yeah?'

'Again, couldn't say . . . I clearly remember being in the store, then it's all a bit vague. Blank, even. Maybe my memory will return bit by bit.'

'But at the moment, nothing?'

Henry nodded. His skull rattled.

'Marvellous,' FB said, clearly annoyed.

'Sorry, boss.'

FB shook his head. 'Like I said, a good kicking.'

'But are you anywhere with it yet?' Henry asked.

'Not so far.'

'Did the policewoman see anyone?'

'She said the alley was empty when she ran in and found you. They must have legged it moments before she arrived.'

Henry took this in. 'Shame.'

'Right, well.' FB slapped his chubby thighs. 'Need to get back to the station. If you do recall anything worthwhile . . .'

Henry nodded. 'Any chance you could arrange a couple of

mugshot albums to be dropped off for me to peruse?' he suggested. 'Could jog my memory.'

FB dithered for a moment, then said OK and left.

Henry had a series of visitors over the course of that day: members of his SU team, none of whom showed any signs of sympathy, as was the usual case with fellow cops. One even showed up bearing a punnet of rotting grapes. Banter and bluster covered up how concerned they had been, and Henry would have been extremely worried if they'd come in all sad-faced and tearful. He would have suspected they knew something he didn't. Their presence cheered him up considerably. A very young CID admin lady came from the police station bearing a couple of hefty photograph albums containing mugshots of hundreds of local crims, which she got him to sign for, and he promised on his life he would guard and return them.

After that, the policewoman who'd found him in the alley came on to the ward and shyly said, 'Hello.'

Henry had the photo albums on his lap, but he'd drifted off into a slight doze and had to force himself to open his eyes. He'd slithered down the bed and quickly pushed himself back up into a sitting position, wiping away the drool from the corner of his mouth. He knew he didn't look great.

'Hi.'

'Sorry to bother you . . .'

'No, it's fine, sit down, sit down,' Henry said.

She was in full uniform, tunic and skirt, and she looked immaculate. She sat.

'It's Julie, isn't it?' Henry asked. He knew really, but his mind was still a bit fuzzy and he wanted to make certain. He also knew she had been in to visit him a couple of times previously, but he'd been more or less out of it.

'Yes, that's right . . . I thought I'd just check in on you.' She removed her hat and shuffled the chair up to the bed as she said, 'See if you're recovering.'

'I'm doing fine . . . I really need to thank you for what you did for me. I haven't had the chance yet.'

'I didn't really do anything,' she said modestly.

'I beg to differ . . . Anyway, thank you.'

'My pleasure.'

'You can't have been far behind the offenders,' Henry said. 'They must only just have scarpered by the time you came into the alley.'

'I suppose so . . . there was just you lying there.'

The two officers looked at each other: Henry, battered and ugly; Julie, way beyond attractive as far as Henry's good eye could see. He had never met her before the attack, but now knew she was mainly a town centre foot patrol officer.

She coughed to clear her throat. 'I've heard you don't remember anything.'

'Not so far – that's why I'm going through these, just to see if I can jog the mind.' He indicated the photograph albums. 'I recall bits. Remember being in the store. Then – splat! – zilch until I woke up in casualty half an hour later surrounded by people in white coats. Thirty minutes of my life is pretty much a blank.'

She blinked and her shoulders seemed to drop slightly in a way that Henry could not quite understand. 'That's really a shame,' she said. 'They need catching. They almost killed you, Henry.'

'Ah, but unless I get a blood clot on my brain,' he joked badly, 'I'm still here . . . just – thanks to you.'

'Well, let's hope you don't get one.'

Henry settled down again after she left and closed his eyes as a wave of tiredness overwhelmed him. He'd had enough of work-related visitors and looking through mugshots, and his one good eye was feeling strained.

His next visitor arrived during official visiting hours.

It was Kate, his wife.

She kissed him carefully on the less battered side of his head, then perched on the edge of the bed so she could hold his left hand, the one without the cannula pierced into his vein.

'You actually do look better,' she admitted. 'Bashed, but better.'

'Improving all the time.' He tried a weak smile; even that hurt, although looking at Kate through one eye did not. He knew she had been at his bedside for two whole days after the assault, sitting there, holding his hand, whispering things to him, keeping him going.

'How's the investigation going?' she asked. She knew FB had been in to see him earlier. She, too, knew the DCI, having encountered him in Rossendale.

'No progress, as far as I know.'

'Damn.'

'I know. Hey, look, sorry.'

'Sorry for what?'

'The one thing I do clearly remember: it should've been our date night.'

'Ah, yes, date night.' Kate looked tenderly at him.

'I'm assuming I was on a promise?'

'More than a promise,' she said tantalizingly. 'It would have been Vesuvius erupting.' She looked him in his good eye, took a breath, about to say something, then hesitated.

'What?' Henry asked.

'Er, look . . . I have something to tell you. I wanted to wait. But it won't wait any longer. There's always somewhere better than a hospital ward to say something important, but I need to tell you, and you need to know, Henry,' she said seriously.

Henry's lubricated mouth suddenly went dry. He knew the precursor to a 'ditch' speech when he heard one. She was going to leave him, to end it – he just knew. Already she'd had enough of being a cop's wife.

'Hey, I know it's been a tough few months – moving across here away from your mum and dad, even though your dad despises me. The new house, new job, no friends . . . but it'll settle, I promise.'

Her grin of wry amusement at his desperate waffle made him realize he was way off the mark.

'Everything's fine between us,' she assured him.

He swallowed. It hurt. His throat was only just starting to improve after the near strangulation. 'I thought you'd had enough,' he said meekly.

'I'll never have enough,' she promised him.

Inside, Henry was pretty sure that his heart had literally melted. They had married only a couple of months after she had followed Henry across from her home in Rossendale, where she lived with her parents. Henry had been promised a move to uniform in Blackpool, but that had not happened and he found himself, more by accident than design, on the western team of the newly formed Support Unit based at headquarters. He was acutely aware that while he was still ensconced in the comfortable world of being a cop with so many colleagues, Kate was completely alone in a new environment with no local friends, in a new job and new house in Blackpool. He knew it was hard for her.

He wouldn't have been surprised if she'd been about to give him an ultimatum of some sort; or maybe no ultimatum at all, just, 'Bye.'

'Same here,' he said in response to her declaration of love.

'So, coming back to our *ruined* date night,' she emphasized, teasing him, 'there was something I needed to tell you, preferably at home, preferably lying naked on the rug in front of the fire . . .'

'After Vesuvius?' he guessed. Even with just those words and despite his condition, Kate had the ability to make the blood stir in his loins.

'But here will have to do because I'm bursting and I can't wait any longer.'

Henry's good eye blinked. His other was too heavily gunked-up to do anything.

Kate was still holding his left hand, still perched on the edge of the bed. She took his hand gently and laid it softly, palm down, across her belly and smiled at him with a tear in each of her blue eyes.

The concept of becoming a father wasn't something Henry had ever really contemplated, but as he lay back in the hospital bed that night, he knew one thing for certain: his life was about to change in ways he could never imagine.

He was in a state of blissful turmoil as he tried to wrestle with the enormity of it all.

One thing he did know for sure was that he didn't care if the baby was a boy or a girl.

Either would do, thank you very much, and he didn't want to know what sex it would be before he/she actually came into the world.

Whatever the sex, he and Kate would take it from there.

Finally, after a couple of hours thinking, wondering how you actually burped a baby, and swallowing as many painkillers as he was allowed, he managed to settle back and apply his mind to the important matter of recovery, getting back to work and catching the people who had put him here.

On that thought, he sat upright and reached for the album of mugshots and flicked through the pages of slot-in photographs of prisoners – frontal shots and profiles, each with a custody reference number and a name underneath.

He found the one he was looking for, slid it out of its pouch and took a closer look at it through his good eye.

The thing was, in spite of the battering he'd taken, which really had mashed his brain, he actually did remember everything about that day: the lad entering the store, the theft of the perfume, the foot chase – the lad's face, all clear in his mind – and then finding him and another youth in the back alley behind the shops. He remembered right up to the point where he was about to reach out and grab the little thief and the realization there was someone behind him. That was the point at which it all went blank and the next thing he knew was waking up in hospital.

He looked at the photograph he'd extracted.

'Yes, I remember you, you little git,' he said to it.

He hadn't revealed any of this to anyone because he wanted to be the one who laid hands on him.

'You're mine, you little bastard.'

TWO

Even though he was in an unmarked cop car and wearing a bomber jacket over his uniform shirt, Henry Christie knew there could be some danger attached to cruising single-crewed – i.e. just by himself – around Shoreside, the most notorious council estate in Blackpool. There had recently been a big increase in tensions between the criminal fraternity on the estate and the police. There had been a series of pretty forceful crime operations, and then a couple of lone officers had been lured into ambushes in which their vehicles had been trapped in cul-de-sacs, attacked and trashed. The officers had escaped unscathed but the vehicles were write-offs.

There was now an edict from above that all police patrols going on to the estate had to be double-crewed and that comms had to be informed of any officer venturing on to the estate for whatever reason.

Which was a slight problem for Henry because his foray on to Shoreside was completely unauthorized, and he was also using his inspector's car without the guy's knowledge.

He wasn't going to let any of those things bother him too much; they were chances he was willing to take.

Because he was on a mission.

A personal mission.

But as soon as he turned on to the estate from the main road, he knew he'd been clocked by two teenagers sitting on a low garden wall, drinking from cans of Irn-Bru. Their conversation stopped abruptly and their eyes levelled on him, identifying the maroon-coloured Vauxhall Cavalier as a police car – which wasn't hard: the two aerials on the back wings screamed *cop car*.

Just so Henry could be certain, he drew in alongside them and wound his window down.

Their heads tilted back and they sneered at him suspiciously.

Henry guessed they were on lookout duty and would be skilled in hurtling through gardens and down alleyways to deliver warnings to their mates and bosses within seconds.

'OK, guys?' he called affably.

They did not reply, but at least it threw them into a bit of confusion.

Henry smiled. 'Yep, you got it: I'm a cop.' Then he pointed at one of them and said, 'Damian Costain, yeah?' Then he transferred the pointing digit to the other and said, 'Ben Flynn – am I right? Yep, I'm a cop and I'm coming on to my patch, not yours, so tell your mates if you want to . . . I'm PC Henry Christie, by the way.'

'Fuck d'you want, cuntstable?' the one with the Costain surname snarled.

'Arf, arf! Never heard that one before. Good joke.' Henry clapped his hands mockingly, knowing he was probably poking a tiger with a shitty stick. 'Can you tell me where Poland Drive is, please?'

It wasn't where he was going, but he thought he'd ask anyway, just for fun and to further the confusion.

'I can tell you where Fuck-Off Drive is,' Costain said and jerked up two fingers at Henry.

Henry gave him the thumbs-up and said, 'Second on the right, then?'

Costain's gesture then turned to one which suggested Henry was keen on masturbation.

He gave the lads a nice smile and a wave, wound up his window and drove on to the estate.

As much as anything, he'd wanted to get a closer look at the pair to check if either of them – or both – were the people he was after.

Neither was, but he had recognized one of them as being a younger member of the Costain family who, Henry had learned, pretty much ruled the roost in this neighbourhood, much to the chagrin of all law-abiding residents on Shoreside.

In his rear-view mirror, he saw the two lads stand up and watch the car, then Costain lobbed his drinks can into the road, turned and sprinted down a ginnel between two houses.

Definitely lookouts: the early-warning system had been activated.

Henry gave a mental shrug, knowing that in minutes his presence would be known across the whole of the estate and that, depending on the mood of the moment, he could find himself in a situation. However, he didn't intend to stay long – just long enough to arrest at least one of the lads who'd kicked his head in some four weeks earlier.

Henry's convalescence had been fairly swift. The head swellings had reduced quickly, his facial, neck and bodily bruising from the assault had turned from a livid purple colour to a sickly yellow, and the broken ribs had knitted together well. As much as his skull felt as if it had been fractured after his attackers had repeatedly kicked his head like a football, somehow it wasn't, even though the doctors had suspected it initially as the first X-rays had been inconclusive because of the swellings.

He was discharged after a week, and ten days after that, having been cared for at home by Kate and his mother – all too much faffing for Henry who didn't like fuss – he was itching to get back to work and make some arrests, although he did continue to maintain he still had that 'five-minute memory loss' which, try as he might, meant he could not recall vital information.

He was lying.

However, as a doctor's note forbade him from returning to work until four weeks had passed and he'd been thoroughly checked over and given the all-clear, he spent a lot of his recovery time fawning over Kate and her newly revealed pregnancy – which drove her to distraction and to the toilet a lot – and doing some very low-level DIY around their new home, a terraced house on the outskirts of Blackpool, which eventually drove *him* to distraction because he was not great at any form of manual labour.

All the while, he was in contact with FB about the investigation into the assault, only to be regularly informed it wasn't getting anywhere fast. Henry picked up from FB's tone of voice that it had lost all momentum, which both annoyed and pleased Henry in equal measure. Annoyed because the enthusiasm had waned; pleased because no arrests had been made – because that was something Henry wanted for himself.

When he finally did resume work, deployments with the Support Unit – which included several football matches and a two-week-long crime operation in Blackburn – kept him occupied, though all the while he was looking for the opportunity to sneak back to Blackpool and try to collar at least one of his attackers.

He managed it after a Support Unit training day.

Following a morning of gritty public order training and an afternoon of physical training at the headquarters gym and running track, Henry found himself alone in the SU office which had once been a police house within the grounds of headquarters. The rest of his team had cheekily taken an early dart in compensation for all the unpaid overtime they'd worked recently.

The vehicles belonging to the unit were parked up behind the house: two personnel carriers and two plain cars, one of which was allocated to the inspector, who had also sneaked home early.

Henry had ambled through the empty house, now converted into offices (which was to be the ultimate fate of all the police houses on the campus) and entered the inspector's office to see the keys for his car tantalizingly splayed out on the desk blotter, just waiting to be snaffled.

He took them, shrugged his bomber on, slid his handcuffs into his belt, his staff down the inner trouser pocket, strapped a radio around his neck, and took the car.

Just for a look around.

Thomas James Benemy.

By now, the lad's name, date of birth, address and previous convictions were seared into Henry's mind – the personal details of the shoplifter – and he was going to pop round, see if he was at home and if he fancied coming for a ride with him to Blackpool nick. With mummy, obviously, because young Tommy was only thirteen years old, old enough to beat a cop senseless, but a juvenile in the eyes of the law, required to be accompanied by an appropriate adult.

If Benemy was at home, and Henry managed to collar him, he hadn't quite decided how he would explain the arrest (and the unofficial use of his car) to his boss, but he would cross that bridge if and when he came to it.

Henry had also taken time out to learn about Shoreside estate and its denizens.

Even when he had been stationed over in Rossendale on the opposite side of the county, he'd heard of Shoreside, just as he'd heard of several infamous council estates in other towns across Lancashire. Each town had one or more, and there were other troubled estates in Blackpool, but Shoreside was the one with the real bad reputation. It was a product of misplaced 1960s ideals about social housing and what people wanted, and in the 1970s and 1980s it had become rundown and lawless.

Although Henry's posting to Blackpool had not materialized as he'd envisaged – he'd been hoping to negotiate a swap with a bobby who wanted to come across to East Lancashire, but the move had fallen apart at the last moment – the sideways step on to the Support Unit was good and he was enjoying travelling around the county's hotspots. He was still determined he would eventually end up as a uniformed cop, then a detective, in Blackpool where a superintendent had once wearily and philosophically explained to him, 'There's only one thing you can be sure of in Blackpool, lad: the tide comes in and goes out twice a day.'

On the basis that he would eventually engineer a posting there, in the meantime he had taken it upon himself to learn about the resort and its trouble spots, about the people and, in particular, the criminals. So whenever he had the chance – and the Support Unit was a regular visitor there – he took his refreshments while perusing photograph albums or mooching in the collator's office, reading intelligence files, or in CID, learning about bad people.

Who were the biggest criminals? Who ran the arcades? Who ran the drug trade? Who fenced stolen goods? Who were the best armed robbers? Who was Top Dog?

He intended to hit the ground running when he got there on a permanent basis.

So he already knew more about Shoreside than just its reputation.

He had been part of a couple of police operations on the estate already and was getting a feel for the place.

What he did not know at the time, though, was how deeply he would become involved with the estate and, in particular, the Costain family – all he was interested in then was anticipating the pleasure of locking up Thomas Benemy, who, with at least one more yet-to-be-identified youth, had almost killed him.

He drove slowly past other kids hanging around, all of whom clocked him as quickly as the first pair he'd encountered, and he began to wonder if something out of the ordinary was brewing that afternoon. Maybe he was imagining it, he thought, trying to brush off the sense of unease, but his continually developing cop instinct, which would serve him well in years to come, told him different. It also told him he would perhaps be wise to make his enquiry about Benemy as quickly as possible, then get off the estate unscathed, report his feelings to the on-duty inspector and hope he wouldn't get mocked too harshly.

He drove into Clement Close, a cul-de-sac with a turning circle at the far end. Just a normal street, mainly semi-detached council houses, sturdy but decrepit, with front gardens littered with old furniture and appliances and smashed-down fences. It had an air of defeat about it, and Henry could sense how much the good people on the estate – and there were many – had been browbeaten by thuggery.

As he drove to the end, he felt a touch of despair for these decent, non-violent folk who seemed to have no voice.

In those moments, he decided that if he did end up posted to Blackpool, he would do his bit to help the downtrodden. Not that he saw himself as a social reformer, but he was canny enough to realize that by doing his job well, he could play some small part in the regeneration of this place.

He swung the car around and drew up outside number seven, which was no different on the outside from any of the other houses. He took a moment to check it out while reminding himself about Thomas James Benemy, thirteen-year-old thief and wild child.

By the age of twelve, Benemy had four arrests for shoplifting under his belt, all dealt with by severe bollockings or cautions, but never a prosecution. He had also been arrested for two assaults while with a gang, but there had never been enough evidence even to caution him. One interesting arrest, which also didn't go further than a few hours in a cell, was for allegedly kidnapping a young girl, holding her in his bedroom and, again allegedly, sexually assaulting her. No further action was taken when the girl, via her parents, refused to lodge a complaint.

'Quite a mosaic,' Henry murmured to himself, wondering where Benemy would end up in life. Nowhere nice, he guessed as he opened the car door with his little finger and climbed out, walking around the car and pausing at the foot of the path leading to the front door. Glancing up the cul-de-sac, he caught sight of two youths sprinting across the entrance, some fifty yards from where he stood.

He frowned, then decided it might be wise to inform someone of his whereabouts.

Just in case.

He called it in – that he was a lone SU officer on a short enquiry on Shoreside and didn't expect to be long. He didn't bother to voice his inner disquiet about the atmosphere on the estate.

The call was acknowledged by the comms room operator, but almost as soon as the short conversation was over, another voice came over the radio.

'PC Christie, what exactly is the nature of your enquiry, please?' It was FB, who obviously had a radio on his desk so he could earwig what was going on out on the streets, and his tone was highly suspicious, confirmed when he added, 'Or can I guess?'

Henry frowned again.

'You wouldn't have had some miracle memory recall, would you?' FB said snarkily.

'Um . . . sorry, boss, your transmission is breaking . . .' Henry didn't finish his own transmission to emphasize the point he was making, then set off up the path to the front door of the Benemy household.

'Don't try to kid a kidder,' FB warned him. Then, 'Whatever, be careful up there; it's a tinderbox.'

Henry saw a movement at one of the upstairs windows, just a shadow, but then the window itself opened a few inches and the barrel of a small-calibre rifle was pushed out between net curtains, aimed at him.

From where he was standing, about halfway up the path, Henry was vulnerable and exposed. In his mind, he suspected the weapon was probably an air rifle, but could not take the chance. It could have been a proper .22 with proper bullets. Being hit by an air pellet was obviously the more favourable option, even though he had dealt with a young girl who'd had an eye shot out by one. Being hit by a pellet could still be potentially very dangerous, whereas a .22 bullet could kill.

Henry heard the 'phht'.

It was an air rifle and the pellet hit him on his chest, pinging off his personal radio with some force.

Henry staggered back a couple of feet and weighed up his options. He could either leg it back to the safety of the inspector's car or

– and it was equidistant – run to the front door and flatten himself under the cover provided by a canopy designed to give callers some protection from the weather. Given the very tight angle down from the window, it would be impossible to get a second good shot without leaning a long way out.

At that stage in his life as a cop, Henry Christie would never have chosen the retreat option. He was hardwired to go in, hard if necessary, and he would never back down or show weakness.

That did not mean he was unkind or unfair. He was neither, but even in his relatively short career, he had encountered many people who equated kindness and fairness with weakness and tried to take advantage.

However, that day, under fire, albeit from an air rifle, he didn't feel inclined to be at all kind.

Keeping his head tucked in, he sprinted to the door, flattened himself up against it, tried the handle – locked – and kicked it hard with his heel.

At the same time, he sneaked a quick look around the canopy up to the window and had to snap back out of sight as the person holding the rifle was actually leaning out and trying to get into a shooting position.

It was Thomas James Benemy.

Henry felt the whoosh of a pellet zing diagonally across him, centimetres away.

He twisted his head, cupped his hands around his mouth and shouted, 'Come on down, Thomas. We need to talk.'

'Fuck off!' the lad screamed back.

'Not gonna happen.' Henry continued to back-heel the door – which opened suddenly to reveal a ferocious woman – Benemy's mother, Trish.

She shrieked, 'What the fuck's going on here?'

Henry spun to her. 'Mrs Benemy, I'm PC Christie from Blackpool nick,' he said hastily, keeping things simple. 'I need to talk to Thomas.'

Trish Benemy glared at him. 'Why? Fuck's he done this time?'

She was almost the stereotypical female council house dweller: badly dyed hair scraped back from her forehead, very pale skin, many studs in her ear lobes and attired in cheap, shimmering shell-suit leggings and a too-big T-shirt cut down to display her large boobs. She took a deep drag of the cigarette dangling in her nicotine-stained fingers and blew the lungful of smoke at Henry, engulfing him in the cloud. That said, she looked no older than Henry, which made him fleetingly wonder how old she must have been when she'd had her son, currently ensconced in the front bedroom, shooting at a cop. And behind the rough edges, she was quite pretty to Henry's eyes, although her own eyes were challenging and intimidating, probably brassed off with having cops knocking on her door.

'Him and his mates set about me about a month ago and gave me a good hiding after he'd stolen stuff from a shop.'

Mrs Benemy gave Henry a critical once-over. She seemed to quite like what she saw. '*He* beat *you* up?'

'Yes, ma'am, he did. Being whacked on the head from behind didn't help.' Henry could tell she wasn't quite believing her son could have pulled this off – Henry, all six foot two of him, slim but athletic – and comparing him to her son's very slight physique.

Still with her appraisal of Henry going on, the corner of her mouth opened and she shouted, 'Tommy, you get the fuck down here, laddo!'

She looked at Henry. He looked at her and smiled. 'He's got a gun, by the way. Been pinging shots at me.'

'Tommy,' she bawled again. 'Down here, lad.' Then to Henry she said a slightly sheepish, 'Sorry.'

'We'll work it out,' Henry promised, suddenly quite liking her from that single-word apology. 'Even though he nearly killed me.'

There was a pause.

Henry heard something from upstairs. He looked over Trish's shoulder from where he could see part of the way up the steps and saw a pair of feet in trainers coming slowly down, then the crouching form of Tommy still clutching the air rifle which, as he came fully into view, he brought up to his right shoulder, wrapping his forefinger around the trigger.

'Watch out!'

Henry shoved Trish to one side while he sidestepped niftily the opposite way, taking cover provided by the front of the house just as Tommy pulled the trigger. The pellet whizzed through the gap between Henry and Trish, missing them both.

Henry dinked back into view, cowering slightly just in case there was another tiny missile in the breach, but Tommy swarmed down the stairs, hurled the empty rifle at Henry, turned and fled towards the rear of the house.

Henry raised his forearm to deflect the rifle as it cartwheeled at him; unfortunately, it bounced off into Trish, clattering her head. Henry did not hesitate. Using the door frame to propel himself into the hallway, he went after Tommy, who had, by this time, reached the kitchen, shoved the door closed behind him and exited through the side door, slamming it shut.

Henry powered down the hallway, yanked open the kitchen door, almost pulling it off its hinges, then half skidded on the linoleum floor, righted himself and went out through the side door after Tommy, who had turned left and hared across the back garden, vaulted the low fence into the garden beyond and ran through the deep grass of that unkempt garden.

He was moving fast.

Henry recalled just how fast the lad could move, so he changed up a gear, his arms pumping as he followed Tommy's trail, taking the back fence without breaking his stride.

In a parallel train of thought, Henry realized this bit of exercise would be a good test of how well he had recovered from the assault. He'd done that day's training workout at headquarters at his own pace, but he would have to put everything into this foot pursuit or risk losing the chance of dragging Tommy into the cells.

And that was something he didn't want to miss.

His pace increased. He was feeling good.

Tommy ran down the side of the house. By the time Henry reached the back corner of that property, he was out of sight.

Henry dug deep and put on an extra sprint, and as he emerged, he saw Tommy running hard and fast down the avenue, a good fifty yards ahead of him.

Henry gritted his teeth, gave chase, completely focusing on the capture, his vision seeming to close down as though he was looking through a telescope, and he started to quickly reduce the distance between himself and Tommy second by second. It became obvious that the young lad, whose initial turn of speed was incredible, didn't have the stamina to outrun Henry this time, not in a straight race. He was constantly looking back over his shoulder and Henry could tell he was flagging, whereas Henry hadn't really broken sweat.

Finally, after much swerving and journeys through several more gardens and alleyways, Tommy gave up, sagged to his knees, gasping for air. When he caught him, Henry was breathing heavily but was nowhere near out of breath.

'Face down, hands behind your back,' he said to the gasping boy. 'You're under arrest for assaulting me, among other things. Say nowt,' Henry advised him, by way of a caution.

Slowly, Tommy went from all fours on to his chest and complied with the instructions. Henry snapped on the cuffs, then manoeuvred Tommy to his feet, spinning him around so they were face to face.

'Got ya!'

'No idea what you mean.'

'Let's chat about that down the nick, eh?' Henry gave him a shove and they began to walk back to Tommy's house with Henry gripping the lad's upper arm. 'We've got a lot to chat about.'

'Don't think so.'

They'd gone about thirty yards when Henry heard a shout from behind.

'Oi, what you think you're doing, cop?'

Henry glanced over his shoulder. Four youths were standing across the avenue. Two were the ones Henry had spoken to on his arrival on the estate, the other two those he'd seen dash across the mouth of Clement Close.

Their appearance gave Henry a bad feeling.

'Come on,' he urged Tommy, 'get a move on.' He upped the walking pace just a touch.

'I said, what're you doing?' another of the little gang shouted.

A couple of yards to Henry's left, half a house brick crashed to the ground, bits splintering. Then another hit the ground to his right. Henry glanced back and saw another arcing through the air, this time on target. He jerked Tommy to one side out of the path of its trajectory and it landed harmlessly.

Two more youths filtered in from somewhere.

Six in total now and they took up a 'Uh! Uh! Uh!' war chant.

'Move faster,' Henry said, dragging Tommy along. 'What's the name of this avenue?' he asked him.

'Eh?' Tommy said dimly.

'Fuck's the name of this avenue?'

'Uh, Tennyson, I think.'

Still bustling Tommy along, Henry spoke into his PR. 'PC Christie, Support Unit, to Blackpool.'

'Go ahead.'

'I've made an arrest after a short foot chase and I'm currently on Tennyson Avenue making my way back to Clement Close with my prisoner . . . Argh!'

One of the half-bricks launched by the gang landed squarely into the centre of Henry's back, right between the shoulder blades, and it hurt.

'PC Christie, are you OK?'

'Yep – just being stoned by a mob.' Henry turned and counted. 'Now about a dozen strong. I require some assistance.'

Rather like a volley of arrows fired by a medieval army, a hail of bricks and large stones then rained down around Henry and his prisoner, both of whom ducked and cowered but somehow were not struck. Henry took a vice-like grip of Tommy's arm and ran him back to his house on Clement Close, crossing through several gardens until they were almost at the back of Tommy's house.

All the while, the gang had increased in size but didn't seem to be significantly gaining on them, so Henry kept pushing and kept comms up to date with the evolving situation. Henry knew he had to reach his car and get off the estate fast, except that when he and Tommy ran through the garden that backed on to the lad's house, he saw smoke spiralling up from the front of the house, and even before he knew for certain what was on fire, he was sure that his inspector would be very displeased with him indeed.

Henry's worst fears were confirmed as he propelled Tommy down the side of the house, stopped abruptly by the front corner and looked down the garden path.

The car that Henry had borrowed had been torched and was now burning fiercely.

'Oh, shit,' Henry said in a very understated manner.

Looking up the avenue, he saw that the gang had made its way through the gardens of other houses, had regrouped and was now trudging down towards Henry, their 'Uh! Uh! Uh!' seeming to gather volume and momentum.

'Officer!'

Henry turned. Trish Benemy was standing at her side door, beckoning urgently. 'Get in here if you want to live.'

They circled the house like a pack of hyenas around an injured lion, too scared to go in for the kill just in case the lion got lucky. However, their presence was frightening and intimidating up to the point where Trish Benemy stated, 'I've had enough of this shit,' and went to her front door, stepped out and stalked boldly down the path to her broken gate. So far, none of the pack had dared to set foot on her property, and as she approached them and the now smouldering shell of the police car, they backed off even further when she hurled a tirade of abuse at them.

Henry watched with awe from her front window, particularly when one of the youths – wearing a scarf to keep his identity hidden – strutted up to her, gesticulating and screaming abuse into her face. She simply stood her ground, hands on hips, and responded in kind.

'Crikey,' Henry said to Tommy who was still cuffed, although his hands were now in front of him, and sitting sullenly on the settee. 'Your mum's a brave woman.'

Tommy looked at Henry, said nothing. Henry shrugged and looked outside again as suddenly, as one entity, the gang stormed down the cul-de-sac towards the turning circle, split up and disappeared through the house gardens. Two police vans and a patrol car screeched into the avenue.

Henry's assistance had arrived, but he winced when his eyes took in the remains of his inspector's car. He was going to have to do a lot of explaining and grovelling, even if his trump card was a good arrest.

THREE

I t wasn't the first time Henry Christie had been paraded in front of Robert Fanshaw-Bayley, and even then he somehow doubted it would be the last. The first time had been when FB was Henry's DI in Rawtenstall and Henry had made a complete hash of transporting a prisoner from Dover back up to the valley; such a hash that the prisoner, a very well-known and prolific burglar, had escaped en route.

So things were not boding well for the young cop, who already knew that FB did not suffer anyone gladly, fool or otherwise.

He stood in front of FB's desk in the DCI's office at Blackpool nick, not exactly to attention but certainly not at ease, and awaited the very loud dressing-down that Henry suspected the rotund detective was about to unleash.

FB was seated, hadn't even glanced up when Henry entered the office, but had sort of gestured for him to stand on the opposite side of the desk and wait while he appeared to sign off some paperwork, which he finally placed in the out-tray. He then laid his bulbous fountain pen down with exaggerated care and raised his face to look at Henry.

Who swallowed.

'Is this scenario becoming a bit of a habit?' FB asked quietly.

'Which scenario, sir?' Henry asked cautiously.

'The one where I have you parading in front of me to explain your . . . let me see' – FB pretended to gather his thoughts, though Henry knew the DCI had already gathered them – 'reckless actions, your shitshow.'

'B–b–b . . .' Henry stuttered.

'No b–b–b's,' FB snorted mockingly.

Henry's mouth snapped shut.

'Is this going to be a feature of your police career? Acting without thought or consideration? Putting investigations and people – your colleagues – in danger? As well as valuable police property? Going on unauthorized jaunts? Completely disregarding the chain of command?'

Henry once again tried to say something in his own defence, but his protestation was cut short by a karate-like slice of FB's hand through the air, brooking no further discussion.

'I seem to recall you want to be a detective?'

'Yes, boss.'

'No, no, no . . . you don't have the right to call me "boss". At this juncture and for the foreseeable future, it remains "sir" – OK?'

'Yes, sir,' Henry said mutedly.

'You don't really like authority, do you, PC . . . PC . . .?'

'Christie, sir,' Henry added helpfully, even though he knew that FB had a habit of pretending to forget names in order to belittle officers of lower rank, or any civilians.

'Yes, PC Christie.'

'It's not a matter of not liking it, sir. I wholeheartedly accept it because that's how the police operate . . . more or less,' Henry said unconvincingly.

FB's chubby lips puckered, then twisted. 'So let me get this straight. You decide to nick your boss's car and then, knowing that a full-scale investigation was underway to identify the persons who assaulted you, you went, without authority, or telling anyone, or running it past me, to try to make an arrest *off your own bat*!' The last four words came out in a staccato burst, like a machine gun. Henry tried to say something, but FB raised a finger to halt any protest and said, 'Uh-uh!' He paused a moment, then said, 'And in so doing went on to an estate where relations between the police and public are fragile to say the least and, single-handedly, caused a fucking riot and managed to burn your inspector's car to nothing more than a shell.'

FB waited.

Henry said, 'I did make a good arrest.'

'You should have told me. I mean, when exactly did your memory miraculously return?'

Henry's lips tightened on his teeth as he struggled to think of a realistic answer.

FB ventured, 'You never lost it, did you?'

'No, sir,' Henry said meekly.

'You were going to have that arrest all along, weren't you?'

Henry nodded: busted.

'Jesus!' FB gasped. 'Not exactly a team player, are you?'

Henry didn't want to get into a debate about that – mainly because he knew he'd been wrong and found out when it all went pear-shaped. Instead, he said, 'I apologize, sir. I did want to make that arrest and I can see my lack of judgement in this respect.' The words were very hard to spout, but he knew he'd been cornered and only a grovelling apology would suffice.

'I should put you on paper,' FB told him.

Henry gulped. If he was formally disciplined, this misdemeanour would go all the way to the top and it would be a toss-up which way it went. It was unlikely that he would be asked to resign or be sacked, but a formal disciplinary appearance before the chief constable might happen, and that would entail an entry on his personal record which would hamper a transfer on to CID for years to come.

He waited for the axe to fall.

But FB's expression changed as he said, 'However, I'm not a total git.'

Henry's mouth went dry and his heart began to pound. 'I didn't think you were, sir,' he said. 'Not a total one.'

Shit! Why did I have to say that? he demanded silently of himself as he saw, like dark clouds scudding across a sky, FB's face change back to anger for a moment, then back to not being a git.

'Thing is this, PC . . . er . . . Christie . . . I kinda like something about you. Can't put my finger on it. It's not as though you're a likeable sort of bloke at all, because clearly you're not. You don't necessarily have to be, in this game, but it does help and you need to know how to play it, and at the moment you don't seem to be good at the game. So I'll tell you what . . .'

Henry braced himself.

'Even though we've wasted well over a full month of manpower on this investigation, I'm prepared to pretend you only just got your memory back and were just being a bit gung-ho – y'know, the enthusiasm of youth and all that palaver – if, and only if, you get an admission of guilt from the lad, plus the names of the others involved, obviously.'

'Thank you . . . er . . . sir. I'll do my best with him.'

FB nodded the nod of a dictator. 'I will smooth it out with the patrol inspector who, because of your incursion on to Shoreside, had to bring in reinforcements to quell a riot – he may well wish to have a word in your lughole; however, I'm not sure I can placate your own inspector whose cherished vehicle you managed to destroy. He may wish to skin your bollocks.'

'Yes, sir,' Henry said smartly.

'Right – fuck off out of my sight.'

The patrol inspector was waiting to ambush Henry as soon as he stepped out of FB's office. He was a chubby, balding guy, baby-faced but with a hint of steel about him, and Henry knew he was in for a severe roasting, the scale of which he had never before experienced in spite of what FB had promised.

The inspector pointed to an office and ushered Henry into it.

Ten minutes later, perspiring heavily and suitably reprimanded, Henry emerged.

It had been one of the best tellings-off he had ever been subjected to, so good that partway through he almost offered to smash himself about the head with a tea-tray.

But he was basically unscathed.

However, his own inspector was waiting for him when he stepped out.

This, probably, was the one he felt worst about because Inspector Jameson was truly one of the nicest guys he had ever met – a true gent, mild yet firm – and Henry could see the man's bottom lip trembling as he spoke about the loss of his beloved car.

'I cleaned it inside and outside, lovingly, at least once a week; vacuumed it, polished it . . . my pride and joy. Every other car I've had access to in my career has been a rattling shithole on wheels.'

'I know, sir, and I'm sorry.' Normally, Henry would have called him 'boss', but decided that formality might be the best move in this case.

Jameson's lips clung together and his chin wobbled as he considered Henry.

'Sir, if – when – you get a replacement, I'll look after it, clean, polish everything, and I won't ever take it without permission,' Henry offered.

Jameson shook his head sadly, lost for words, then waved Henry away, unable to speak.

Henry went down to the custody complex on the lower ground floor and took his place in a short line of other arresting officers waiting to be given access to their prisoners. The new Police and Criminal Evidence Act (PACE) had come into force the previous year and custody offices across England and Wales were still getting familiar with its vagaries, the main one being that detainees could only be held for a minimum of twenty-four hours without charge (though there were exceptions) and their detention had to be reviewed every six hours by an officer of the rank of inspector or above, not connected with the case. That meant prisoners could no longer be left to stew in cells for hours or days on end and were given the chance to have legal representation and, for juveniles, to be accompanied by appropriate adults.

It also meant that Thomas James Benemy was in a juvenile cell, which had a wooden door and a toughened glass viewing panel instead of the adult steel and sliding metal hatch.

Henry finally made it to the custody sergeant who had a gaoler bring out the lad and take him to an interview room where Henry sat opposite him and waited for Tommy's mother to be brought in.

Henry decided to say nothing, although he had to bite his tongue. The lad kept his eyes from meeting Henry's.

Henry knew not to judge people from their appearance, but he couldn't help but think that Tommy looked like a decent kid. Good looking in an inoffensive way, maybe a bit soft in his manner now that he wasn't armed with an air rifle.

Finally, Tommy's mother, Trish, was shown into the interview room by WPC Clarke, Henry's alleyway angel (as he called her, though only to himself), who gave him a nice smile. Henry caught the briefest look between Trish and Tommy, almost nothing, but one Henry did not quite understand . . . but then it was gone and Mrs Benemy was sitting across from him, next to her son. Clarke withdrew from the room, giving Henry another nice smile, then she was gone.

Henry regarded mother and son.

'Before we start,' he said to Trish, 'I want to say thanks again for what you did back up there on the estate. Pretty sure I'd've been hung, drawn and quartered without your intervention.'

She shrugged as if it was nothing. 'Just a bunch of little shits.'

'But thanks.'

'OK . . . doesn't mean I like you, or any other cop for that matter.'

'Totally get that.' Henry straightened out his paperwork, then looked at young Tommy, reminded him he was still under caution and could have legal representation if desired.

Trish spoke. 'We're fine.'

'OK, in that case, let me summarize. I was on duty in Marston's Department Store when I saw you' – he pointed at Tommy – 'come into the store, steal a large amount of perfume and leg it from the shop, and I gave chase.'

Henry saw Trish give her son a quizzical look. She asked Henry, 'How much perfume?'

'About two grand's worth.'

Trish blinked and her head rotated slowly to her son whose mouth popped open as he cowered. She said, 'Where was mine?'

Tommy gulped audibly but said nothing.

Trish's jaw rotated angrily.

'It was good stuff, too,' Henry added helpfully, hoping to fan a few flames. 'Chanel, I think.'

She looked back at him, and Henry could see she was simmering, maybe about to blow like a pressure cooker.

'You mean he didn't bring any home?' Henry asked innocuously, seeing the possibility of stirring up the situation to his advantage. It always made interviewing surly juveniles so much easier when the adult was furious with the kid for whatever reason. Usually, it was just because of the inconvenience of being dragged from home into a cold interview room, sometimes because they were genuinely shocked and distressed by the behaviour of the fruits of their loins, or, as in this case, because they did not benefit from the crime.

'No! Only thing he brought home was this . . .' She grabbed his arm, shoved his sleeve up and twisted his forearm so Henry could see a recently etched tattoo which looked like a small house – just a square with a triangle on top to represent the roof, and with a diagonal slash through the square. 'A friggin' tatt! And not a good one at that!' She threw his arm away in disgust.

Averting his eyes from the string of tattoos around Trish's neck and the double standard applied here, Henry said, 'So what happened to the perfumes, Tommy?'

'I didn't steal anything. It wasn't me,' he protested.

Henry said, 'Let's not go down that road of drivel, eh? I saw you, I chased you. I caught you, I got assaulted.'

Tommy looked down at the table. 'No comment.'

Henry glanced at Trish who had folded her arms haughtily underneath her bosom; evidently, her son's lack of generosity was gnawing at her. Two grand's worth of expensive perfume and not a single bottle coming in her direction must have been painfully galling.

'I will be going back to your house and seizing the clothing you had on that day – the red jacket and blue jeans and those grey trainers – which you're wearing today, actually.' Henry had seen that Tommy was wearing them when arrested. 'I'm pretty sure they'll have my blood on them from when you were kicking my head in.'

'No comment.'

'So, before we come to the assault properly, let's just backtrack slightly to the perfume. I mean, a lad like you, stealing that amount of perfume? Were you stealing to order? Is that it?'

'No comment.'

'You went into the shop, stole a fortune in perfume – none of which ended up with your mum, although' – Henry glanced at Trish – 'I will have to have a look through your room, y'know?'

She nodded tightly. 'Be my guest. He brought fuck all back.'

Henry turned back to Tommy. 'So was that other lad the one who handled the stolen property and was he the one you were stealing for?'

'No comment.'

'And, of course, whoever snuck up behind me and smacked me on the head. Who was that and were you stealing for that person?'

'No comment.'

That final 'No comment' must have been the one that sent Trish Benemy into a frenzy. Before Henry could stop her, the simmering rage within erupted into a volcanic fury. She spun where she sat and clobbered Tommy very, very hard across his head with such force he went tipping backwards, sprawling off the chair and rolling into a tight ball in the corner of the interview room, covering his head with his hands and forearms as Trish rose majestically and started to kick him.

Momentarily, Henry was stunned, then was up, dashing around the table, trying to pull her off without actually grappling her – and later being accused of indecently assaulting her, which was always the problem when wrestling a woman. However, he barged her sideways and managed to place himself between the two, making placating gestures while Tommy sobbed.

The interview room burst open and WPC Clarke rushed in.

'Are you OK, Henry? I heard a commotion.'

Henry eyed Trish warily, and although she glared at him and said things like 'Little cunt' under her breath about Tommy, she nodded to indicate that hostilities were over.

To Clarke, Henry said, 'Can you just take the lad back to the detention room? Me and Mrs Benemy need a little chat.'

The follow-up interview was much less fraught, but just as unproductive as far as Henry was concerned.

It remained 'No comment'; even so, Henry persisted so that all the ground was covered and there could be no get-out when it came to court. If Tommy didn't want to answer, that was his prerogative and so be it. Henry just had to make sure he asked the right questions anyway so as to negate any future defence that a certain question was not put to him. Even if he chose not to answer, Henry still had to ensure that all avenues of escape were closed. Tommy also refused to name the other people involved; Henry noticed that Tommy looked afraid when questioned about them, but that was all.

After photographing and fingerprinting Tommy, Henry went with him to the custody officer who released him 'pending further enquiries'.

Throughout the time in custody, Henry had kept in contact with WPC Clarke who volunteered to drive mum and son home and also carry out the search of the house for any stolen property and seize any of the clothing Tommy had been wearing at the time of the assault.

As they walked Tommy and Trish out to the car park, Trish said to Henry, 'I do actually love him, y'know.'

'I'm sure you do, Trish.'

'Some smelly would have been nice, though,' she said wistfully. 'But that's not it . . . It's just me and him, y'know? Fuck knows where his dad is, so, yeah, me and him trying to eke out some kind of life, which means we both have our part to play and his is *not* getting involved in crime – unless it's bank robbery, and he isn't cut out for that.'

Henry nodded and asked, 'What is he involved in?'

She sighed. 'I don't know . . . but I get a bad feeling about it.'

'Is it more than just nicking to order?'

She shrugged. 'Like I say, dunno.'

Clarke had drawn a police car up and was waiting with the doors open.

'We'll chat next week, eh?' Henry suggested.

She nodded, then hustled Tommy into the back seat of the car. Henry watched them drive away with Trish's face half in the shadow as she looked back at him. Henry thought she looked sad.

He gave a shrug, wandered out to the far reaches of the underground garage where he knew he would find Inspector Jameson's car which had been recovered and brought – for some reason that escaped Henry – into the station car park instead of being towed straight to a scrapyard.

It really was a burnt-out shell, blackened, scorched, all four tyres having seared away to nothing on naked wheel hubs.

'Oh dear,' Henry said out loud.

Not only that, but he now also had the additional problem of somehow hitching a ride back to the Support Unit office at headquarters to pick up his own car, then drive all the way back to his home in Blackpool.

He didn't notice FB coming up behind him – he moved silently for a big guy. He slapped Henry between the shoulder blades.

'Did you get a cough from the lad?'

'Not quite.'

'Ahh, a euphemism for "no".'

'Hmm, OK . . . but he's coming back in next week for further questioning.'

'With a detective alongside you this time, I hope?'

'If that's what you want, sir, of course,' Henry conceded gratefully, feeling he'd ruffled too many feathers that day, even though this felt like lack of faith in his ability to do the job.

'Good.' FB stood alongside Henry and surveyed the wreck of the car. 'And now you're wondering how you're going to get back to base camp?'

'Something like that.'

'Oh, just out of curiosity, how well do you now recall the faces of the other people who assaulted you?' FB asked, changing tack.

'I'd know the other lad, the one Benemy was with in the alley, but I didn't see who came up behind and walloped me. I've looked through the photo albums, but I haven't seen the face of the lad, though.'

'That's not an exact science, as we know.'

'No.'

'Anyway, how do we get you home?'

'I was going to go up to comms and see if anyone was heading out that way and cadge a lift now that Shoreside's quietened down.'

'I'll give you a ride. I live out that way these days,' FB said, to Henry's surprise.

'That would be great, boss, thanks.'

The following week was extremely busy for Henry and the rest of his Support Unit team who were deployed right across the county, including a very long weekend in Blackpool when their feet didn't touch the ground. It was exhilarating work supporting the local cops and dealing with everything Blackpool could throw at them.

On the final, busy Sunday night in the resort, Henry and the team managed several arrests for public order offences and, finally, around four a.m. as a new dawn arrived, they were done.

Henry had been dropped off at the custody office to process his prisoner – an unpleasant eighteen-year-old youth who had lobbed a few bricks at the personnel carrier. Led by Henry, the cops had swarmed out of the carrier. Henry had caught him easily and, holding him by the collar, he'd tiptoed him back to the van without breaking sweat.

There was no need to interview him – just to photograph and fingerprint him, and type up the charge forms, followed by the actual verbal charging in the presence of the custody officer who bailed him to appear at court in three weeks' time.

An easy prisoner and one to add to Henry's ever-increasing tally.

Henry escorted him out of the custody office, all the way to the rear doors of the garage, letting him step out through the side door. He watched the lad walk miserably away.

Henry exhaled a long, weary sigh and looked up at the dawn sky. He had radioed his team to come and pick him up and there would be a ten-minute wait before they arrived, so he sat on a low wall on Richardson Street to enjoy a bit of peace and quiet which, he was coming to realize, was something unusual in Blackpool.

'We meet again.' Henry turned to see WPC Clarke walking towards him across the public car park from the direction of the town centre – her beat. He rose from the wall as she crossed the tarmac. She was dressed in her uniform – just a skirt and blouse as the night had been warm enough to dispense with tunics. Henry liked what he saw.

'Hi,' he said.

'Are you stalking me?' she chuckled.

'I could ask the same question.'

She stepped over the low wall and was alongside him, stumbling slightly and, seemingly accidentally, falling against him. He caught her gently.

'Oops,' she giggled, looking up at him.

'You OK?' He backed off slightly, moving his open hands quickly away from her.

'Yeah, yeah, Little Miss Clumsy.'

Henry smirked. 'Glad I bumped into you, actually.'

'Me too.' Her eyes played over his face and he watched them dance with a certain tightness in his chest.

He fought to bring himself back on track and dismiss all inappropriate thoughts. 'I haven't had the chance to catch up with you and I'm off for a couple of days now, then back over here to deal with Tommy Benemy.'

'I know.'

'I take it you didn't find anything of interest at his house when you took him back?'

She took her hat off. Her hair was pinned up neatly under it. She eased out the grips, ruffled her hair with her fingertips and shook it free so it fell naturally into a bob that framed her face, making Henry's mouth go dry.

'No, nothing,' she said. 'No bloodstained clothing, no perfumes.'

'What did you think about Tommy?'

'What do you mean?'

Henry shrugged. 'You think he's into anything more than shoplifting? Is he stealing to order for a gang or something?'

'What makes you think that?'

'The fact that he stole a ton of perfume – and didn't give his mum any.'

'Is that all? I wouldn't necessarily believe her.'

'Maybe not . . . I got the impression he was hiding something behind the "no comment".'

'Such as?' Her face had a puzzled look to it.

Henry's mouth turned down at the corners. 'Don't know; can't quite put my finger on it . . . just that maybe he didn't want to say anything because if he opened up, he'd start blabbing on about something and not be able to stop. Something dark.'

'Henry . . . you're being dramatic,' she teased him, but tenderly, a soft smile on her face. 'I didn't get that impression. All I saw was a daft lad, maybe doing a dare.'

'And then beating the crap out of me with others?'

'Well, yeah, a bit OTT on that one,' she agreed.

'Anyway, thanks for helping me out – taking him home and that.'

'Not a problem.'

She looked at him again. He coughed uneasily.

'I'll really get into his ribs when he comes back in . . . I'm pretty sure I can get him talking.'

'I'm pretty sure you can,' she said, a flirty half-smile playing on her lips. 'What are you up to now?'

'Just waiting to be picked up by the guys and then get back to HQ to finish for a couple of days. My first job back will be dealing with Tommy.'

'When I said, "What are you doing now?" I didn't quite mean that.' She arched her finely lined eyebrows enquiringly. 'I meant when you get off duty.' She made a show of checking her watch. 'I'm off in an hour . . . that should tie in with how long it'll take you to get back to HQ, then get back here . . . I'm in a flat on Devonshire Road,' she concluded.

Henry tried, but he could not stop his bottom lip from bubbling open like a loose tyre. He managed to shut it.

'Up to you,' she said.

At which moment, the personnel carrier full of Henry's team turned into Richardson Street, and as soon as the cops on board spotted him talking to a pretty female officer, a raucous roar and accompanying whistles rose from the van, which even Henry and Clarke could hear from fifty yards away.

'Like I said, I'll leave it with you,' she said, then turned to the oncoming van, gave its passengers a 'Hello boys' wave with a twinkle of her fingers and headed towards the side door to the police car park.

Good-naturedly fending off a barrage of inappropriate comments, Henry climbed into the van and told them all to fuck off.

By the time Tommy Benemy was an hour late turning up to answer his bail at Blackpool police station, Henry had almost paced a groove into the linoleum at the back of the public enquiry desk.

Finally, and in frustration, he stomped into the CID office where the detective delegated by FB to assist Henry in interviewing Tommy was at his desk, elbow-deep in paperwork, surrounded by a cloud of cigarette smoke.

He was a heavily jowled old lag called Phil Brand, a decent, hard-working detective.

'Take it the lad hasn't shown his fizzog,' Brand said as he watched Henry walk in.

'No sign.'

'Tried ringing?'

'They don't have a phone.'

Brand sat back. He was one of the old-school jacks, all of whom (to Henry) seemed to have thick moustaches and monobrows. Even then, Henry recognized them as a dying breed, especially with the introduction of PACE. Many struggled with the new law, but Henry realized it was here to stay, and although he too was used to dealing with the way things had been, he understood that the only way forward was to make it work for you.

Brand stroked his moustache with his thumb and fingertip. 'You got transport?'

Henry shook his head. 'No.' He'd been dropped off at Blackpool by Inspector Jameson – who'd now been allocated a decrepit pool vehicle until a new one was sourced – while the remainder of his team were on a crime operation in Morecambe.

Brand picked up a set of car keys from his desk and lobbed them across to Henry. 'It's a bleedin' Maestro – not exactly sure where it's parked. Go and see if the lad's at home, or whatever.'

Henry caught the keys. 'Last time I went on to Shoreside, I caused a riot.'

'Well, don't this time, eh?' Brand resumed his reading of a stack of crime reports.

Fifteen minutes later, Henry was on Shoreside and managed to drive without incident to the cul-de-sac on which the Benemys lived, spun around in the turning circle and stopped at the house.

The grubby net curtain twitched at the living-room window: Trish Benemy looking out.

Henry wondered what wonderful excuse there would be as he walked up the path.

The door opened before he could rap on it.

'We had an appointment,' he said to Trish. 'You, me, Tommy, down at the cop shop.'

'I know.'

Henry thought she looked beyond tired. Pale eyes, sunk deep into their sockets. Vulnerable, even.

'What's the problem?'

'Tommy,' she said haltingly. 'I haven't seen him for three days and nights. He's gone missing and I'm really worried about him.'

FOUR

1986 – Twelve Months Later

'Wow, you look smart, Henry.'

Henry tugged down the hem of the jacket of his brand new, dark-blue suit and grinned proudly. 'Thanks, boss.'

The praise had been heaped on him as he walked through the door of the CID office at Blackpool nick by FB who had a slightly contemptuous smirk on his face and tone in his voice that Henry didn't really notice because today was his first day as an official, fully fledged detective constable. *DC Henry Christie.* It had a certain ring to it, he thought – an authority, a gravitas. It also gave him, he assumed, the right to call FB 'boss' instead of 'sir'.

Because Henry was now in the inner circle. Or at least on the outer rim of it, but definitely part of the – mostly – boys' club that was the Criminal Investigation Department. That very powerful inner movement within the cops that answered to no one. Even the chief constable kept them at arms' length. It wasn't that Henry had been promoted. He was still just as much a constable as anyone in uniform, but in reality he was much, much more.

At least in his own mind.

A fucking detective.

For real.

At fucking last.

He had been a CID Aide for a short time at Blackburn a few years earlier, but that had ended inauspiciously when, in a fit of immature temper, he'd raised his fist to a DI and almost punched the guy's lights out – and he'd been back in uniform so quick that, yes, his feet didn't touch the ground.

But he'd grafted hard since. Mostly kept his head down, made numerous arrests, many low level, but some decent ones, and his record was exemplary – with the occasional glitch – and eventually his move on to CID was irresistible.

FB surveyed him critically.

FB in his turn was less than spic and span. His weight had continued to rise in the few years Henry had known him, but he seemed convinced his clothes still fitted comfortably, even though each seam seemed to be straining, each button ready to ping off.

'Office,' FB snapped.

Henry glanced around the room. It was Monday morning and most of the desks were occupied by detectives, all watching Henry and FB with bemusement. Smoke rose from several cigarettes, and the aroma of bacon baps and fresh coffee permeated the office. Henry had hoped he would have been shown to his desk by the DS, given a bit of an induction and then maybe a partner and some jobs to deal with.

It looked as if FB wanted to bend his ear before anyone else did.

FB pushed past him and Henry followed like the good lad he was. The CID office was situated in a low-level annexe to the main building of the police station and the DSs and DIs had their offices in there, but the DCI's office was on the fourth floor of the main building, on the level where the higher ranks in the division hung out, such as the superintendents and the chief super, or, as Henry liked to call them, 'the big nobs'. This was the level to which FB took Henry, which meant having to share an awkwardly silent ride up in the creaky lift.

'Sit down,' FB said, circumnavigating his desk and plonking himself down on his office chair, which hissed in protest and sank an inch or two on its hydraulic strut.

Henry sat, glancing out through the narrow floor-to-ceiling toughened-glass window overlooking the public car park at the side of the nick and the bottom third of Blackpool Tower. As an office, it was nothing special: poky, grim, very much like the rest of the building, which was a crumbling mass of steel and concrete, even though it had only been up for a decade. However, Henry already fancied himself sitting on the opposite side of the desk now occupied by FB. Not that he was especially ambitious, and even then he recognized it as a passing whim.

Henry adjusted his suit so as not to wrinkle it and even straightened his trouser creases and smiled at FB . . . who said, 'The tache – get rid, eh? Doesn't do you any favours.'

Henry felt a chill run through him. His thumb and forefinger came up to the growth under his nose, specially cultivated so that he might look like one of the more experienced jacks. It hadn't grown terribly well – more bumfluff than anything and certainly nothing like the Walrus that dominated FB's top lip.

'Yes, boss.'

'So – welcome to the department, DC . . . er . . . Christie.'

'Thanks, boss, good to be here.'

'Maybe hang fire on the "boss" thing for now. Let's stick to "sir" for the time being, see how things pan out.'

'Sure, sir,' Henry said, feeling slightly deflated.

'So, you did it?'

Henry nodded sagely. 'I did, sir.' His mind flashed back to the gruelling application form which Kate assisted in completing, followed by the tense weeks wondering if he'd made the cut or been binned; then the local interview at headquarters because the Support Unit came under that remit; then the tough interview facing a panel consisting of FB, the ACC (Crime) and a detective superintendent, who collectively asked some of the most ridiculous questions imaginable, including 'Which daily newspaper do you read?'

But Henry had been prepared for that one. He'd done his research and confidently replied, '*The Daily Telegraph*,' even though that was a fib. He didn't read newspapers, didn't have the time or inclination, especially with a newly born daughter on the scene, but he had spent the last fortnight reading the said broadsheet.

There was a supplementary question to that on the *Telegraph*'s recent leader on world poverty which Henry winged his way through because he didn't really know what a 'leader' was.

He was on firmer ground when asked about his best arrest and who he thought was the top criminal in Lancashire. And he knew his legal definitions by heart so he could answer any questions about criminal law.

He was perspiring heavily by the end and was glad to get out of the room and down to the canteen for a cup of tea, which he took over to an empty table. He had sat down shaking, convinced he'd failed.

He'd been staring out of a window at the headquarters social club, clasping his brew for comfort, when he became aware of a figure standing to one side of him: FB.

'Hello, sir.'

'Thought I might catch you here, lad.'

'Just settling the old nerves,' Henry admitted.

'Well, you got through.'

'Really?'

'Really.'

'Wow – thank you, sir.'

'Obviously, I fought against it all the way, but y'know, democracy and all that, so I had to capitulate. You start at Blackpool CID in two weeks' time or thereabouts, and you'll get an initial detective course sometime later in the year. Is that OK with you?'

'More than OK. Thank you again.'

'Don't thank me; thank the ACC. He saw something in you I didn't. The paperwork's in the correspondence,' FB said, and with that he rotated on his heels and walked away with the metallic clipping noise Henry had come to associate with FB who had steel heel protectors on his winkle-picker shoes, which, Henry realized, meant he must have sneaked up on him.

And even as he sat facing him three weeks later, Henry wasn't certain if FB had meant any of the things he'd said in the canteen. Did he really not want Henry on the CID?

'Yes, yes, you did it,' FB repeated gravely. 'But the thing is, now you're on your probationary period, so it's only fair you should know what I expect of you.'

Henry nodded.

'OK, keep your head down, make arrests – lots of them. I want to see burglars of all shapes and sizes in those minging cells downstairs. That's your focus – fuckers who wreck people's lives. Anything else is a plus, OK?'

Henry nodded again. Burglars it would be.

'You've got to be a team player, not go off doing your own thing whenever you please. So, burglars, clear-up rates and team player.'

Henry nodded. Team player. Got it.

'And if you do all that, you can call me boss, now, OK?'

'Yes, boss.'

'All that said, head back down to the CID office and liaise with the DS. There's a search warrant being executed this morning; your ex-mates from the Support Unit are assisting.' FB checked his watch. 'They'll be briefing about now, so get your skates on.'

'OK, boss.' Henry began to rise.

'One thing – piece of advice from a seasoned detective to a tyro – never wear a suit you don't want to get shit up. And definitely shave that tache off . . . it's unpleasant to look at. Oh, and that haircut . . . do they call 'em mullets, or something . . . meh!'

Henry returned to the CID office less than motivated by FB's welcome speech, which felt more like a warning than anything, but he tried to shrug it off as he threaded his way through the narrow corridors of the police station, which was now his home base at last, favouring the concrete stairs rather than the lift, although, even if it never felt quite safe, he was pretty sure no one had ever been trapped in it. There were actually two lifts in the station, neither of which seemed fit for purpose.

When he arrived in the office, it was almost deserted.

The only person remaining was DC Brand, the detective Henry had liaised with when he should have been interviewing Tommy Benemy. Brand was sitting back, expertly blowing smoke rings.

'Where is everyone?'

'If you leg it down to the garage, you might just catch 'em before they set off,' Brand said. 'They got sick of waiting for you.'

Henry was almost on his way before Brand had finished speaking, rushing – not running – down to the garage where a small convoy of police vehicles was about to set off, including the personnel carrier used by his now former SU colleagues assisting that morning's raid.

Henry heard a muffled cheer from the van as he tried to jog as quickly as possible across the garage without appearing to be stressed out or concerned he was going to be left behind for his first ever job as a DC.

He saw the DS and another DC pull out of a parking space in a plain car and drive towards the exit, followed by the section van, so it was pretty clear his new workmates weren't about to wait for him.

Fortunately, his old ones saw his predicament and the side door of the van slid open for him and several pairs of hands gestured for him to hurry up and jump aboard as the vehicle started to roll.

He was heaved in, the door slammed shut behind him.

'Thanks, guys.'

He then had to endure a journey full of good-natured abuse about his new status, new suit, haircut and moustache (which they hadn't seen because he'd grown it secretly while on leave for the past two weeks). He took it all in good heart. His posting on to the Support Unit had been more by accident than design, but he'd hugely enjoyed it for many reasons. The camaraderie had been great, the varied work fun, and, not least, it had taken him to parts of Lancashire he would probably never have visited if he'd stayed as a response PC. His knowledge of the constabulary had increased significantly; in a fairly short space of time, he had been to almost every police station in the county.

The carrier followed the two local vehicles on to the promenade where the convoy turned left and made towards South Shore, an area which, behind the façade of the seafront, had a grim reputation for drug dealing, violence and general criminality. Henry knew that this was a place he would come to know intimately as a DC in Blackpool.

He was looking forward to the relationship.

They veered left off the prom on to Lytham Road and drove towards the maze of streets behind the Pleasure Beach, drawing to a halt under the shadow of the railway bridge where the DS and the DC got out of their car and walked back to the Support Unit with street maps in their hands. The carrier door slid open and the DS, whose name was Ronson, came to the opening, slightly surprised to see Henry in among the unit, who were all kitted out in dark-blue overalls.

'You made it, then?' he said to Henry.

Henry would have quipped something back, but just nodded.

'OK, folks,' Ronson said. 'You know the drill. The house we're going for is down the next street' – he jerked his thumb over his shoulder – 'number thirty-five, on the right, three doors down. It's divided into flats and the one we're interested in is the basement, so that makes it easy for us. Three of you to the back yard, two to deal with the soil pipe and a third to watch the back door to deal with anyone who scarpers. Everyone else, down the steps at the front and in through that door. OK?'

Henry assumed that he'd missed the main briefing at the station and this was just a reminder for everyone.

Hesitantly, he held up a hand.

Ronson said a slightly contemptuous, 'What?'

'What are we looking for, just so I know?'

'Anything we can find. Mainly drugs and money, possibly firearms.'

'Cheers.'

Ronson didn't have to 'tut'. It was in his eye-roll.

It would be wrong to say that cops don't like kicking down doors: they do. Henry had grown to love it while on the Support Unit. The unit had quickly become specialists at entering properties, constantly practising and refining the art, and during his time on the unit Henry had been part of teams that had entered numerous houses, flats and business premises.

Sometimes a knock on the door was sufficient. People often just opened up and let the police in; sometimes, because of the nature of the warrant and especially when drugs or guns were involved, there had to be a direct quick entry. Drugs often ended up being flushed away; hence the cops covering the back today, their task to smash the soil pipe – the thick downward pipe that was the toilet outlet – and get a sieve under it. It could be a messy affair. Henry knew that drug dealers often left their shit in the toilet bowl in case they were raided, just so the sieve would end up full of it, as well as drugs.

That was the less sexy part of a house raid.

'Henry, you go with the guys doing the back, will you?' Ronson instructed him as the team climbed out of the carrier with their gear.

In spite of the possibility of actual shit being mixed with the drugs, there was also the chance that a suspect might do a runner.

Hiding his disappointment at not being able to go through the front door, Henry tagged along with the three cops tasked with the rear-end job, one of whom carried a sledgehammer and another a fishing net. They jogged down the back alley, crouching by the wall behind the target property, waiting for the 'Go'.

Which came via the PR about thirty seconds later as the team went to the front door.

Henry stood aside and let the 'shit collectors', as they were colourfully known, run up to the rear of the house to deal with the soil pipe, although they were slightly flummoxed to discover there was no such thing. As it was a basement flat, the soil pipe as such was inside the property – so no shit, no drugs, and no one did a runner.

They had to stand around and wait for the back door to open, revealing the face of Ronson who beckoned them inside.

'Two arrested, man and woman. Drugs and money by the bed, plus a knackered revolver, still capable of blowing your head off.'

'Nice one,' Henry congratulated him.

'Yep, good result.'

Henry followed Ronson into the flat which consisted of a kitchen and toilet at the rear, leading through to a bed-sitting room at the front, which was below the level of the road outside, accessed by steps. Two handcuffed prisoners, looking the worse for wear, were being led out by Support Unit officers, and Henry only glimpsed them.

The bed they had been caught on was nothing more than a very old, used, lifeless mattress laid directly on the floor, covered in a grubby sheet with stained pillows; it all reeked of weed, the stench of stale sex and cigarette smoke – the usual aroma of a type of property Henry was already familiar with.

'Scenes of crime are on their way,' Ronson said. He squatted down and carefully lifted the corner of the mattress so Henry could see underneath. The mattress was on floorboards and he could make out a hatch of some sort in the floor. 'I'm interested in what might be down here, Henry. Looks like a cellar, maybe,' Ronson said. 'You hang on here and wait for SOCO, then have a look down with a proper lighting rig.'

'You reckon there's a stash down there?'

Ronson shrugged and pointed to a set of shelves by the wall on which were a set of weighing scales and several Tupperware containers that looked to be packed with green foliage. 'Even if there isn't, there's enough here for a supplying charge. I'm going back to the nick to book the prisoners in. You stay here and manage the scene search, will you?'

'Sure.'

Ronson let the grimy mattress fall back into place, then stood up, gave Henry a wink and said, 'Welcome to the CID . . . we'll speak later.'

Searching property was a fairly logical process – ceilings, walls, floors, cupboards – and Henry ensured it was done in order and thoroughly when a scenes of crime officer arrived. They found a lot more than just what was in the Tupperware containers. Bagged-up cocaine, more cannabis, amphetamines and a lot of cash stashed around the flat – almost £10,000 in crumpled notes. He also found another gun – a sawn-off shotgun and ammunition – so this really was turning out to be a good arrest, and the couple, whoever they were, had an awful lot of awkward questions to answer.

When Henry was finally happy everything had been done, it was time to slide the mattress to one side and raise the hatch underneath, which was flush with the floor by means of a ring-pull imbedded in the surface of the hatch itself. Henry hooked his finger in and slowly began to raise the hatch which was about two and a half feet square.

It came easily, but even when it was only open a crack, the stench that poured out invaded his nostrils, made him rear back and cover his nose by cupping his free hand over it.

He knew the smell.

Rotting flesh.

He glanced up at the SOCO and the cluster of Support Unit officers who'd gathered to observe. They had all taken a few steps back at the smell and reacted in the same way as Henry by covering their faces and uttering various expletives.

This was a heightened version of the gases released when a pathologist sliced open a cadaver at the beginning of a post-mortem of a body that had been dead more than a couple of days. In his service as a uniformed patrol officer, Henry had attended numerous PMs and he knew the smell well.

He removed his hand from his face and continued to lift the hatch on its hinges, laying it back flat.

'Torch.'

Someone handed him a Maglite which he switched on and pointed down through the hatch into the cellar below. Henry guessed this was probably where coal had been delivered in the not-too-distant past – what he would have called the 'coal-hole'.

He crouched, leaned in slightly and flashed the strong beam into the space below, which was accessed by a metallic ladder affixed to the edge of the hatch.

At first there seemed to be nothing, just the horrendous smell of putrefied flesh which had lost some of its initial intensity now that the hatch had been open for a few seconds. It was as though it had wanted to escape, to be released from whatever horror it emanated from.

The torch beam criss-crossed the cellar.

Then stopped suddenly and retraced its arc slowly.

Henry's stomach tightened as he moved the beam back and saw what the horror was.

He didn't say anything even though 'Shit!' was on the tip of his tongue.

He glanced at the SOCO who, peering down, had also seen what the torch had illuminated.

'Start taking photos and video,' Henry told him, 'as I climb down the ladder and describe what I see when I get to the bottom, OK?'

The SOCO gulped, nodded, tried to manage his horror.

Henry decided to go down the ladder on his heels, facing into the cellar, treading carefully until he reached the bottom rung and stepped off. Above him, the SOCO filmed him with the unwieldy video camera.

Henry flashed the torch around the dark room.

He had already become immune to the stench and no longer needed to cover his nose. The smell was no longer important.

As a cop, he'd learned the ability to reset himself immediately after a shock. That's how it was. Otherwise, he knew he would be of little use to anyone requiring his help.

Time for reflection and introspection could come later.

Finally, he stopped with the torch and aimed the beam on to the two figures he had seen when he'd opened the hatch.

Two corpses now.

Young kids chained to the wall with manacles on their wrists and ankles. He thought maybe twelve, fourteen years old at most.

Both sitting on their backsides by the cellar wall, their arms chained high above them like prisoners in a medieval dungeon. Both were naked, and Henry could not be a hundred per cent sure if he was looking at a boy and a girl, or two boys, or two girls.

Their faces, necks, chests, stomachs and groin areas had been eaten away by rats, and all Henry could now see, closer up as he shone the torch, was a horrendous mass of squirming maggots devouring what remained of the flesh of these two kids. Even though he knew maggots in themselves were silent creatures, he could actually hear the collective noise of them, hear the disgusting squelch of them as they writhed en masse and intertwined with each other with a kind of slurping, water-slushing, saliva-swallowing kind of noise that belonged in a horror movie.

Instead, it was here . . . in a cellar in Blackpool South Shore.

Henry watched, transfixed.

'Are you OK, Henry?' the SOCO called down.

'I am,' Henry replied. 'Fine and dandy.'

The words suppressed the dreadfulness of what he was looking at and the cold rage that had already begun to fester inside his chest.

FIVE

Ronson shook his head.

'And you needn't look at me like that,' he said to Henry, whose expression was a gnarled mash of anger and frustration, even though he was trying to control himself and stop himself from exploding.

'I was first down that ladder. I was first to see those two kids. I want to get into the ribs of both those bastards in the cells. I want to have that chance,' he pleaded.

Ronson smirked.

Henry could already tell that he and the DS were unlikely to become a smoothly flowing crime fighting duo – just something in the air between them.

'Henry, it's your first day as a detective, for a start. And even I won't be interviewing these two . . . a couple of Murder Squad detectives are being brought in to run it, so us locals are pretty much out of the picture anyway. This is serious stuff and not something to get cocked up by a rookie jack baying for blood.'

Henry seethed. He knew he was seething, could feel himself seething because his jaw was clenched and the air hissed out of his dilating nostrils. Not only that but he felt his hands start to bunch into coiled fists, which even he knew wasn't a good sign. He needed to control this shit very badly – and he knew that, too.

'OK,' he conceded.

'I get it. I get you want to interview them.'

'It's not about getting something over someone else, Sarge, or getting to the front of the queue . . . it's about . . .' Henry struggled to find the words without sounding trite and pathetic, to say that he wanted to be there for those two dead kids, to fight for them and be part of giving them justice.

'Tell you what, go chill. I can see you're having a control issue here. Go and have a walk on the seafront, let the wind blow some sense into you and, more importantly, let it blow away the reek of death from your shiny new suit . . . yes, you smell like a mortuary.

Be back here in an hour and I'll give you your first job as a detect-ive on my team – some burglaries to look at.'

Henry was about to protest.

Ronson held up a hand. 'Do it.'

Henry backed off, knowing the DS was right: he was getting well and truly wound up.

He had spent several hours at the scene. That was taken away from him when two cocky detectives landed from headquarters, a DS and a DC, who declared they were the crime scene managers now and that Henry could piss off – the exact term used to dismiss him.

Back at the station, all access to the two prisoners was denied as more of the headquarters team were now circling, and Henry's demand that he be allowed into the investigation fell on deaf ears.

And he had to accept it. His time would come, he knew it, but that didn't stop his frustration.

He and Ronson had had their head-to-head in the CID office, so Henry retreated to the desk he had been allocated in the far corner. It was probably the oldest desk in the room, and even as he walked towards it, he could see it had a bit of a lean on it, and that it was stacked high with boxes and files that should have been in storage or the waste bin. The desk was pushed right back into the corner of the office and the chair that went with it had seen better days. Much better days. The location was also adjacent to the brewing table, stacked with unwashed pots on one side, and a toilet door on the other; it was not conducive to being able to concentrate on work.

Henry looked at it all and shook his head. Not that he was surprised, being the rookie, but the first day had not gone anywhere near as he'd envisaged. No generous welcome, no time to get his feet under the table, get to know a few of his colleagues and have his workload allocated.

Not that he had a problem helping out with a warrant, but it just didn't fit with his hopes and expectations.

He took a deep breath, spun on his heels and left the CID office, went along the corridor, dropped down a level to the custody office and entered.

Amazingly, there was a lull in activity and Henry managed to get straight up to the desk, behind which the custody sergeant was hunched over a binder containing all the records of everyone currently in the cells – fourteen men, one woman.

The sergeant looked up wearily, pulled his glasses from the top of his head and refitted them on the bridge of his nose. 'Help you?'

'Hi – DC Christie, just started this morning.'

'Congratulations,' the sergeant said, clearly not meaning it.

'I – uh – went on the warrant this morning . . . two people locked up, bloke and a woman . . . just wondered if I could see them?'

'See as in interview? That would be a no.'

'No . . . literally just see them. Look through the hatch at them. That's all.'

'For what reason?'

'Curiosity. Want to see what two people look like who have murdered two kids.'

'Morbid curiosity, I'd venture.'

'Maybe,' Henry conceded.

'Hmm.' The sergeant considered the request. 'OK. You'll have to go down the female cell corridor with the WPC who's been brought in to supervise the woman prisoner.'

'That's fine.'

'She's down there now.' The sergeant cocked his head. Henry nodded and went to the female section of the custody office which was completely separate from the male side.

The iron barred gate into it was slightly ajar. Henry pushed it open and stepped into the corridor. It was grim and unwelcoming, as he supposed cell corridors should be, and the atmosphere was a mix of the usual aroma of cells probably the world over, but with the addition of cheap perfume.

He walked towards the ninety-degree turn, hearing a low whispering voice somewhere ahead. He turned into the actual cell corridor and looked along to see a uniformed policewoman bending over at one of the cell doors with her fingertips wrapped over the bottom lip of the open inspection hatch and her face right up to the gap, saying something to the occupant, the only female in custody at that time.

Henry recognized her as the same WPC who had nursed him in the back alley after he'd been assaulted the year before, the one who had later visited him in hospital to see how he was progressing. He hadn't seen her since but remembered her name was Julie Clarke.

Henry watched her for a few moments, quite liking the profile of her slim body, even in uniform.

She had her mouth up to the hatch and he could see her chin moving as she spoke quietly to the occupant.

Henry walked towards her, trying to eavesdrop, interested in what was being said in such hushed tones. His hearing was pretty good, but the sound was muffled as her voice was projected into the cell.

He was about six feet from her by the time she realized he was approaching. She drew her face out of the open hatch and looked at him, startled.

'Hey, Henry Christie, what're you doing here?' As she turned, she slid the hatch up with her fingertips to close it, allowing the bolts to spring into place, ensuring it was locked. Her eyes took him in and widened. 'Gosh! You look smart.'

'First day CID.'

'Welcome to the madhouse.'

'Good to be here, even though it was a baptism of fire. Is that Cressida Leyland in there?'

'Certainly is. Why?'

'I was on the warrant this morning . . . not involved in how it's all panning out now, though.'

'Oh, God. Yeah, awful. What a bitch!'

'I just wanted to have a look at her. The custody sergeant said it would be OK if you were here.'

'Sure . . . just been talking to her . . . just had to change her cell because the one she was in originally had a duff toilet.'

'OK . . . mind if I . . .?' he asked. 'I only saw her back as they locked her up.'

Clarke stood aside and let Henry open the cell hatch to peer in.

Cressida Leyland was forty, thin, scraggy, and had a drug-addled look about her. She was now kitted out in a forensic suit, having had the clothes she was arrested in taken away from her following the discovery in the cellar underneath her bed. She had wiry, blue-tinted hair and the expression of a terrified animal, and when Henry shoved his face into the hatch, she drew back into the corner of her cell.

Henry simply looked at her long and hard, wondering what was in her mind.

Finally, he withdrew.

'Have you any idea what this is all about? I mean, dead kids – Christ alive,' Clarke said. 'What sick mind . . .?'

'Yeah, absolutely. Anyway, I've seen her . . . and now I'm going to have a look at her partner.'

'Husband, you mean?'

'Terry Leyland, is it? I just want to see his face, look into his eyes. I'd like to punch him out, obviously; do him harm.'

They were ambling back down the corridor towards the custody office.

'But you might get blood on your nice new suit,' she said.

'After this morning, it already needs a dry clean. Reeks of death.'

Clarke stopped and turned to face Henry, taking hold of his jacket lapel and bringing him towards her. She tilted down a little and sniffed at the material. Then from that angle she looked up at Henry who was watching her, enthralled and perplexed at the same time.

'All I smell is you,' she said.

Henry's mouth went dry as he looked down into her eyes, which looked up at him from an angle that made them appear bigger and rounder and more seductive than they probably really were.

'Well, that's a good thing,' he croaked.

'Yes, it is.'

With a wicked grin, Clarke released the lapel and pushed him playfully away from her, and, with a strange, unsettling undertone, said, 'Men! So easy.' She gave him a wink, then set off ahead of him.

The custody sergeant allowed him to go down the male cell corridor along with a stern warning not to say even one word to the prisoner. He went to cell number ten, dropped the hatch, looked in.

Terry Leyland was very much the mirror image of Cressida, his wife. He was scrawny, untidy, unshaven and had a scraggy neck. He too was in a forensic suit and was sitting on the bed, backed up tight into the corner of the cell. He raised his eyes and stared sullenly at Henry.

In spite of the sergeant's warning, Henry said, 'Just wanted to look into your face.'

'Well, now you can fuck off.' Leyland's voice was as harsh as his appearance. He laid himself out on the reinforced plastic mattress, clasped his fingers behind his head and stared at the ceiling of his cell.

Henry didn't trust himself not to say anything out of order. He slammed the hatch shut and stalked away.

He took Ronson's advice and went to let the seafront breeze blow some of the cobwebs – and the smell of death – away. He walked from the police station to the promenade. The afternoon had turned chilly and his suit wasn't really the right clothing to protect him from the icy wind now coming in from the Irish Sea. He walked with his hands thrust deep into his pockets and meandered to the sea wall, leaning against the railings with his lower belly, looking out across the white-topped grey sea which was coming in.

He had calmed down, which was one thing, and he wasn't sure what he'd achieved by going in to look at the two prisoners. Perhaps it was just to gloat, to sneer, knowing that, all being well, neither would ever set foot outside a prison cell again. He visualized once more the sight that had greeted him in the cellar, then skipped to his minor skirmish with Ronson when he'd tried abysmally to explain his desire to be part of the investigation into the double murder.

Leaning on the railings, he attempted to iron out that concept in his mind.

Suddenly, he knew what it was: having seen those dead children, he knew what was driving his desire to become a detective.

The search for truth. And maybe justice, though he doubted his ability to achieve that every time.

He wanted to be the one who did that for the victims, any victim, even if it was 'only' victims of burglary.

Yet, as he stood there with his face in the wind, he knew he had a lot to learn. This was his first day as a detective. He had skills to acquire, knowledge to apply and attitude and behaviour to sharpen. Some of that would come with the residential detective course he was due to undertake, but mostly it would be learned by dealing effectively with the bread and butter of being a detective on the ground.

Be the steady detective who came on duty and dealt with overnight prisoners in the cells; the one who attended the day-to-day sordid crimes that had significant effect on the victims, even if they were low-level offences. He needed to catch those burglars and thieves who stole cars, and scummy robbers who picked on the vulnerable in the streets. And even if he couldn't realistically catch every villain, he had to be the detective who listened to and reassured and fought for the victims of crime, no matter how small and inconsequential the crime might be.

Then, when he'd learned his trade, when he'd experienced different avenues of detective work – maybe getting on the Regional Crime Squad, which he quite fancied – he knew that ultimately he wanted to be a Murder Squad detective.

That, to him, was the ultimate role.

He knew it wouldn't be an easy route. He knew that life would chuck up obstacles and he would have to work hard to achieve that aim.

But that day, standing on Blackpool promenade, he determined he would take the first baby steps towards it. That was his vague plan as he turned away from the sea and walked inland into the resort centre because he needed a coffee.

He didn't quite get one.

It was a nice coffee shop, an old established business which had yet to embrace the creeping culture of the cappuccino and latte, but still served hot, frothy, milky coffee that was a delight. Henry ordered a large one and took it to a seat close to the window so he could watch life tootle by. Which it was doing by the bucketload in Blackpool.

He had taken a couple of sips of the coffee, leaving a foamy moustache on top of his real one, when he noticed a woman who seemed to be a homeless tramp walking down the street, deliberately stepping in front of people, stopping them while she showed them something about the size of a postcard. Henry assumed it was one of those *Help me I'm homeless/penniless* kind of cards, begging for money, which tended to infuriate people when such things were shoved under their noses.

This woman was annoying almost everyone – and that included Henry who watched with growing irritation as she moved herself into the path of yet another shopper and stuck the card into the woman's face.

Henry took a quick sip of his coffee, rose from his seat, calling to the lady behind the counter and pointing to his drink. 'I'll be back for this.'

He left the café and went directly to the woman who was brandishing the card at another unsuspecting victim. Henry fished out his warrant card and he got to her as the latest shopper sidestepped the tramp.

From behind, Henry said, 'Excuse me.'

The woman's shoulders slumped; she turned.

From a distance, Henry thought she looked oddly familiar, and when he saw her close up, he recognized her immediately. Although she was dressed in rags and had let herself go, she was not a tramp, nor was she homeless.

'I come into town every day,' Trish Benemy said to Henry. 'Every single day. To do this because I don't know what else to do.'

She and the tyro detective were back in the café in which Henry had left his milky coffee. He'd bought an additional one for her and they were now sitting at a table at the back, Henry ignoring the snooty looks of the owner who had baulked at Henry bringing an apparently homeless person in. There was no doubt that beggars and the homeless were a problem on the streets and many places wouldn't tolerate them, but Henry had flashed his warrant card and the owner backed down, grumbling.

Trish slid the crumpled card across the table to Henry. It was face down. Henry slowly turned it over.

It wasn't a plea for money or food.

It was just a photograph.

Of her son. Thomas James Benemy.

'He's never, ever, ever come back home,' Trish said.

'You've never heard from him?'

'Not a peep – which is why I think he's dead.'

If Henry was honest with himself, he hadn't really given much thought to Tommy Benemy over the last year, ever since he'd visited the house when he'd been expecting the lad to answer bail, only to be told he had gone missing from home. He'd treated the news from Trish with a large dose of salt. Maybe Tommy had done a runner from justice, which wasn't quite the same as going missing from home. Henry had scoffed at Trish and demanded to be allowed to search the house, which he did and found nothing.

Tommy certainly wasn't there at that time.

Henry had been pretty annoyed and left the house in a huff,

telling Trish to report him officially missing if he wasn't back home
in a few days.

From that point on, as frustrating as it was for Henry, he didn't
get the satisfaction of dealing with Tommy and putting him before
a court and identifying the other people involved in the assault. The
nature of his work with the Support Unit did not really give him
the chance to spend much time trying to track Tommy down. Henry
was all over the county, having huge amounts of fun, and only
checked in occasionally at Blackpool to look at the missing-from-
home (MFH) report that Trish made.

The report was kept in the sergeants' office on a pro-forma with
additional forms attached on which all further enquiries were logged
in longhand.

It seemed clear that after the initial flurry of activity by the local
officers, Tommy's file wasn't revisited very often and not a lot was
being done to trace him. Occasionally, a patrol sergeant would
allocate a PC to go and visit Trish, but that was about as far as it
went.

Kids went missing in Blackpool. Most turned up, but some never
did – and after a year it looked like Tommy was on the latter list.

Henry frowned at Trish.

'Are you seriously telling me that Tommy never contacted you?'

'Never.'

He looked at Tommy's crumpled photo, one of those school ones
with him wearing a shirt and tie and a blazer, hair neatly trimmed,
looking smart, smiling.

'That was last year,' Trish said. 'Didn't spend much time in
school after that.'

'Where do you think he is?'

'I don't know, but every day I come into town and show people
this picture. Someone must have seen him. Someone must know
where he is.' She was starting to get distraught. 'He couldn't have
just vanished into thin air. That's why I think he got in with the
wrong people. I think he's . . .'

She didn't complete the sentence. Henry watched her face
wracked by emotion and he was touched by this brash, harsh woman
who was the product of a tough environment, had brought up a kid
by herself, tried hard and possessed true love for the lad.

'So here I am. Every single frickin' day,' she said simply.

Henry nodded thoughtfully and let it all run through his mind. A thirteen-year-old boy missing from home for a year or more? Unusual and extremely worrying, but not unheard of. If he was still in town, Blackpool was a great place to lie low in the shadows of the underworld. It was crowded with other kids, holidaymakers and an itinerant population surging through year on year. So many possibilities, most of them unpleasant, and the most unpleasant prospect of all, the one Trish feared the most, that Tommy was dead.

'So you're a detective now, are you?' she asked Henry, appraising him.

'First day.'

'And you're finding time to have a brew?'

'Long story, Trish.' He encircled the coffee mug with his hands and leaned towards her slightly and picked up a reek of body odour – even over the whiff he could still smell coming from himself – which meant she really did need a shower. 'You still at the same address?'

'Till I get booted, yeah. Not paid rent for a while.'

'Look – go home, OK? I can't tell you how to live your life and certainly can't tell you how you should deal with Tommy being missing for this length of time – must be very tough, must eat you up. But go home and let me have a look at his file, let me do some digging, and I'll get back to you in a few days. I promise, now that I'm here full time, I'll keep him on my radar – not least because I want to arrest him myself for what he did to me.'

'You promise? I haven't heard from the cops in six months.'

'I promise.'

Henry had brought his PR along with him, slotted loosely into his inside jacket pocket with the volume turned down, but now, as he was conditioned to do so, he still kept an ear to what was going on, which is how he heard the urgent transmission from comms: 'Patrols town centre, report of a building on fire in Abingdon Street off Talbot Road, exact address not known but fire brigade in attendance . . . repeat, building on fire, Abingdon Street.'

Henry took the radio out and transmitted, 'PC . . . er, sorry, DC Christie to Blackpool. I'm on foot just near the Winter Gardens . . . am I close by?'

'If you stand at the Winter Gardens front entrance and look north, you're looking along Abingdon Street. You might see the smoke from there.'

'I'll make my way.'

'Roger that.'

Henry heard other patrols responding, including WPC Clarke who was also on foot in the town.

'Look, got to go, Trish. Go home, pamper yourself if you can and leave Tommy to me for a few days, OK?'

She nodded.

Henry gave her a couple of pounds and left her in the café to make his way along Abingdon Street. He could see smoke rising and, in the distance, he heard the mixed sound of police and fire engine sirens getting nearer and nearer.

SIX

The flames ripped up the front of the house, whooshing out of the front window, and as Henry ran up the street, he could feel heat pulsating towards and over him, even though the house was at least another hundred yards ahead.

The fire brigade had arrived – two tenders – and as Henry jogged towards the scene, his Support Unit colleagues had also arrived. Some immediately began to feed cordon tape across the road to keep the quickly growing crowd of onlookers back; others rushed to nearby houses to try to evacuate them.

Henry pretty much had to let it happen, just stand back and watch proceedings.

The firemen – they were all blokes – arrived kitted up and within moments were dousing the flames with forceful jets of water from two hoses.

Two local mobile patrols were also on the scene, plus the patrol sergeant. Henry sidled up to him. He knew the sergeant, not well, but was aware he'd been in Blackpool for most of his service.

They stood and watched the fire brigade try to extinguish the fire, but it had taken hold with ferocity and the flames now licked out of the front window of the middle floor of the three-storey house.

Henry nodded and said, 'Hi, Sarge,' to the PS.

'Ahh, DC Christie – new kid on the block.'

'New but already slightly tarnished.'

'Hmm – quite a find this morning,' the sergeant said.

'You could say that,' Henry agreed. 'You know anything about this house – occupants, et cetera?'

The sergeant shook his head, making his jowls wobble. 'Derelict, I think. Was a DSS doss house, but I think it was in the process of being done up as flats – the ground floor was boarded up, but it could easily have been a haunt for the homeless crowd to bed down in.'

'Anyone likely to be inside now?' Henry asked.

The sergeant shrugged. 'Not sure, but I bloody hope not.'

Despite the best efforts of the fire brigade, a new set of flames whooshed out of a top-floor window, confirming the whole building was ablaze. The heat was incredible, like standing in front of an open furnace door.

Mesmerized, Henry watched for a while before turning to the sergeant and saying, 'Leave it with you.'

'No probs,' the sergeant said.

Henry began the walk back to the station just as he was called up on his PR. It was FB. 'DCI to DC Christie, receiving?'

'Go ahead, boss,' Henry replied, knowing he was pushing the 'boss' aspect of their relationship maybe too much.

'Get back in here now – my office,' FB said tersely, straight to the point, adding, 'and it's "sir", not "boss".'

And with those words, Henry guessed he was in the mire.

Henry knocked a bit timidly at FB's office door.

He had put a spurt on to get back to the police station from the fire and now was sweating heavily in his nice new shirt under his nice new suit, agonizing over what FB could want from him; maybe he was always so offhand on the radio. That would not have surprised Henry based on his experiences of the guy so far.

'Enter.'

Henry opened the door and stepped into FB's domain.

The DCI was at his desk with his head in his hands, bringing his face up slowly and dragging his loose features with his fingertips.

'Boss?' Henry said.

FB considered him, jaw rotating and teeth grating. 'Where have you been?'

'Just on the town . . . been to that house fire.'

FB nodded. 'Before that?'

'Here – in the nick.'

'What did you do in the nick?'

'Boss? What are you getting at?'

'I want to know *exactly* what you did in the nick.'

Henry was still frowning, confused. 'What do you mean?'

FB rose slowly from the chair, which creaked with relief. 'It's a simple enough question, isn't it?'

'Yes, but—'

'Tell me. Exactly. What. You. *Fucking*. Did!'

Henry wracked his brains. 'Er . . . got back from the search warrant job and, uh . . .' Henry began, finding this quite hard, feeling some unaccountable pressure without knowing why.

'And "uh" what?'

'Spoke to DS Ronson who told me I wouldn't be taking any part in the investigation, who then told me to go and chill out.'

'So – you were angry? At finding those kids?'

'Yeah, suppose so . . . boss, what is this?'

FB tilted his face. 'I think we can definitely return to the "sir" situation, don't you?'

Nonplussed, Henry said, 'Sure, sir.'

'OK – what did you do between speaking to DS Ronson and going out for this "chill", as you call it? Something, I might add, no one else around here seems to have time to do.'

'I went to look in on the two prisoners, Terry and Cressida Leyland.'

FB's already broad nostrils flared. 'What did you say to them?'

'Why?'

'Answer the question.'

'Nothing to Cressida. I told Terry I wanted to see his face. He told me to fuck off. That was it.'

'Anything else?'

Henry shook his head.

'You sure? What did you give them?'

Henry shrugged. 'Like what?'

'Let me take this back a step,' FB said, making an anticlockwise circle with his finger to indicate what he was saying.

'Hang on, sir – take what back?'

'How much did you hate those two prisoners?'

'Hate? I didn't hate them.'

'I think you might have done,' FB insisted.

'Right, sir,' Henry said firmly, 'I don't know what's going on here, so perhaps you should be upfront with me and then we can take it from there, because just at this moment, I feel like you're trying to trick me into saying something to suit your agenda, though I have no idea what that agenda is.'

FB's face, from being flaccid, suddenly went rigid. 'You'll answer my questions, sonny.' His voice was nasty, authoritarian.

Henry remained silent, but inside everything was tightening up, with the exception of his heart which was expanding, ready to split open with every beat.

FB finally, dramatically, revealed all. 'Those two prisoners are now both dead. The woman slit her wrists with half a razor blade and bled out in about a minute. The man hanged himself from the cell door hatch with a length of garden twine.'

Henry was dumbfounded. 'What? You think I gave them string and a razor blade so they'd kill themselves?'

'Did you?' FB's face was uncompromising.

'No!'

'They came into this nick and they were searched thoroughly. Their clothing was removed and replaced with forensic suits and slip-on shoes. There was no way they could have taken anything into a cell with which they could have committed suicide.'

'So I gave him a length of garden twine, and her a razor blade? Not being funny, but either of those items could already have been in the cell before they landed.'

'Both cells were searched before the prisoners were put in them.'

'In that case, they had the items secreted on their persons.'

'Nah – they were searched.'

'Underpants, knickers removed? Bra? Arse cracks, vagina, mouth cavities?' Henry said. He had searched enough people to know that concealing objects, drugs, money and almost anything else they might use to self-harm or as a weapon to harm others was an art in the criminal community. Only the most diligent and sometimes intimate searching could find such things . . . so unless an intimate search was ordered, which was not a common occurrence, items could easily be hidden.

'You were the only non-custody person to visit them both,' FB said.

'And I gave them the tools to kill themselves?' Henry said cynically. 'Course I did. I wanted to see both of them dead for what they did to those kids.'

'I fucking knew it!' FB said triumphantly.

'Duh – no, I didn't.' Henry put him right. 'This is fucking preposterous. I'll tell you what I wanted for those two child killers – for them to go through the justice system, to face evidence that would put them away for life; not to let them kill themselves, because that's too good for them.'

He and FB stared hard at each other.

Henry could see a pulse thumping wildly at each of FB's temples. Then FB relented. 'I had to ask, put you under pressure.'

Although relief flooded through him, Henry was still wary and did not like FB's bull-in-a-china-shop approach one bit.

He said simply, 'No, you didn't. You just had to ask me a straightforward question which I would have responded to in a straightforward, honest way. Instead, you bashed me around the head.'

FB shrugged. 'We do things my way around here.'

'My way or the highway?'

'Very definitely.'

There were more tense, stand-off moments between them then. Finally, Henry nodded, then said, 'I get that. So what happened?'

'They killed themselves between cell visits. He strung himself up to the hatch and she slit her wrists.' FB held out his left arm and turned it out so the forearm was uppermost. 'But not just slashing across the wrists, oh no.' He demonstrated by slicing the soft edge of his right hand across his wrist in a sawing motion. 'She went for the professional approach.'

Even before FB's demonstration of that, Henry knew what he meant.

Suicide attempts by wrist-slashing were not always successful and were more often than not just cries for help anyway.

However, someone serious about taking their own life would slash upwards, cut deep into the wrist and follow the line of the veins up the arm, like slicing a sandwich baguette; even if they were discovered quickly, the damage done was so severe that quickly applied first aid might not be enough to save life.

That was the professional approach.

'They were on fifteen-minute visits,' FB said, 'and both timed it just right so by the time they were visited again, she'd bled out and he'd strung himself up and garrotted himself.'

'Shit,' Henry said.

'Indeed. Two deaths in police custody – not a good look. Independent Police Complaints Committee already on the case.' FB was trembling, very annoyed. 'Anyway, anything in that fire?'

'Just a derelict house. Hopefully, no one was inside.'

'OK – dismissed.'

And that was it. He waved Henry away with a contemptuous flick of the fingers.

Henry backed out of the office, sidestepped and went up to the top floor of the building to the canteen where he grabbed himself another coffee to take down to the CID office in lieu of the one he'd left behind in the café in town: another thing he had promised himself was that his time on CID would never, ever be short of coffee. He decided it was time to do a bit of nest-building at his new-old desk in the grotty corner of the office.

There was a short queue at the counter, which gave Henry a little time to glance around and see WPC Clarke sitting in one corner, huddled over a mug of something, staring dejectedly down into the liquid.

Henry bought his coffee and wandered over to her. She didn't look up or even seem to notice him.

'Join you?' he asked. She seemed deep in thought, and Henry could take a stab at why.

She raised her head as if she had not properly heard him, then recognized him. 'Henry! Yeah, yeah.'

He slid into the chair opposite and looked at her.

She was pale and shaken.

She explained: 'Just trying to get my head around what happened in the cells,' she began, Henry guessing that she assumed he knew what she was talking about. 'I just . . . can't believe it. On my watch, too.' She sucked in a deep breath. 'I'd just come back from my refs . . . God, so much blood – it felt like I was wading through it to get to her. She was on the bed, her arm dangling down and' – here she closed her eyes tightly, reliving the dreadful scene – 'she'd just cut herself open so badly it had cascaded out of her.'

'Hey,' Henry reached across and touched her arm. 'You're not to blame.'

'I will get blamed, though. Not a thorough enough search, they'll say – even though it was, as far as I could do.'

'If you know you did a good job, it'll work out fine. Hindsight is what us cops always get battered with . . . I've more or less been accused of giving them both the tools do themselves in.'

'Really?' She looked Henry in the eye, appalled.

'FB launched into me – all bollocks, obviously.'

'But you did go and see both of them, didn't you?'

'Uh, yeah – don't you start – but I didn't give them anything. They sneaked the twine in and the razor in – those people have stuff like that on them all the time . . . they bloody practise hiding it just in case they get nicked.'

'Yeah, suppose so. God – weird.'

'Anyway, I'm sure you'll have nothing to worry about, Julie.'

'Thanks.'

'Hey, I bumped into Tommy Benemy's mother in town.'

Clarke frowned.

'The lad I chased after he'd nicked all that perfume.'

'Ahh, one of the ones who assaulted you?'

'One and the same.'

'He went missing, didn't he?'

'And never turned up, case never solved . . . one I'll have to put down to experience,' Henry said philosophically. 'His mum was in town showing pictures of Tommy to people, stopping them in the street.'

'For real?'

Henry nodded.

'So you reckon she wasn't just covering for him?'

'If she was – is – then she's taken it a bit too far. No, I'm sure he's genuinely gone missing, gone off the grid, which is more than a tad worrying for a thirteen-year-old. I told her I'd look into it, keep checking.'

He was about to say something more when comms called him over the air: 'DC Christie – can you make back to the house fire, please?'

'Affirmative – but for what reason?' Even as he asked the question, he realized it was a bit of a daft one. It meant the fire was not accidental, that it was arson maybe or perhaps a body had been found, and in both cases he would be required to attend.

'Where are you now?' the operator asked him.

'Station – canteen.'

'I'll ring you.'

The fact that the operator didn't want to say anything over the air was another clue.

The internal phone on a table in the far corner of the canteen rang almost immediately.

Henry gave Clarke a thin smile – the weary look of someone who was always busy – pushed himself up and went to pick it up.

* * *

Henry leaned back against the wall of the public mortuary with his arms folded across his chest, wondering if his new suit would actually have to be binned when he finally got home sometime later that evening – the right side of midnight, he hoped.

So far the lovely material had been permeated with the aroma of two dead children (whose bodies were now lying in a chiller in an adjoining examination suite), the reek of smoke from the house that had burned down and the smell of charred human flesh from the body that, once the flames that had consumed the house had been extinguished, had been discovered in a ground-floor room.

Now the material was about to be assailed by a further stench of death as the Home Office pathologist got to work on that particular body to perform a post-mortem.

Henry knew it would stink.

Death did.

At that moment – eight fifty-seven p.m. according to the large clock on the wall above the door – the body on the slab was being circled by the pathologist, a spindly young man with very large ears (like the FA Cup, Henry thought), who seemed to be stalking the unmoving body as he made his verbal observations first, watched by Henry, WPC Clarke and a mesmerized mortuary assistant who had obviously not seen a pathologist move in such a manner before.

The pathologist was called Professor Baines and he didn't seem much older than Henry. The two men had never met formally.

The body on the slab was that of a male, about five feet eight inches tall, medium build. He had been severely burned and reminded Henry of someone putting up their mitts for a fight.

'What's all that about?' Henry had asked Baines, pointing to the dead man's arms.

'Ah,' the young professor answered, 'the pugilistic attitude.'

'What – as in boxer?'

'One of the characteristic features of bodies exposed to intense heat.' Baines continued to loop the slab, his thin arms and legs bringing to mind a praying mantis. 'It's called heat stiffening. Arms extended from the shoulders and the forearms partially flexed. And yes, like a boxer. Legs, as you can see, also flexed. Doesn't happen every time – there are no fixed rules – but it is common. It's the coagulation of the muscles on the flex or surface of the limbs.' He finished his explanation with a smile.

'Oh, right, thanks,' Henry said as if he was expected to understand such terms.

Baines said, 'A bit like pulling a longbow.'

'Indeed,' Henry said, now slightly understanding.

'But, obviously in this case, I would suggest the vital question that needs to be answered is whether this poor soul was alive or dead when the fire started. Blood samples will help: do they contain traces of carbon monoxide or not?'

'Meaning?'

Baines turned to Henry. 'Meaning that if carbon monoxide is present, the victim was breathing *after* the fire started.'

'Ah.'

'Also, the presence of particles of soot in the lungs and air passages is a similar, supporting indicator. There are other ways to tell if burn injuries were suffered before or after death,' Baines babbled on, engrossed in his puzzle, 'but I won't even try to explain that to you, officer, uh, DC . . .?'

'Christie.'

'DC Christie . . . except to say that burns received after death will show no signs of vital reactions. Anyway, let's take a closer look.' The pathologist stopped suddenly, walked over to Henry and said, 'My name is Baines, by the way. Very pleased to meet you. This is my first solo post-mortem, incidentally. I'm quite new to this game.'

After a very detailed examination – including directing a scenes of crime officer to take photographs and record the progress of the PM on video – Baines meticulously plotted everything on pro-forma diagrams of the human body and then, speaking out loud into a microphone hanging above the body, he began the dissection.

Henry had once overcooked a chicken in the early days of his marriage to Kate – trying to impress her with his culinary prowess – and it had come out of the oven black and smoking, almost in flames, and try as he might not to think it, the body of this unfortunate man on the slab reminded him of that particular Sunday roast.

In that instance, Henry had chucked the bird away and he and Kate gone out for lunch instead.

Today's roast would be minutely examined.

This was the first time he had attended the PM of someone who had died in such a manner. He'd been to countless others, and if he was honest, this one, so far, was up there with the worst.

However, he expected the cause of death would be smoke inhalation in this case and that it would become just a job for the uniform branch to sort out and report – hence the presence of WPC Clarke who had been deployed to it for such an eventuality.

He guessed this could well be a homeless guy who'd hunkered down in a dilapidated building, maybe tried to light a fire for warmth, fallen asleep, maybe drunk, and the fire had got out of hand before he'd even woken up.

Sad, but these things happened.

He glanced at Clarke. She seemed fixated, staring at the scene being enacted in front of her eyes, mesmerized with horror.

'You don't have to stay,' Henry said quietly.

She spun ferociously to him. 'Because I'm a girly?'

He was taken aback and his face must have registered horror. 'No,' he backed off, 'because you don't have to.'

'I'll be fine,' she said dryly and turned back to watch the proceedings which began as Baines, assisted by the mortuary attendant, began the slow task of peeling away the clothing worn by the victim. Some sections were easier to remove than others; in particular, the dead man's shirt was problematic.

'Nylon,' Baines said to Henry. 'It's just melted on him.'

Finally, he was ready to do some cutting.

It began with Baines selecting a dissecting knife from his range of shiny instruments, which reminded Henry of a very neat cutlery drawer. His bony fingers had fluttered over the array of cutting instruments which included a brain knife, scissors, saws – including an electric saw with oscillating safety blades – a skull key, scalpels, forceps and chisels. Baines's fingers quivered like a classical pianist about to slam his fingers down on to the ivories, although in this case he picked up the knife and moved across to the body, making an incision down the centre of the torso from neck to pubes, veering around the navel. The pathologist's concerto.

While he did this, the mortuary assistant, under Baines's direction, used a scalpel to trace a cut around the dead man's probable hairline, then carefully peeled the scalp forwards with his fingertips, rolling it over the facial features to expose the skull underneath which was cream-coloured and unaffected by the fire.

Meanwhile, Baines had gently eased the body cavity open to reveal the ribcage and internal organs.

At that point, Clarke fainted.

Two hours later, Henry was standing outside the mortuary at the rear of Blackpool Victoria Hospital. He was with Baines, who was leaning nonchalantly against his dinky little sports car, a British racing green Triumph Spitfire, smoking a large cigar.

'A rain of blows to the skull,' Baines reiterated, just so Henry could take it in again; and just to make sure Henry was also scribbling it all down in his pocket notebook. 'Bludgeoning, and from the indentation of the impact, the shape of the wounds on the skull itself, a sustained attack – initially from behind, I would say, with a weapon similar to a baseball bat, perhaps.'

Henry nodded, wrote feverishly, hoping he'd be able to read his own scrawl later, even though he knew Baines would fax in a copy of his typed report in detail.

'Skull very badly fractured with many splinters of bone embedded in the brain itself, as I showed you.' He puffed on his cigar.

Indeed, Henry had seen this.

But that had been after Baines had done his work on the bodily organs. After removing the lattice that was the sternum and ribs, he had removed the heart and lungs, transferring them to the dissecting table. He had lifted the lungs up like an old cardigan and then laid them out neatly before slicing into them. At that point, Henry had given up any hope of keeping the smell out of the fabric of his suit and had gone to watch the procedure closely, with Baines happy to explain what he was doing and seeing and how he drew his conclusions.

Clarke, in the meantime, sat out in the corridor with her head in her hands.

The lungs had shown cancerous growths in the bottom sections of both, but, more importantly, there was no evidence of the man having inhaled smoke from the fire.

Then there was the brain to examine after the skull cap had been removed, but before Baines did this, he pointed out the damage done to the bone by a weapon.

Once the skull cap had been removed, Baines inspected the brain closely in situ. Henry joined him and it was clear to see how much damage had been done to the grey matter. Baines then removed the brain and carried it over to the dissecting table as if carrying a pet rabbit, then dissected it methodically.

'So the fundamental questions to be asked,' Baines said, pausing as he mulled things over. 'No, actually, I'll jump to the answers. Number one: the injuries to the brain were not caused by the fire; number two: the injuries we saw were caused before the fire; three: these injuries to the brain were the cause of death. Five: they are homicidal injuries.' He took a few more puffs of his cigar and exhaled the smoke. 'Clearly, the blood will have to be tested for carbon monoxide, but even now I know the result – negative.'

Henry, with his pen poised eagerly over his notebook like a keen journalist about to get a scoop, said, 'Which means?'

Baines threw down the stub of his cigar and crushed it underfoot. 'It means, DC Christie, that you have a murder on your hands and somewhere out there' – he waved a hand towards Blackpool – 'is a very brutal killer.' And with that, he gave Henry a smile, clambered into his soft-topped car like a stick insect negotiating a branch, fired it up and skidded away while Henry checked his notes and wondered what had happened to answer number four.

SEVEN

'Fuck me! The direct entrants are getting older and older!'
Henry Christie's mouth sagged open with a popping sound
as he came to a hesitant stop on the threshold of the office
in which he would be working for the foreseeable future. He had
been about to knock on the open door and announce his arrival –
his first day at work – but before he could speak, the woman in the
chair closest to the door, who must have either heard him coming
or sensed his presence, had spun around and delivered the dispar-
aging one-liner, taking Henry aback.

'I take it you are the new guy, yeah?' she asked.

Henry paused in order to regather his senses and checked the
laminated sign Blu-Tacked to the door which, in varying sizes and
colours of fonts read, *Lancashire Constabulary Cold Case Unit.*
Above that sign was a National Health Service rainbow poster, with
the words *Save Our NHS* written below. It looked like a kid had
done it.

Henry said, 'I assume so . . .'

She spun back to her desk, tilted forward and sprang to her feet,
gathering up a file as she did. 'Been waiting for you to land. Got
a job on. Where've you been?'

'Er . . . with the detective chief super.'

'Oh, Ricky boy.'

'Mr Dean, yes.'

'That's what I said, Ricky boy . . . fancies himself sooo much,'
she said and took two strides across the room, grabbed a faded
denim jacket from a hook on the wall, then two more strides across
to Henry, pushed the file into his chest, making him take hold, while
she inserted her arms into the jacket which, to Henry's conservative
mind, looked slightly incongruous over the extremely short skirt,
flowery blouse and silk scarf she was wearing around her neck,
though it did align nicely with her tanned bare legs, Doc Marten

ankle boots and close-cropped hair with a purple flash across her right temple that reminded him of a David Bowie album cover.

She shouldered her way past him – which is when he noticed she was just as tall as he was – and said, 'C'mon, then, been bloody waiting for you just in case I need a bit of macho back-up.'

On those last words, she stopped abruptly and gave Henry a quick, derisive yet amused once-over with very, very blue eyes and a crooked half-smile playing on her lips as she surveyed him. She uttered a snort of a laugh and said, 'Yeah, right.'

Then she was past him, heading down the corridor, leaving him abandoned.

The office he was looking into had four desks in it and a man sitting at one of them. He was wearing a face mask. He looked at Henry, who couldn't discern his expression, but the guy shrugged, then returned to the typing he was engaged in at a desktop computer which, Henry noticed, was about the size and depth of an old TV. This observation gave Henry the clue that this was a slightly forgotten corner of the constabulary.

He wheeled around and followed in the slipstream of the woman who had not slowed down and was already exiting through the door at the end of the corridor.

Henry upped his pace and managed to contort through the pneumatically closing door before it shut – but she was already outside the building and striding headlong through the landscaped grounds towards the large car park used by the Constabulary Training Centre at Hutton Hall, situated several miles south of Preston.

The building he'd just entered and exited was a former student accommodation block that had been converted into offices many years before to house the Force Major Investigation Team (FMIT) initially and now the more recently formed Cold Case Unit (CCU) which had a ground-floor office in one corner.

Henry gave chase and tried to catch up with the woman without losing too much of his dignity and trying not to wheeze.

'I park across here so I can walk through the trees,' she explained for no reason. 'Then I can see squirrels, rabbits and birds. Did you know that the rabbits here once had myxomatosis?'

'Really?'

'Oh, yeah – gunked-up eyes . . . yuk! Horrible sight.' She shuddered as she walked along.

Henry did know – it was a disease that came and went. He'd seen a lot of dead or suffering rabbits in his time on FMIT.

'I'm not a direct entrant, by the way.'

'I know that – it was a joke. Well, the direct entrant bit was because, to be fair, you do look a bit long in the tooth.'

'That would be because of my age.'

She grinned at that one, but then asked, 'How much are you on?'

'What d'you mean?'

'Daily rate . . . y'know? Dosh.'

'That's between me and my maker,' Henry responded. He was startled at her rudeness, but not really bothered because he had already decided in the two or three minutes he'd known this woman that he would be giving as good as he got, even if technically she was his boss.

She gave him a sly look as they reached the tarmac of the car park and took a diagonal route which ended up with her pointing a remote lock at an old Mini Cooper with a Union Jack painted on the roof but also a Ban the Bomb logo on the bonnet.

Henry saw his chance for a dig and said, 'And I thought we'd be going out in a 2CV.'

She stopped abruptly. Henry carried on a couple more steps and almost collided with her.

'Stereotyping or being cheeky?' she pondered.

'Holding my own.'

She surveyed him critically once more. 'Riiight,' she said, drawing out the word, then nodding her head. 'I admire that, but don't get me wrong. In that office, I'm the boss and I'm the only one allowed to overstep the mark because I'm female and I will always use the sexist card.'

'Fair enough. Mine's the ageist card.' Henry smirked. 'You get that when you're over sixty.'

'Sixty? Jeez – I put you more round the seventy-two mark.'

She sidestepped past him, went to her car and got in behind the wheel, saying, 'Get in,' as she did.

Henry shook his head in disbelief, bit his bottom lip, found his face mask in his pocket, put it on and, wondering why he was bothering at all, got into the opposite side, dropping into a sporty bucket seat which felt just a bit too body-hugging for his girth, by which time the engine was revving.

After a few ferocious revs, the woman turned to Henry – she was now wearing a pink face mask and her voice was slightly muffled.

'I'd offer to shake your hand, but as I don't know where you've been and you're not in my bubble, I'd just like to say I'm pleased to meet you. My friends call me Debs, my enemies call me "deadly" and there is no in-between. And I'm your DS, so get used to it.'

'Gotcha.'

'I know exactly who you are, what you were, what you are now,' she said. 'One thing I've learned in life, and it was a harsh lesson, is to prepare, get to know your adversaries and, well, you'll probably find out other shit in due course.'

'And what are we up to now?' Henry tapped the folder which was on his lap. It had the name *Clanfield* scrawled across it in thick felt tip.

'Well, with any luck, we're going to arrest a rapist. How does that sound?'

'I'm up for that.'

Henry Christie's day had actually started much earlier, at five a.m., when he'd had to put a few things in place before he even set out.

He lived in a village called Kendleton and jointly owned the rural inn in the village, The Tawny Owl, known locally as Th'Owl. And days there always began early, or at least they had done until the pandemic closed everything down. The shutdown had actually come at quite a bad time for Th'Owl because in the previous year horrific moorland fires had ravaged the countryside around the village and decimated trade, and things were only really getting back to normal after a good Christmas when the virus came to town.

The plus side was that the business was debt-free and Henry could afford not to have to furlough his staff and was able to continue to pay full wages, though he knew it was something he couldn't sustain indefinitely.

He was also – personally – in the fortunate position of being in receipt of a police pension, which kept the family side of things ticking over – family meaning Ginny, the stepdaughter of his late fiancée, Alison, with whom he ran the business fifty-fifty.

Even so, he knew that any extra cash coming in would go a long way towards keeping things afloat, so it was a good thing when he took a phone call from Rik Dean, the detective chief superintendent in charge of FMIT – actually one of a series of calls – asking him to consider coming back to work as a civilian investigator.

Henry had steadfastly refused the offers even if they were quite lucrative because he had recently found himself involved in two complex multiple-murder investigations and decided he'd had enough of policing.

But purely from a mercenary point of view, Henry changed his mind after much finger wrangling because every little would help to keep the business afloat.

In his past life, a life that seemed so long ago, when Henry had been a cop, he'd risen to the less-than-dizzy heights of detective superintendent on FMIT, and now the force was reluctant to lose his skills and expertise. Rik Dean often badgered him to consider a civilian investigator role, especially after his success on the investigations he had become embroiled in during the previous year which had involved organized crime, money laundering and brutal killings – and especially as Henry had also managed to save Rik Dean's life into the bargain.

But Henry hadn't been sitting by the phone waiting for it to ring.

If the call had never come, he would not have bothered, and no doubt the business would have survived, unlike many other pubs and hotels which were closing down, unable to weather the storm of the virus and the attendant lockdowns.

When the actual phone call had come, he had been in the bar of Th'Owl. He was dressed in overalls, splattered with a cream-coloured emulsion and balancing precariously at the top of step ladders as he daubed an intricate ceiling cornice with a brush that sent spatters of paint across his cheeks and forehead.

Observing him was Diane Daniels, a detective sergeant on FMIT, who was on a slow recovery trajectory from serious gunshot wounds received in the line of duty the previous year. She'd been critically injured, almost died, and was still too weak to return to work. She was sitting in the bow window of the pub, her legs stretched out across the long seat, watching alternately Henry's antics and the herd of deer grazing brazenly on the village green out front.

As the pandemic bit into the human population and everything had ground to an abrupt stop, wildlife from the surrounding countryside seemed to sense the opportunity to invade areas normally shunned because of unpleasant people.

'Haven't seen Horace today, must be hiding,' Diane said. She was sipping a cup of green tea flavoured with orange and ginger and was referring to the huge red deer stag which frequented the area and was regularly seen during the pandemic strutting cockily through the village streets. Henry had called him Horace and the name had stuck.

'He'll be down.'

Henry overstretched himself slightly and almost lost his balance, making Diane lurch towards him to rescue him if he fell – a conditioned reflex, but a move she could never have completed if Henry had gone flying. She winced in agony.

'Sorry,' he apologized.

'You're too bloody old to be going up ladders,' she chided him, getting comfortable again.

'Needs must.'

Diane turned to look back out of the window and saw Horace emerge from woodland on the opposite side of the green. 'Ooh, he's here,' she said happily, watching the magnificent animal wade across the stream and bound up on to the green where, muscles shimmering, he surveyed the grazing females, most of which seemed to give him sidelong coquettish looks. 'Looks like he means business,' Diane commented. 'I quite envy those ladies.' She gave Henry a wistful look.

He didn't respond to the jibe.

His mobile phone, which was on the table in front of Diane, began to ring. He knew it was his rather than hers – which lay alongside – because of the ringtone. For a while he had stopped using Rolling Stones songs but had resumed and now 'Living in a Ghost Town' sounded out loudly, with Jagger's wailing vocals a very appropriate soundtrack to the pandemic gripping the world.

Diane winced again as she leaned forwards, tilting the phone to see who was calling.

'Rik Dean . . . should I answer it?'

Now that she was on FMIT, Rik was her boss, but he was also Henry's brother-in-law and former colleague. Henry had identified Rik as a good detective many years before and had got him on to CID way back; he had moved up through the ranks without any further assistance from Henry and had finally stepped into Henry's shoes on FMIT as Henry retired. It was something that still left a sour taste in Henry's mouth, but he was learning to live with it.

'Nah,' Henry said from his perch.

'It might be important. It might be to do with . . . y'know?' Diane said.

The phone continued to ring. Henry liked the tune.

She was referring to the investigation Henry had become involved in which had resulted in Henry and a guy called Steve Flynn bursting into a deadly hostage situation in Rik's house and shots being fired. Even now, months later, the legal and court wranglings were still trundling on with no end in sight. Henry expected Crown Court dates soon and a trial that would be long, aggressive and emotional.

That said, Henry also enjoyed winding Rik up.

'If it's important, he'll call back or leave a message.'

He did ring again about half an hour later when Henry had had enough of painting and had moved to sit alongside Diane in the window with a fresh brew each as they watched the wildlife. Horace had disappeared, but the herd was still there.

'How're you feeling, babe?' Henry asked her, probably for the tenth time that day. Since the shooting and the time spent in hospital, she had been staying at The Tawny Owl under Henry's watchful, overprotective gaze, plus the care of the local GP, Dr Lott, who had taken her on board as a personal case, not least because he was a Tawny Owl regular and wanted to keep on Henry's good side, as did many of the villagers.

She sat up again and Henry watched her flexing everything from her neck down. She winced again and finally declared, 'Better each day.'

Then the phone rang. Henry answered this time and put it on speakerphone so Diane could eavesdrop.

'I knew you wouldn't answer first time,' Rik Dean barked without precursor.

'What do you want, Rik? Is court coming up?'

'No, not much happening in the justice system with the pandemic.'

'Nothing new there. OK, so what do you want?'

'How's Diane?'

'I just asked her that – doing as well as can be expected when recovering from a near-death experience.'

'Good. Hey! Y'know – tell her not to hurry back.'

'She isn't going to.'

'No, no, you're right.'

'So what do you want? You got my sister, you got my job,' Henry teased him. 'This isn't just a welfare check, is it?'

'No,' he hesitated. 'Look, Henry, I know I keep pestering you . . .'

'Yes, you do,' Henry interrupted him. 'And yes.'

'Yes, what?'

'Yes, I've thought about it. I need the money for the business and to keep myself in the luxury to which I have become accustomed. I'll do a six-month contract.'

When Rik had managed to entice Henry back for a very short spurt the year before, because Henry hadn't really wanted to do it, he had stuck out for an extortionate amount of money – and got it. Now he was prepared to accept the going rate, whatever that was, for civvies in that role.

Henry could almost imagine Rik blinking in astonishment.

'Really?'

'Yep.'

'That would be great because one of my cold case investigators just upped and left and we're a bit short.'

'Cold case? Not ongoing ones?'

'Cold case,' Rik confirmed.

Henry had a little moment's thought about it, then said, 'OK.'

'You'll be working under the DS based in the FMIT block at Hutton.'

'DS who?'

'Blackstone. I'm sure you'll get along like a house on fire.' And with that, Rik hung up.

Henry looked at Diane. 'You know this DS Blackstone?'

'Oh yeah.' And she began to giggle.

It took a while for things to fall into place, with the result that Henry's first day as a Cold Case Civilian Investigator actually coincided with the tentative reopening of The Tawny Owl under pretty strict but seemingly ever-changing government guidelines to be adhered to by pubs reopening for business following the COVID lockdown. That was why he was up particularly early.

There was a much-reduced service, but he still wanted to be open for the breakfast trade, and as soon as he unlocked the front door, two local gamekeepers came in, sat at a table and ordered the Tawny Full English which they habitually ate every day prior to going to work on a local estate, but hadn't been able to do so for several months.

When it was time for Henry to set off for work (a thought that slightly appalled him, not least because he was returning to a world in which he had to ask someone for permission to take a day off), he had to be shunted out by Ginny who insisted she could manage things. Henry knew this but it was still a wrench to get into his new Audi A5 and head for the motorway.

Blackstone tore off the car park, leaving marks on the tarmac, but slowed as she drove along the drive from the training school towards headquarters, then out through the exit under the rising barriers.

Henry opened the Clanfield file and fished out the meagre contents.

Before he had a chance to start reading, Blackstone said, 'Stranger rape from ten years ago; ten-year-old girl approached by a youth on the banks of the River Ribble near Avenham Park in Preston. Dragged into bushes, raped at least twice, half strangled, but survived.'

Henry forced himself to think, remember. Then it came to him. 'She was called Melanie . . . Melanie Wooton, school kid on her way home.'

'Good memory.'

'Big investigation . . . a few suspects thrown into the pot . . . pretty good e-fit of the offender if I recall. Wasn't one of my jobs, though.'

'*Very* good memory. So what were you doing at the time?'

'Chasing terrorists, I think. I remember the girl was very badly traumatized.'

'Very badly, which was only to be expected. Horrific ordeal. I think the force did a pretty good job with her in terms of support,' Blackstone said.

'But no arrests.'

'No DNA matches – although the lad's spunk is still on file, which makes it look like the offender didn't have, and still doesn't, a criminal record or cautions.'

'So why has this been resurrected?' Henry asked.

'It hasn't really.'

Henry arched his eyebrows.

'Not officially; not officially as in "Please look at this, DS Blackstone, because some new evidence has come to light". I just want to look into it, is why it's been resurrected, as you say,' she admitted.

Henry shrugged. 'OK.'

'I remember it happening, too,' Blackstone said. 'I wasn't involved, either. I was based in Lancaster back then, but I read newspaper reports, spoke to detectives on the job and it sort of resonated with me. When I landed this godforsaken job on the CCU, I checked up, saw it had never been solved, and there it was, stacked up, festering away and no one's even looked at it for five years, far as I can tell. I thought I would.'

'And you've uncovered something?'

'On a wing and a prayer,' she said.

They were on the road into Preston now, driving along the newly built by-pass towards the city.

Blackstone explained that the offender, a white male, maybe around fourteen to sixteen years, with no previous criminal convictions due to the lack of a DNA match, was probably a local resident and may have known or stalked the victim (although she maintained she did not recognize him). She went on to say that it was unlikely this would be a first offence, so Blackstone had done a couple of things.

First – and this impressed Henry – she had drawn a circle on a map with a compass of a two-mile radius of where the rape had occurred and noted the name of every street and road within that area. She had then looked at the voters' register which listed the occupants of every house, from ten years ago up to and including the current list.

She had cross-referenced these details with the house-to-house logs that were completed in the aftermath of the rape, and then meticulously compiled an Excel spreadsheet which included details of all the houses and their inhabitants against what was recorded on the logs.

'Obviously, it's not *that* scientific,' she admitted as they crossed the bridge over the River Ribble just before rising up to Preston itself.

'Thing is, and you'll know this, sometimes cops doing house-to-house enquiries are not always as meticulous as they should be because it can get a bit tedious, and, of course, there is always the possibility of residents lying to them, believe it or not.'

'What were you looking for?' Henry asked, intrigued.

'Well, basically,' she said, banging on the horn and swerving the Mini around another driver who had the temerity to signal well in advance before pulling out in front of her. 'Dickhead,' she snarled. 'Anyway, if the offender was a lad under voting age, which would seem to be the case, his name would not have appeared on the voters' list at that time, and, don't get me wrong, I know people move home all the time . . . anyway, I just kept looking for males appearing on subsequent voters' lists in the streets in the area, males who have obviously turned eighteen at some time in the last ten years.'

Henry nodded, got the logic.

'Not rocket science, as they say,' she admitted.

'I take it you found something. A name?'

'Yep . . . four households in that compass circle have had male members of the family registered since the offence took place.'

'Nice one,' Henry said appreciatively.

'I've already spoken to three and ruled them out for various reasons – not least because all willingly provided DNA samples which cleared them. But I've been having a real to-do trying to pin the fourth lad down.'

'And now you have?'

'I most certainly have. The original family still live at the same address they did ten years ago – mum, dad, daughter. They were all listed on the voters' register at the time of the rape. The son's name appeared on the list four years later, which fits in with the possible age of the offender, if you will.'

'Fourteen becoming eighteen.'

'Yep, and he's still on the register for that address, making him about twenty-four now; however, the son no longer lives with mum, dad and big sister. He left home under a cloud.'

'What sort of cloud?'

'One that included violently assaulting his mother – pushed her downstairs, broke her arm.'

'Not reported?' Henry guessed.

'Correct. And he assaulted his sister sexually over the years, though never raped her, apparently.'

'Also not reported?'

'Correct also.'

'And the father?'

'He's on the voters' register, but has not been with the mother for years.'

'And what about the house-to-house?' Henry asked.

'The mum doesn't remember the police calling, even though the form says they did . . . not sure if I want to go down that route, though,' Blackstone confessed and eyed Henry. As she drove along, she unwrapped a stick of chewing gum which she slid into her mouth.

'Hmm.' Henry thought about that. The implication would be that it might unearth the falsification of a document and land someone in deep trouble for claiming they had done a job which they hadn't. Henry was slightly conflicted about it, but said nothing.

'Tch! Families!' Blackstone tutted, having moved on. 'Anyway, the lad gets kicked out when he was nineteen, but the family never kept track of the little shit's whereabouts, had nothing to do with him. Thing is, I've also looked at all sexual offences committed by strangers in the Preston area for the last six years and there is an intermittent series of indecent assaults which have been growing in the severity of violence used but have, unfortunately, left no DNA behind. Strangling. Girls dragged into trees, gloved fingers inserted, plus some indecent exposures. The descriptions fit an older version of our rapist. See the file.'

Henry sifted through the paperwork as Blackstone explained, 'I got the e-fit guy to do a bit of ageing, best guess, adding ten years to the original e-fits.'

Henry was again impressed.

'His name is Ellis Clanfield. He's on jobseeker's allowance, which is how I found him. He lives alone in a grot-box bedsit just off the city centre; I'm not saying it's our guy, but if nothing else, I'm going to get his DNA for elimination today . . . but I just have this' – Blackstone juddered her shoulders – 'feeling. And if it is him, we need to get him off the streets because I suspect that if we don't, Mr Christie, the next time we find any DNA, it'll be on a dead victim.'

'Call me Henry.'

'Henry.'

'Pretty good hunting ground for a sexual predator,' Blackstone said as she pulled up on a less than salubrious cobbled street in the east of Preston, quite close to the city centre, not far from where the original rape had taken place.

Henry understood what she meant.

From his own knowledge of the area, he remembered there were a couple of primary schools, a secondary school and a college nearby, and a maze of back streets as well as a plethora of grotty businesses; it was a vicinity in which a fairly clever offender could easily go to ground without too much trouble. A stalker's paradise, he thought, and an area in need of much development.

'I'm not going to play funny buggers with this guy. I'm not going to play word or mind games with him. I'm going to tell him exactly where I stand and that I expect his full cooperation in providing a DNA sample, and if I don't like the look or feel of him, I'm lifting him.'

'Best way,' Henry said.

'Mask up, Zorro.'

They walked along the street.

'He's in a flat over a tattoo parlour . . . you could've guessed, really,' Blackstone said.

'Course he is.'

'So why are you coming back, Henry?' she asked him, her face mask muffling her voice. 'Can't be short of dosh, surely? Not on your humungous pension.'

'I was asked,' Henry said, 'and the money will be useful.'

'Fair dos.'

'And you're an investigator down, I'm informed.'

'Oh, yeah, that wanker.'

There was obviously a story to tell there, Henry thought, but he didn't push it because he'd already had an inkling from his earlier meeting with Rik Dean who'd alluded to a personality clash between the recently departed investigator and the CCU DS, who turned out to be Blackstone and who seemed to Henry, even in these early moments, to be an abrasive whirlwind and a little quirky to boot.

Then he found himself feeling uncomfortable at labelling her like this, wondering if he would have pigeon-holed a man as quickly.

There was no doubting, though, that she came across as a very determined character who took no bullshit.

And he was also very impressed by her because even if this inquiry into Clanfield came to nothing, what she'd done to track him down should be applauded. It was this kind of determined, unflashy, basic detective work that Henry had loved seeing from the people who worked for him in the past. Bread-and-butter stuff that caught villains.

The tattoo parlour was on a street consisting of small, terraced houses, most converted into flats, and some shops, including the tattoo parlour, an off-licence and what looked like a brothel.

The door to Ellis Clanfield's flat was next to the tattooist, right on the pavement. Henry looked up, feeling constrained by his face mask, to the first-floor window above the shop which he assumed was the flat. Torn, grubby curtains hung down inside, and on the outside the glass was so dirty Henry could have made a trail through the grime with his finger.

'Nice,' he said.

Blackstone banged loudly on the door.

Henry visualized maybe a small vestibule beyond the door leading immediately up a steep set of stairs to the flat. Tight, steep, hard to negotiate, room for only one person at a time.

There was no reply. Blackstone banged again: louder.

Henry glanced up, caught a glimpse of movement behind the window grime, plus a twitch of the ragged curtain.

'He's in.'

'I saw.' Blackstone had looked up, too.

Henry was liking this, even if he was feeling slightly nervous. Although he'd fairly recently been involved in two interconnected, fast-moving investigations, they'd had a life of their own, a vortex he'd been sucked into and hadn't had much time to reflect on; he'd been caught up in irresistible storms which eventually spat him out.

This was totally different.

Back to basic coppering. Within half an hour of walking into a new office, he was knocking on the door of a possible suspect, about to talk face to face, which he always firmly believed was the bottom line for a detective: speaking to people.

He was bloody excited by this prospect.

Blackstone rapped her knuckles on the door, which Henry noticed wasn't the sturdiest of structures and looked quite susceptible to being kicked easily off its hinges. If necessary.

Something else he liked doing.

Booting doors down.

Blackstone bent over to the letterbox, flipped it up and peered through it with one eye, then put her mouth to it and shouted, 'Mr Clanfield, this is the police. Please open up; we wish to have a word with you.'

She stood upright and said to Henry, 'You got your cuffs and baton?'

Henry patted his pockets, pretending to look for the said appointments. She smirked.

'I was hoping you'd have that sort of thing. I'm just a civvie,' he said.

'Fortunately . . .' she began, but stopped talking abruptly. Footsteps on the stairs.

'Who is it?' a deep voice asked from behind the door.

'Police. I'm DS Blackstone from police headquarters and this is . . . er . . .' She turned to Henry, frowning as she tried to think of a way of introducing him. 'Another detective.'

'Quick thinking,' Henry quipped.

It made her grin.

'Prove it,' the voice demanded.

'Open the door and I'll gladly show you my warrant card,' Blackstone said.

'Show me through the letterbox.'

'OK – flip it open.'

The flap opened and Blackstone took out her ID and showed it to the gap. 'Like I said, DS Blackstone.'

The flap clattered shut.

But there was no movement or noise to suggest the door might be about to be opened.

'Mr Clanfield, please open up,' Blackstone said with a steely hint of warning.

They heard footsteps going quickly back up the stairs. It did not seem as though he was going to comply with the request.

'Stand back!' Blackstone said dramatically. She scythed her arms

back to give some space, lined up and flat-footed the door with the
sole of her right boot. The door capitulated without almost any
resistance and they caught sight of Clanfield's heels disappearing
into the door of the flat at the top of the flight of stairs.

Blackstone emitted a sort of roar and set off after him with a
powerful surge, then a 'Bastard!' under her breath. Henry was close
at her heels.

There was a tiny landing at the top of the stairs with two doors
off it, one straight ahead and one to the left, which was the one
Clanfield had run into and closed behind him.

Blackstone twisted in the narrow space while Henry held back
four steps down to give her room. She rattled the door handle –
locked – but the whole door frame rattled. Blackstone glared deter-
minedly at Henry, then put her shoulder to the door and barged it
open with ease, breaking a poorly affixed bolt and entering the flat.

Across the squalid bedsit, Clanfield had rushed to the settee
and hefted up a laptop computer which he was balancing on the
splayed fingers of his left hand while he dabbed desperately at
the keyboard with the tip of his right forefinger.

Blackstone shot across to him as she realized he was trying to
delete files.

Henry came in behind her to see Clanfield look up and hurl the
laptop across the room with the intention of chucking it out of
the front window. It was beyond Blackstone's reach, but Henry
dinked across and managed to deflect it from its trajectory so it
landed on the floor. The lid unhinged itself from the keypad as it struck
the hard laminate.

Blackstone tried to grab Clanfield but he swerved, avoiding her
fingers, and ducked towards the door. Henry managed to push him
aside, making him stagger against a small table on which Henry
had seen a stack of photographs; a brief glimpse told him they
were all obscene.

Blackstone turned quickly as Henry managed to pin Clanfield
against the wall, holding the struggling man there as Blackstone
took out her handcuffs. Between them they forced the man's hands
behind his back and cuffed him before Henry spun him around and
manoeuvred him to face Blackstone who was adjusting her face
mask which had gone cockeyed.

Henry held on tight as Blackstone looped the elastic around her ear, but it flipped out of her fingers. Clanfield spat into her exposed face and screamed, 'I've got COVID, you bitch. I've got the fucking virus and now you have, too!'

From his point of view across the man's shoulder, Henry saw the spittle shoot out of Clanfield's mouth and spray across Blackstone's eyes, nose and mouth.

She withdrew with an 'Ugh!' of utter disgust, wiping her face with her now scrunched-up mask and staring ferociously at Clanfield.

She didn't stare for long.

Even so, Henry recognized her expression as one he'd seen on many a copper's face before. It had probably been on his own face from time to time.

It was only the briefest, most transient of expressions, but one that said – and warned of – so much.

Henry wanted to shout, 'No!' but the world seemed to slow down and the word would not come out quickly enough, though as he gripped Clanfield's upper arms as he stood behind him, he did manage to duck down and brace himself at the same time.

Blackstone hit Clanfield. Very, very hard. A direct punch to the face.

Clanfield's head snapped back and Henry felt two things, one immediately after the other.

First, the shudder of Clanfield's body as the shockwave following the punch shimmered through him; second, the splatter of blood from the busted nose which went both ways, back over Henry and forwards over Blackstone.

In spite of the hotspots across his face, Henry kept hold of Clanfield, whose head bobbed and rolled uncontrollably as Henry eased him down to the floor, while he looked up at Blackstone who stood there shaking, now wiping the blood splatter off her face with her mask, growling, 'No fucker spits at me and gets away with it, especially not during a pandemic.'

'Fucker!'

It was a word often repeated by Blackstone through her new face mask, even after assistance had been summoned and Clanfield had been dragged and dumped into the back of a police van to take him to Preston police station.

Two local detectives had turned up and taken over the scene to allow Blackstone and Henry to follow their prisoner, despite the guy's continual bleating that he should be taken to hospital because he was a victim of police brutality. Blackstone wanted him booked into the system before that happened, so that a full record of her side of the story could be written on the custody record. She told nothing but the truth.

After that there would be no choice but to have him taken to Royal Preston Hospital by uniformed officers, leaving Blackstone and Henry to chat to Rik Dean, who had been informed of the arrest (and the kerfuffle) and had hurriedly turned out from headquarters. He spoke to the pair in an empty office at the nick.

'He fuckin' spat at me, boss,' Blackstone said, still snarling.

Rik looked at Henry, who said, 'He did. Unprovoked. Under any circumstances, he got what he deserved; under the present circumstances, he definitely did.'

Rik took this in, weighed it up, then said, 'OK, make sure it's written up fully on the custody record, then get yourselves cleaned up and disinfected – whatever you need to do.' He looked at Henry whose nice new, first-day-back-at-work suit now had specks of blood around the shoulder. 'Have you got a change of clothing, Henry?'

'In the back of my car.'

Then Rik looked at Blackstone, who was still visibly seething and covered in more blood than Henry. 'You live down at the docks, don't you?'

'Yuh.'

'Do you want to nip home, get a shower and a change of clothing? Then get back here. Clanfield's going to be at RPH for a while, I think.'

'Thanks, boss.'

'Henry – I'll run you back to Hutton Hall and you can shower and change up there.'

Henry was about to say OK, but Blackstone cut in, 'I'll run him up, boss, then back down to my place where he can grab a shower, too. Then we'll head back here.'

'Fine by me,' Rik said. 'Henry?'

'Yeah, yeah,' he said a bit cautiously.

'No need to worry,' Blackstone said. 'I won't shag you.'

*   *   *

It was a good apartment, one of only two on the top floor of a converted warehouse overlooking Albert Dock. It had a large sliding window opening on to a wide balcony, large enough for a table, chairs and potted plants.

Blackstone had driven Henry up to HQ where he'd gone to his car and grabbed his change of clothing from the boot (one thing he hadn't forgotten was that a detective – and even a civilian investigator – always had a spare set with them) and she took him back to her place on the docks and let him get a shower first.

He sat by the open balcony window while she then went in, emerging ten minutes later, muttering to herself; more disconcerting for Henry was that she came back into the lounge wearing only a pair of tight cropped trousers and a lacy black bra.

Henry averted his eyes.

But not before he had seen the myriad of tattoos on her arms and across her midriff and the swathe of something which ran like the map of a silver/red river and its tributaries from the front of her left shoulder, across the top of her chest with fingers shaped like spikes halfway up her neck. At first Henry thought it was another tattoo of some sort, but then he realized exactly what it was.

A very serious acid burn.

EIGHT

They were back at the station in time to be in the reception committee for Clanfield, who had, despite his continuing bad behaviour, been cleaned up at the hospital. His nose had been realigned by a burly, no-nonsense doctor with no time or inclination to mess about, who clamped the broken nose between the palms of his hands and straightened it with a gristly crunch that made the patient scream.

Henry and Blackstone watched Clanfield's arrival back into the custody office, soon after which he was in a cell, demanding food, drink and a solicitor.

By then it was well into the afternoon.

Rik Dean had scarpered back to headquarters, so Blackstone and Henry briefed the local DI who suggested it might be better if a couple of his detectives interviewed Clanfield, which didn't seem to bother Blackstone too much.

'Way of the world,' she said philosophically to Henry. 'We do the graft and hand it over, as you know. They'll interview him, take the DNA swab and probably bail him unless he coughs the job. When the sample comes back, if it's positive, they can nail him as far as I'm concerned. As long as he ends up in front of a Crown Court judge, I'm happy.'

'But you did the legwork.'

'Whatev,' she said. They were walking along the main corridor that formed the spine of the police station, Henry nodding at one of two folk he recognized from the past, including Chief Superintendent Lee, one of his old friends; they touched elbows. 'God, you know people,' Blackstone said. 'And they even seem to like you!'

'Very funny.' He glanced at her, and his eyes dropped slightly as he saw the new scarf she'd wrapped around her neck as a replacement for the one splashed with Clanfield's blood, which she had binned. Now he understood why it was on, what it was covering and that it wasn't just pretentiousness.

She went on, 'We'll write up our part, and they can have it . . . but I do have one thing I'd like to do. I know his hovel's being searched, but I want to go back and have a quick look around myself.'

'Why?'

'I have my reasons.' She narrowed her eyes and waggled her eyebrows which, Henry saw for the first time, were tattooed. 'One of which might actually keep him in custody.'

A Support Unit personnel carrier was parked on the street outside Clanfield's flat. Henry and Blackstone had to ease their way up the stairs as two cops wearing overalls came down, one carrying three laptops in sealed plastic evidence wallets, bagged and tagged; the other had two large bin bags.

'What's in there?' Blackstone asked him.

'Photographs – thousands of them, found in a space in the ceiling.'

'OK,' she said. 'I won't bother guessing just yet.'

'They're grim,' the cop said, his face tight with disgust and emotion.

In the living room – which had been turned upside down while being searched – Blackstone paused for a moment, then led Henry into the equally squalid bedroom. It was small and the three-quarter-sized bed almost filled it. The bed had been stripped, and eventually the bedding and mattress would be seized for evidence because, Henry guessed, there would be lots of traces of sexual activity that would be worth analyzing. The bedhead was made of pillars of cheap pine with a narrow shelf along the top, on which were several items including an overflowing ashtray, a pack of condoms (some had been used and were discarded in among the cigarette and spliff butts in the ashtray), a nasal spray and a small round tin with a push-on lid that had the words *Boozy Chocolate Cake* on the side of it.

Henry stood back and watched Blackstone stalk the room. He could tell she knew what she was looking for, and as she hadn't yet revealed this to him, the new boy, he let her get on with it.

There wasn't really too much room to stalk, though. Just enough to edge around the bed.

Henry could see her eyes continually returning to the small cake tin which was about three inches tall and maybe four in diameter with a small domed lid, something that might have been in a hamper at some stage.

Finally, she pulled a pair of latex gloves out of a pocket and snapped her hands into them, then picked up the tin and tilted it so she could see its base.

'Chocolate and Champagne cake,' she said, reading what was printed on the underside. 'Got cherries on it.'

Gently, she shook it. Something rattled – definitely not cake, something metallic. She eased the lid off and peered into it.

Henry watched her face closely, saw the miniscule change of expression. A change he knew meant *Victory!*

She placed the lid down on the bedhead shelf, held the tin on the palm of her left hand, while the fingers of her right delved into the tin like a bird's beak and came out with something between finger and thumb.

A necklace. A delicate open-heart shape embellished with tiny stones that could have been diamonds on a silver chain.

She held it up for Henry to see.

'Not necessarily conclusive, but Melanie Wooton was wearing a necklace made by Pandora like this one, which the offender tore from her neck during the assault. There are several family photos of her wearing it. Her mum bought it her for a birthday – and it could have her DNA on it still – and her blood, because when it was ripped from her, it cut her neck slightly.'

'Trophies,' Henry said.

'And there are others in here,' Blackstone said and shook the tin gently. 'Which is a big worry.'

'He will have some very tough questions to answer.'

Blackstone carefully put the tin down, rooted out an evidence bag from her pocket and eased the necklace into it, sealing the bag.

'If I were you, which I'm not . . .' Henry began.

'What would you do?'

'Well, bearing in mind we have semen samples from the rape and you now have this, I would get back to Preston nick, ensure we get some very fast-track DNA comparisons done and make damn sure that guy goes nowhere for a few days. Because if he walks out of that door in the next twenty-four hours, he'll be on the wind.'

'Sounds like a plan, old guy.'
She gave him a quirky smile.

By the time everything was coordinated, it was eight p.m. Evidence samples had been bagged up and submitted into the hands of a traffic motorcyclist who then blazed a trail to the necessary laboratories which were on standby to receive the packages.

As it happened – and although good evidence would be required for corroboration – Clanfield began to crumble towards the end of the first round of interviews.

Henry and Blackstone watched two very cool, experienced detective constables dismantle his story and his protestations of innocence bit by bit.

'It's like boiling a lobster,' Blackstone commented at one point. They were in the CID office watching a live audio-visual feed from the interview room down in the custody complex. 'Drop him into cold water, turn the heat up gently . . .'

'And before he knows it, his goose is cooked,' Henry said.

'Not to mix metaphors,' Blackstone chuckled.

Henry grinned and watched proceedings unfold. He'd taken a break to call Ginny and Diane at The Tawny Owl to check on how the first day was going; their response made him feel guilty. After a slow, hesitant start, the locals had poured back in for pre-booked food and drink; it had been very busy, but actually, because of the COVID measures in place, manageable.

He told Diane about his baptism of fire with Blackstone and heard her laugh, which was a sound he had grown to love.

In the interview room, the two detectives, who had pre-planned the interview meticulously, began to put things to Clanfield. Not in a threatening way but in such a manner as to make him feel very comfortable and then very, very uncomfortable.

The fact that the police still had semen samples from Melanie Wooton's rape.

'Definitely his spunk,' Blackstone had said at that point as she watched Clanfield squirm.

And that – obviously – the police had now taken DNA swabs from him which would match those from the victim if he was the offender.

'Like a fish on a hook,' she then said.

And that various items – not yet specified – had been seized from his flat that could also link him to the rape, not to mention what might be found on his computer and the numerous obscene photographs also seized.

'Bastard's fucking wriggling like a fucker,' Blackstone said.

At that point, the pressure on Clanfield was so intense that he said simply, 'I might as well tell you.'

Blackstone twisted to Henry and offered up a palm for a high five.

Henry was about to respond, but before their hands actually met, they both realized it was something they were not allowed to do. Sheepishly, they pulled back and gave each other an elbow instead.

It was ten p.m. by the time they walked out of the police station. Despite Clanfield's admission, he had not been charged with any offences, but his detention had been further authorized overnight. There was a lot more to do with him.

As they walked across to her car, much to Henry's surprise, Blackstone threaded her arm through Henry's.

'I know, I know – the bloody virus, but I feel happy. We did good there.' She smiled at him and added, 'Pal.'

'You did. I just watched, mostly.'

Henry's mobile phone rang. He disentangled himself from Blackstone and fished it out of his pocket. It was Rik Dean.

'Bloody good result today, mate.'

'Not my doing,' Henry said, eyeing Blackstone.

'Whatever . . . Look, are you planning on going home now?'

'Absolutely.'

'Change your plans, then.' Rik told him something, then hung up.

To Blackstone, Henry said, 'Rik Dean . . . he says good job.'

A fierce look instantly descended on her features. 'So why didn't he call me? Why did he have to call his mate? Fucking bosses – I've shat 'em,' she snarled, at which moment her mobile phone rang. She didn't recognize the number, but she answered it. 'DS Blackstone.'

'Debbie? Rik Dean here . . . just a quick word to say: awesome, bloody well done. You probably won't get too much credit – that's the CCU for you – but I wanted you to know from me what a brilliant job you did. I'll be briefing the chief in the morning and I'll let her know.'

'Uh, thanks, boss.'

'Anyway – you have a good night.'

The call ended.

Henry had picked up the gist, tilted his head at her and arched his eyebrows, waiting for a response.

'Well, I'm astounded . . .' Then she looked suspiciously at Henry. 'You told him to ring me, didn't you?'

'You heard my end of the conversation. It was all his own doing. He just had something to tell me that had nothing to do with Clanfield, that's all.'

'I think you spoke in code.'

'I can assure you we didn't. I taught Ricky boy all he knows, including how to be a good manager and the value of patting your staff on the back for a job well done occasionally.'

'Well, whatever . . . like I said, astounded.' The change in her temperament back to one of happy normality was as quick as the change a couple of moments earlier to one of incandescent rage. She hooked her arm through Henry's again and sort of skipped alongside him to her car. 'What did he want?'

Henry told her.

'Oh, right.' Her mood flatlined. 'How about I take you, then you don't waste any time going back to Hutton for your car. The McDonald's drive-through on the docks has reopened, so we could grab a burger on the way, 'cos I'm famished.'

It would be the second dive of a flat Henry would enter that day, a dingy hole above what was once a tobacconist, now just a shop selling tat, on Central Drive, Blackpool, in close proximity to the resort centre.

Two police cars were on the road outside, the occupants standing in a cluster by an open door that Henry assumed was the entrance to the flat. Blackstone parked behind the cop cars, and she and Henry got out of the Mini, binning their fast-food wrappers and walking to the assembled officers.

'Can I help?' one asked, stepping forward.

Blackstone, who did not recognize any of them, showed them her ID. 'DS Blackstone from the Cold Case Unit; this is Mr Christie, a civilian investigator, formerly a detective super on FMIT. We've been asked to attend this by Detective Chief Superintendent Dean.'

He gestured. 'Up the stairs. Can't get the lights working, but if you go down the long corridor to the end, the flat's on the right. Bit grizzly and stinky . . . which is why we're all out here.'

'I believe a paramedic pronounced life extinct?' Blackstone asked.

'That's right . . . and a CSI's been and gone. Just waiting for a body remover with a strong stomach and a big plastic bag. The night detective's been and gone, too.'

'Suspicious circumstances?' Henry asked.

'Just a sad, lonely old lady,' one of the other officers called out. 'Pain in the arse, if anything . . . nobody's interested, just a run-of-the-mill suicide.'

Henry gave him a chilly stare, but said nothing. One thing Henry had never come across in his career was a 'run-of-the-mill' suicide.

Blackstone, echoing Henry's thoughts, said, 'Should I punch him out now?'

The officer looked quickly away.

Henry jerked his head to Blackstone. 'Let's have a look.' To the cop he'd been speaking to, he said, 'Borrow your torch?'

He handed Henry a hefty Maglite torch and said, 'Oh, it's on the gas fire, by the way.'

'What is?'

'The reason you're here.'

Henry nodded and entered. Like Clanfield's flat earlier in the day, there was a steep flight of steps directly behind the door, but without any lighting to show the way. Henry took a grip of the handrail and went up, using the torch.

He went carefully, with Blackstone behind, reaching a landing and then a long, narrow corridor.

'This goes back a long way,' Henry said, flashing the torch beam down it.

Outside, when he'd arrived a few minutes earlier, he could smell death in the air. Up here, the stench was more intense and sharp on the nostrils. Decomposition of flesh – the smell that police officers were obliged to walk towards, not away from.

'You might want to brace yourself,' he said over his shoulder in warning to Blackstone whom he could feel right up behind him.

She had her own torch and had balanced it on his shoulder like a sniper and peered down the beam. She was very close to Henry and he heard her gasp and sensed her body stiffen up.

'Henry,' she whispered into his ear. Her voice was brittle, and although he had only known this woman for a short time, he recognized something completely different in the tone. He knew what it was: fear. He assumed that was a fairly normal reaction to having to walk down a long, dark corridor expecting to see a dead body. Anyone would have been a little bit tense – even Henry who had walked down many such corridors and alleyways. It was only human to be like that, but a cop had to be able to control the fear.

'You OK?'

Suddenly, there was a chilling scream and Henry felt the rush of something between his feet.

Blackstone screamed too and dropped her torch with a clatter.

'Fuck! A bloody cat,' Henry said. He turned to see a petrified moggy hurtling down the stairs. He let out a long gasp.

He picked up Blackstone's torch for her and shone it across her face at an angle so as not to dazzle her, and in the long shadows caused by the way the light spread diagonally over her features, her eyes seemed sunken and frightened.

'You still OK?'

'No.' She shook her head. 'Not really.' Her voice was tiny and fragile, lost even. All her bluster had gone.

'I know it's a bad smell,' he said.

'It's not that . . . Look, I'm sorry, I can't go down there.' She pushed his arm away and took the torch from his grasp.

'OK, not a problem.'

Without another word, she turned and went back down the stairs to the outside world.

Henry frowned as he watched her, not understanding and wary of making assumptions. He turned and looked back along the corridor which, even to him and despite other cops having already trodden this path, was not exactly enticing, not least because of the smell and fleeing felines.

There was a light switch on the wall which he flicked, but nothing happened.

Adjusting his face mask, he began the walk along the corridor, its floorboards creaking. It seemed to take an age to reach the final door which led into the bedsit and from which the overwhelming putrid smell emanated.

He stepped inside, flashed the torch around, now hearing a low, buzzing murmur. He kept his mouth closed tight and pinched his nostrils over his mask – which was not helping to reduce the smell in any way – as the torch beam moved around, past a small TV on a stand, a gas fire, a kitchen sink, a single gas hob and a tiny fridge, past a settee to the bed at the back of the tiny room in which someone had once lived, if one could call it that.

The bed. A shape on the bed.

Then, with a noise like the crack of a bullwhip which made him jump, the lights suddenly came on and he could clearly see what before had only been an outline on the bed – a body, face up.

And with the illumination came the reason for the low murmuring sound he'd heard as a huge swarm of bluebottles rose en masse from the body, disturbed by the lights.

'Ugh!' Henry stepped back, disgusted, swatting them away with his hand, feeling their hard bodies as he wafted them. 'Holy—!' He tried not to swear.

He too wanted to do a runner, but he held his nerve as the flies buzzed around him and he continued to flick them away as he stepped forward to look, feeling nauseous.

And he saw someone who had taken their own life – quietly, desperately, sadly – and who had only been discovered because of the smell.

The head was encased in a clear plastic bag which had kept the woman's facial features more or less intact while the remainder of the corpse rotted away, particularly the lower half of the torso from which the juices spread across the bed and seeped down through the mattress, causing a black viscous puddle underneath the angle-frame bed.

Henry took cautious steps as the flies began to settle back on the body, forcing himself to compartmentalize the horror he was seeing.

He wasn't sure how long he looked at the face – just long enough to know he had let someone down very badly.

Finally, he backed away, turned on his heels and looked at the wall-mounted gas fire which protruded from the wall and acted as a mantelpiece on which items could be displayed.

There was a folded letter propped up on it, leaning against the wall.

Henry picked it up. Scrawled across the back of it in spidery, almost childlike handwriting were the words *For Detective Henry Christie.*

'I'm sorry I bottled it,' Blackstone said. 'I just got spooked . . . can't explain it . . . and that effin' cat! Scared the crap out of me. I just had to do a runner. It was like my throat clogged up and I couldn't breathe.'

'It got worse,' Henry said, 'but no problem.'

They were now sitting in the twenty-four-hour Kentucky Fried Chicken restaurant on Preston New Road, Blackpool. It had recently reopened and social distancing measures were in place but unnecessary at this time of day as it was almost deserted. It was somewhere Henry had frequented in his past, somewhere that could be relied on for sustenance and half-decent coffee at any time of day or night for hard-working cops who were short on sleep but long on hours.

He hadn't been in for a while. One of the last occasions had been when he had proposed marriage to Alison. Not the most romantic of locations but, at that specific moment in time, it had been the ideal spot to slide a ring on to her finger, especially when the answer had been 'Yes'.

It was a future that hadn't happened.

Henry compartmentalized that bittersweet memory when he instructed Blackstone to turn into the restaurant car park on the way back to Preston. She took a seat while he ordered two large coffees and, when he returned with them, she spoke of her sudden loss of bravery.

She narrowed her eyes at his seeming disinterest. 'Don't you want to know why?'

'I'm sure you'll tell me,' he said, obviously distracted. He sipped his hot brew through the tiny hole in the lid of the disposable cup, then decided to peel the damn thing off before noticing Blackstone glaring at him. 'What?'

'I was going to tell you something deep and meaningful. Something I've never even considered saying to anyone . . . but you.'

'Why me? We've known each other less than a day.'

She shook her head, pursed her lips and looked away.

Henry took the letter with his name on it out of his pocket, the one he'd taken from the scene of the suicide but not yet unfolded or read. He placed it on the table.

'What's that?' Blackstone asked.

'A letter from the suicide.'

'I hope you haven't read it yet. The first time a suicide note should be read is by the coroner.'

Henry gave her an 'as if' look. He knew that, technically and procedurally, she was probably right. Practically, however, that never happened. He had never been to a suicide where a sealed note or letter had not been opened by the police. If nothing else, if the death was not suicide but a murder, it could become vital evidence that might be worthless two months later when an inquest opened.

'Is this why Ricky boy asked you to attend?'

'It's got my name on it, so I guess so.'

'Better unfold it and read it, then.'

Henry's mouth went dry. He took a hurried sip of coffee and unfolded the paper without actually touching its surface with his fingers. He hardly dared to bring his eyes to read the words that were written in the same immature scrawl as his name on the back.

It wasn't a long note. It was badly written, had several spelling mistakes and bad punctuation, but was no less heartbreaking for that.

> Dear Detective Christie.
>
> I jus wanned to say thank u for what u did for me. I kept looking. Every day I kept lookin for my boy. Lookin n asking but no one ever seen Tommy. I don no what happened to him. I jus know it were bad. An I was is mum and I cud never find him agen. I knew I never wud. 30 years gone and I dint give up but now I ave dun.
>
> I tried
>
> I know you did to.
>
> But he's dead. Has to be.
>
> I cant look any more. I got to call it a day.
>
> Evry day I miss him.
>
> Now I need to be wi im.
>
> Pleese don't you give up on im.

There was no signature, which Henry found slightly odd, and the bottom quarter of the page was ripped off, which was also strange.

Henry sat back after reading it and swivelled it around to
Blackstone, keeping his fingers off the surface.

'You know when you've let someone down? I mean, really, really
let someone down?' he said.

Now the reason for Henry's disinterest in hearing Blackstone's
excuse for not going down the corridor became apparent to her as
she read the note a few times, then passed it back to him.

Henry gave her the background. The arrest of young Tommy over
thirty years before for shoplifting – not the most heinous of crimes;
the assault on Henry that put him in hospital; Tommy going missing
from home, never to show up again. He told Blackstone about
bumping into Trish, Tommy's mum, a year later as she stopped
people on the streets of Blackpool, shoving a photo of the lad under
their noses.

No one had seen him.

Henry had promised to keep an eye on the case and until a couple
of years before his retirement he did review it annually, checked in
with Trish – whose life had become a constant, dedicated search
for Tommy with the knock-on consequences that she suffered
psychologically and financially because of the never-ending quest,
and that she turned to drink.

Officially, the file on Tommy was shelved. Henry did check it
each year to see if anything more had come to light, but despite
some apparent sightings of Tommy in Manchester in the first couple
of years, the file had gone dead since.

'I think she had a pretty miserable life before he went missing,
but Tommy – the little rascal that he was – was all she had, and
when he went, she had nothing but hope – and hope in me,' Henry
said bleakly.

'Fuckin' 'ell, you're taking this a bit too much to heart,'
Blackstone said. 'Bit OTT.'

Henry looked squarely at her. 'Admittedly we've only known
each other what, twelve, fourteen hours, but I already know you
don't believe those words.'

'Oh? Exactly how do you know that?' she bristled.

'Because I can tell. You might come across as hard as nails, don't
give a flying eff on the outside, but I can see right through you, DS
Blackstone. I know what I see isn't pretty in there' – he pointed to

her heart – 'but I know it cares.' He paused and looked down his nose at her. 'So, go on, tell me why you bolted back out the door, had a panic attack. Walking down corridors is what cops do all the time. Into situations you know are going to be tough. They do it every day of every week. Knocking on a door is like walking down a corridor, yet I know you would have done that without hesitation because you already did it earlier today.'

'You a psychoanalyst or something?'

Henry grinned. 'No, just a psycho and I'm anal.'

He expected the quip to break the tension that had somehow formed between them.

It didn't.

Instead, her face became very serene and expressionless. Her eyes played over him in a challenging way, though Henry couldn't decide if she was challenging him or challenging herself.

He found out.

There were no tears in those eyes in among the thick mascara.

Slowly, her fingers moved to the scarf wrapped around her neck. She unravelled it slowly and removed it, placing it on the table, covering the suicide note.

All the while, her eyes were fixed on his.

He felt himself holding his breath.

Then she unbuttoned the top three buttons of her blouse, each one very slowly, very deliberately.

Then, with the first two fingers of each hand hooked around each side of her blouse, she slowly pulled the blouse apart and downwards and showed Henry her neck and upper chest.

Then her tears fell.

NINE

They sat in silence as Blackstone drove back to headquarters, both consumed by their own thoughts, memories and deficiencies.

In the car park, Henry climbed out – he had felt as if his arse had been dragging on the floor of the Mini and he had to haul himself out – and he gave her a quick wave. She looked blankly at him and drove away. He got into the luxury of his Audi and set off home, calling Diane on the hands-free Bluetooth and talking to her for the whole length of his journey back to The Tawny Owl.

She waited up for him and met him at the front of the pub where they embraced tenderly – he didn't squeeze too hard – and kissed long and soft before breaking off to sit out on the front patio area with a nice Japanese whisky each. There was no sign of wildlife on the village green.

It was only then, as Henry sat there alongside a woman he had come to love – if 'love' was the right word at his age and after losing both his wife and then his fiancée (on balance, he thought it was) – that he finally chilled properly in the balminess of the late night as they talked about each other's day.

Although Diane had only been an onlooker on the first day's proper trading of Th'Owl, she had helped out where she could. It had been a steady day, she said, and she'd seen a wariness in most of the customers, until they'd had a few drinks, at which point all social distancing guidelines seemed to be quite forgotten. The feeling was that they were all very happy the place had reopened, not least because it was the only decent pub in the district and the social hub of the village. Its closest rival in a nearby village had shut its doors well before lockdown, never to reopen again.

Finally, their conversation dwindled into a comfortable silence.

'Hell of a first day,' Henry muttered. He sipped the fine, mellow whisky.

'They never pan out how you expect.'

'No.' His brow creased. 'Never.'

They were sitting side by side on a chunky wooden bench, their legs touching gently.

Diane laid a cool hand on Henry's inner thigh and he slid his hand over hers. He couldn't deny that a little shimmer went through him. He turned and they looked at each other, almost nose to nose.

'Err,' he said nervously and swallowed.

As Diane's recuperation had been slow and sometimes non-existent for weeks on end, they hadn't dared to re-establish any sort of intimacy beyond gentle cuddles and caresses. She had been in too much pain from the wounds, but over recent weeks there had been some progress as the pain diminished a little more each day.

'I know you've had a long day,' she said quietly, 'and I've really missed you.'

'Well, y'know, working man bringing home the veggies.'

'So macho.' She grinned. 'Thing is, I'd like to try something that we've only really done the once.'

Henry swallowed again.

'How do you feel,' she said in a low, seductive voice, 'about you grabbing a shower and then us taking our time over it?'

Henry could already feel himself responding. He nodded eagerly, not trusting himself to actually speak. He finished his drink, got to his feet and held out his hands to bring Diane up to hers.

Ten minutes later, he was in the shower, soaping himself down, when the glass door opened and Diane stepped in alongside him and said, 'I couldn't wait.'

Henry slept soundly for five hours, with Diane tucked up tightly against him for most of that time. He woke at six forty-five, hearing noises from inside the pub which told him the second day of trading had already begun. He rolled quietly out of bed, had another quick shower – alone this time – dressed and made his way to the kitchens where Ginny was already preparing the breakfasts.

'The two gamekeepers are coming in again,' she told him. 'They'll be in at seven and a couple of the Duke's estate workers will be in a little later.' She was referring to the Duke of Westminster's Lancashire estate which was nearby. 'I hear your day was somewhat fraught . . . Diane was telling me.'

Henry saw something cross Ginny's face.

He knew that bringing Diane home had crossed some sort of line with Ginny. The Tawny Owl had originally been owned by Alison, Ginny's stepmother, who had transformed the pub from a neglected wreck into a thriving business; when Alison had died, even though she and Henry were not married, he had inherited the pub but subsequently gave Ginny a fifty per cent share in it . . . so he knew that the spirit of Alison still lived in the place, was ingrained into every fibre of it. Although Ginny had tried hard to accept Diane – whom she actually liked a lot – Henry knew she was finding the presence of the new woman in his life hard to deal with. It perhaps didn't help that in the aftermath of Alison's tragic death, Ginny had started calling Henry 'Dad'.

'Everything OK, darling?' he asked her.

Her nod was rigid.

'Hey, let's talk later, eh?'

He gave her a hug, then said, 'Coffee and a Cumberland sausage bun?'

'Coming right up.'

Ten minutes later, he was on the road, heading south for his second day as a civilian investigator.

'Civilian Investigator Christie,' he said aloud, wondering how best to introduce himself to prospective suspects and witnesses. 'CI Christie?' he tried. 'Or maybe just Christie, Henry Christie, civvie dogsbody.'

Somehow Henry was not surprised to see Blackstone's Mini Cooper in the car park even though it was not yet eight a.m. when he pulled up. Unlike him, he guessed she might have had a troubled night.

He entered the FMIT building, amused that the key code for the door was still the same combination as when his office had been there years before. For all that cops pounded on about security for others, they were often lax with their own. He walked down the ground-floor corridor to the CCU in the corner office and, as expected, found Blackstone at her desk.

This time she did not acknowledge him, busy concentrating on something.

Henry went to the desk he assumed belonged to him – which was stacked with other people's discarded crap, propped against which was a brown A4 envelope with his name on it. He tore it open and tapped out a parking permit and an ID badge on a lanyard with a swipe card, which he knew gave him restricted access to the headquarters building. His temporary computer access code was on a slip of paper.

This was the first time he'd been at his desk, having been dragged out by Blackstone the previous day before he had even set foot in the office.

It reminded him a little of that time, many years before, on his first day on CID: he'd been given the worst desk, in the worst spot, the crappiest chair and, from the looks of it, the oldest computer.

He sat in the chair which hissed down a few inches in protest on its pneumatic strut. When he was almost certain it wouldn't collapse under his weight, he used his feet to spin around and look over at Blackstone who still did not raise her head.

'Morning, boss.'

She continued to read, head down in the documents in front of her, ignoring him. He noticed that, overnight, she had changed the colour and style of her hair. It was now orange and as spiky as a conker shell.

Henry didn't mind a waiting game. He was getting decent enough money for his trouble, so sitting around doing nothing for a few minutes was no hardship, although it wasn't his natural state. He could relax as much as the next person but preferred to be 'doing'.

Presently, she looked up. 'What fucking time do you call this?'

'My contracted hours are nine to five, actually.'

'Just guidelines, those.'

'Ahh,' Henry said.

Her expression had been surly up to that point, but now they both smiled as the ice broke.

'How're you doing?' he asked.

'All good,' she said primly. 'Yourself?'

'Yeah, would say so. You know how it is – old folk don't need much sleep. What's today's plan?'

Henry glanced at the files in front of Blackstone.

'Tell me more about Thomas James Benemy,' she said.

'I thought I'd already said enough.'

'No, I mean from the start. What happened?'

Unsure why she was asking, Henry began again, repeating and filling in the blanks from the story he'd told the previous day. The shoplifting deployment way back in 1985, spotting Tommy helping himself to perfume; the chase through the streets and finding him in an alley, then being beaten unconscious; keeping Tommy's ID to himself, arresting him; then Tommy going missing.

'So you got beaten up, then woke up surrounded by people in white coats and you didn't put much effort into catching the people who did it to you?' Blackstone grimaced.

'There was an investigation, but it dwindled to nothing, and anyway, I was on the Support Unit and we didn't really stay in one place long enough for me to keep following this up. Y'know – join the Support Unit, visit every town and village in Lancashire, cause mayhem, then leave? A great life.' Henry shrugged. 'I was young, carefree! So he got away with it – *they* got away with giving me a good kicking. Shit happens.'

For the first time in a while, his thoughts returned to Robert Fanshaw-Bayley, the man who was his DCI back then, later to become the chief constable and always remain Henry's nemesis. FB was dead now, having suffered a massive heart attack some time ago. Henry had been with him when he died and he kind of missed him now. Not much. Just a bit. He had been a huge part of his life for so many years.

'And he stole two grand's worth of perfume?' Blackstone asked. Henry nodded.

'A lot for a shoplifter – especially a lad.'

'Fenced it on, I assume,' Henry guessed.

'In an organized way?' Blackstone asked.

'What do you mean?'

'Nothing.'

'Don't you mean something?'

Blackstone laid her left hand flat on a stack of A4-sized forms. She said, 'I had an early start this morning.'

'After the hair re-dye?'

'That's a whole different story . . . Anyway, I went over to Blackpool and got the key to the archive building.'

'The archive building?' Henry said in disbelief. 'Didn't know such a thing existed.'

'Well, as you know, there's a new police station just recently opened, and when they were transferring shite from the old one to the new one, they didn't want to fill the new one with boxes and boxes of files and other bollocks, so, in their wisdom, they've somehow acquired a secure industrial unit just off Marton roundabout where they now store all this crap. You know what cops are like for not chucking stuff, even when they can? Anyway, I found all these crime forms for 1984 to 1986 from Blackpool Central.'

Henry wanted to say something to show he was intrigued.

He kept quiet.

'I sifted out all the reports of shoplifting over those years.'

'Ones where offenders were arrested?'

'Yes and no.'

'But shoplifting, if someone isn't caught, rarely gets reported,' Henry pointed out.

'I get that – unless, of course, a whole ton of stuff gets stolen all at once. I mean, if a bottle of aftershave is stolen, even if the store notices, it's not that bothered, yeah? All big stores have a margin to deal with stolen goods . . . but if the volume of goods stolen all at once is substantial, then they will report it. Like, if Boots had two grand's worth of perfume stolen and no one was arrested, they would most likely report it.'

'Possibly,' Henry agreed.

'Anyway,' Blackstone said, gathering momentum and enthusiasm, 'I've looked at all the town-centre shoplifting reports for that era, eighty-four to eighty-six, eliminated any which an offender was arrested and any under five hundred pounds in value, and I've put the results on a spreadsheet.'

Henry's 'spreadsheet' face came on. The one in which his indifference was apparent for all to see. He wasn't great at covering that up. However, he leaned forward, feigning interest.

'Bit of context first . . . there were forty thousand crimes, give or take, committed in Blackpool in that period of time. Shoplifting – or, to give it its official Home Office term, "stealing from shops and stalls" – is one of the minor ones, so it doesn't surprise me that what I've found has been overlooked – and is still being overlooked.'

'And that is?'

'There were over a hundred reports from shops in town with goods worth more than two thousand pounds stolen on each occasion – so quite big crimes, but still shoplifting and not a sexy crime, shall we say?'

Henry calculated: 'Two hundred grand.'

'And mostly expensive perfumes or designer clothing.'

'So, branded goods?'

'All branded goods,' she confirmed. 'So over that period of time, a lot of stuff of high value has been stolen . . . and that includes your incident with Tommy.'

'OK,' Henry said, wondering where this was going.

She looked at him expectantly, as though he should *know* where it was going.

He said, 'OK,' again.

'I thought you were supposed to be a detective?'

'Once . . . now I'm just Christie, Henry Christie, Civilian Investigator.'

Blackstone's head sagged despondently as though she was banging it against a brick wall.

'Just tell me,' Henry said.

She tried to motivate herself again. 'Right, right . . . another thing: how often did the Support Unit go to Blackpool to run anti-shoplifting operations that you can remember?'

Henry shrugged. 'When I was on the unit, maybe half a dozen times?'

'I'll tell you – twelve times.'

'OK, I'll have that,' Henry accepted.

'And with that one exception when you arrested Tommy, not once were any of those high-value thefts ever committed when you guys were in town. I've cross-checked the dates. I mean, shoplifters were arrested but they were just the usual lot because shoplifting's a blight on the town anyway . . . but I'm looking for something different within the dross of it all – some pattern.'

Henry waited.

'So – question – why were none of the "big" offences committed when you lot were in town?' Blackstone posed.

Henry thought about it, then said something that, a moment later, he wished he hadn't. 'You're not one of those who think there's a conspiracy around every corner, are you?'

As soon as he said it, he regretted it from the instant look of horror and hurt on Blackstone's face. A look coupled with disappointment.

She rose from her chair and said, 'Fuck you, Henry Christie.'

Henry watched her storm out of the office, heard her footsteps thudding down the corridor in her pink Doc Marten boots, then heard the door open. She obviously then left the FMIT building in a fury directed at him.

He moved across to her desk, looking at the computer screen still displaying the spreadsheet she had been talking about, plus the stack of handwritten crime forms she had rooted out from the archives, a building Henry assumed must have looked a bit like the warehouse at Area 51. Henry had to admit she had been very busy.

Next to her desk were two bin bags, one of which was sealed around the top with an evidence tag, the other open. Henry recognized them as the bags containing the obscene pornographic photos seized from Clanfield's flat the day before. Henry realized that Blackstone must also have been to Preston police station to get these from the property store, making Henry wonder why. Not only that; he also wondered just how little sleep she must have had if she had dyed her hair, travelled to Blackpool and also to Preston, and then been in work before Henry arrived – and he had been early.

He sat in her chair, then picked a pair of latex gloves out of the box on her desk, pulled them on and dipped his hand into the open bag and carefully extracted a handful of photographs.

He placed them on the stack of old crime reports and tapped them into place so they formed a neatish pile – they varied in size – then began to look at them. He didn't really want to, but knew it was one of the necessary parts of his job.

In terms of the age of the photographs, there seemed to be a lot of variation. Some were in black and white, though most were colour, and some had obviously been taken with a Polaroid camera; some could have been fifty years old, some could have been taken yesterday – and maybe were. Even with the few he had taken out of the bag, it was quite a collection. Henry could only guess how many thousands of images Clanfield had on his computer as well. He was a seriously perverted guy.

Although Henry took in each image he looked at and could only conceive what hell the victims in each were going through, he was curiously detached from what he was seeing, although not desensitized. They were sickening, but over the years he'd seen the likes of such things many times and could handle it emotionally, tough though it was.

What it did to him was give him a drive to bring the offenders down.

The majority of the photos did not show the faces of the abused victims – these were scrubbed or pixelated out – just what was happening to their bodies. Nor were the faces of the abusers ever shown.

He had never thought he would have to look at such things again, yet here he was.

After about a dozen, he'd had enough. He'd started off thinking he had a thick skin, but it was already showing signs of seepage. Maybe he wasn't as tough as he used to be; maybe age had softened him up.

'Enough,' he said. He picked up the stack with one hand, opened the bin bag with the other and dropped the photographs back in – except that didn't quite happen. The latex gloves made his fingers slippy and he lost grip of the photos, flipping them all over the floor and underneath Blackstone's desk as if he was throwing down a pack of playing cards.

Cursing, he slid off the chair on to his hands and knees and started to collect them up and drop them in the bag, not really looking at the images any more, except for the very last one he was about to put in.

Down there on his knees, he went very tense and very cold. He slid the photograph on to the desktop and hauled himself creakily to his feet using the edge of the desk. He stood and looked at the image for many seconds before getting out his mobile phone and dialling Blackstone's number.

'What?' she answered curtly.

'Where are you right now?'

She was in the dining room where the breakfast serving was just finishing for the few residential students at the training centre. COVID had shut down the centre, but as restrictions were eased, one or two courses for smaller numbers were beginning to run again.

She was hunched over an empty plate that may have accommodated a very large breakfast and was drinking a cup of coffee while messing about with her mobile phone.

Henry approached her cagily. 'Can I get you another brew?'

Without looking up, she nodded, and Henry was sure he could feel the heat of wrath radiating from her. She was still mad at him.

He went to the coffee machine, bought two white coffees, and carried them back to Blackstone who, as far as he could tell, still hadn't raised her head, although he guessed she may well have watched him walking down the dining room and fired laser daggers from her eyes into his back.

He pushed a coffee towards her as he sat down opposite, just far enough away from her to avoid the arc of her punches and infection from COVID.

'I'm so sorry,' he said genuinely.

She grunted something; he wasn't exactly sure what.

'I said I'm very sorry.'

This time she raised her head slowly. Henry half expected it to swivel 360 degrees.

'What do you want – a carrot?'

Henry blinked.

'You know what? I've only known you a day and a bit, but even so, in that short space of time, I actually expected more of you today – *much more*. I know you've been a hotshot detective, murder solver, used your gun, got shot, took on paid assassins and terrorists and all that sexy shit . . . yeah, I did my homework on you, and I thought you'd just be a jumped-up dickwit know-it-all. And, this morning, lo and behold, you proved to be just that, Henry Christie.'

'Yeah, OK, I get you,' he said shamefacedly. 'But, y'know . . .' He was struggling to put across what he wanted to say in a way that might mean they could actually continue to talk to each other.

She didn't give him the chance. Instead, she cut in: 'I've been shat on for the last four years, give or take, because I went on about a big conspiracy. I've been kept down, like being fucking water-boarded, just because I had the temerity to suggest that – yep – there's a conspiracy going on that involves cops, businessmen, crims, counsellors, judges – you name it, all pissing in the same pot. And it's fucking organized, too, Henry, and I'll lay odds it's been going on even before, and certainly since, you chased Tommy Benemy out of that shop in 1985. Thirty-five-plus years – and you know what, I got sidelined, told to forget it. And I thought you were better and would listen and take me seriously, Henry Christie. Obviously not.'

She raised her head even more, tilted her chin and pulled down the scarf she was wearing, showing Henry the burns on her neck again – which she still had to explain to him.

'I'm no hotshot analyst, Henry. But I look for repeating patterns, even if they're not frequent. I wasn't any good at maths, but I can add up and subtract, and I read stuff and I see through the dross. Doing that drove me down a dark corridor four years ago . . .'

Her eyes showed Henry she was once again reliving this, but now she was verbalizing it for his benefit. 'Accidentally, more than anything, but I knew I was on the brink of something that had been bugging me, and it led me to an unlit corridor . . . and the screams of a kid . . . and the shadow of a man, I think . . . then the flash and burn of sulphuric acid.'

She took a juddering breath. 'And that's why I had that panic attack last night.'

Henry gulped and said, inadequately, 'Demons.'

'Scarred,' she said. She tapped her temple. 'Up here.' Then she touched her neck. 'And down here.' Then she touched her chest over her heart. 'And in here, too.' Then added, 'For life.'

Henry said, 'Right, OK . . . let me just say something and don't get mad with me.'

'Look, I'm not a flat-earther, for fuck's sake!'

'I said don't get mad.' His voice was calm.

'OK, OK.' She backed off.

'Thing is, conspiracy theories are usually unfounded. You know, like the government child sex accusations in the seventies . . .'

She opened her mouth to interrupt.

Henry held up a finger. 'Mostly, they come to nothing, especially those concerning institutions and organizations. Yep, I'll have it – like-minded, evil individuals linking together, maybe, but not really coordinated, if you get my drift? I get organized crime, I do . . . I've been chasing it all my life, trying to bring it down, and I did wonder about Tommy Benemy and the amount of stuff he stole, but . . . meh.' He shrugged. 'Unconvinced . . . but I do have an open mind – honestly.' He smiled. 'Right – mansplaining section of the day done; now down to you.'

'Bottom line?' she said.

'Bottom line.'

'Cops, businesses, councillors, crims . . . missing children, unde-tected crime waves – yes, coordinated evil. And no one wants to know.'

'Like a modern-day Fagin?'

'Up to a point. Kids stealing to order, being abused, being murdered, maybe . . . certainly intimidated to keep schtum because it's the only thing they know.'

Henry considered her words.

'I haven't done this,' Blackstone went on, 'but I'll bet if you get hold of Blackpool's crime figures for the last thirty-five years, I can do exactly what I did with those from 1984 to 1986 . . . because I also researched them for a two-year period when I was a DS in Blackpool four years ago.'

'You reckon?'

'Yes, because I am not nuts.'

'How far up did you take it?'

'I worked my way up from my DI to the chief constable and they all told me I was seeing things that didn't exist. There was no "real" pattern to the shoplifting figures, just blips. They covered up their ears and sang the "blah-blah" song to drown me out. Didn't want to know. Too scary to even contemplate, especially when I suggested that cops might be involved. "Cops don't do abuse," they said. Looked at me like I was a hysterical woman, because that's the world we still live in.' She looked devastated.

Henry leaned back and rolled the base of his coffee cup on the table. He uttered an expletive quietly and said, 'You think this is still going on? Even now?'

Blackstone also sat back and looked at him. 'Maybe. I just saw . . . similarities, shall we say? Thing is, what if this is true and it's been going on for years in front of our noses and we haven't seen it? Anyway, why did you come and apologize?'

'I had an epiphany,' he said mysteriously.

'Don't talk like a wanker. One thing I don't do these days is suffer dickheads gladly – ask the civvie investigator whose place you took. He was an ex-Jack, up his own fat arse . . . bit like you.'

'Was that my induction-stroke-welcome speech?'

'Part of it . . . so, why?'

'I was going through your things . . .'

She glared at him. 'You went through my things?'

He gave her a nice smile, hoping to deflect any more hostility from her. 'And came across this.'

He dipped his hand into his jacket pocket, took out the photograph he'd picked up from the ones he'd knocked on to the floor under her desk. He checked there was no one else in close proximity to see the disturbing image – the dining room was all but empty now – and pushed it over to Blackstone but kept his hand over it.

'This kind of makes sense of what you were telling me,' Henry said. 'Possibly.'

He took away his hand to reveal it: a naked young boy but with his face scratched out.

She looked at it. 'And?' She shrugged. 'Just like a thousand other photos in that bin bag.'

'It isn't.'

Blackstone waited.

Henry's voice was hesitant, shaky, and his heart began to up its rhythm. 'I can't see the face, but look at his right forearm.'

She picked up the photograph and peered closely at it, seeing a thin arm with some marks on it. 'A tattoo?'

Henry nodded.

Blackstone looked even closer. 'Of what?'

'A house.'

'Just looks like a square with a triangle on it.'

'It is. A box – the house – with a point on it, like a kid might draw, I suppose. And, if you look closely enough, it looks like a line slashed across the box at a bit of an angle. I'll bet the tech people can zoom in on it and make the image clearer if we ask them.'

'To what end? Just another photo of a kid being abused. Clanfield will get charged with possession of them and that's probably as far as it'll go.'

'Not in this case,' Henry said. 'What if we actually knew who the kid was? A name, an identity to work from, something that could open up a can of worms, something that might help to prove or disprove your totally outlandish flat-earth theories,' he teased her.

She blinked at him.

Henry said. 'I'll lay my three-hundred-quid-a-day pay on it – a pound to a pinch of shit, to quote a gambling term – that this is Thomas James Benemy.'

Blackstone rocked forward. 'Are you sure?'

Henry nodded. He clearly remembered Trish Benemy whingeing about her son's stupidity in having the 'house' tattoo etched on his arm. 'What we have now is the confirmed identity of a lad who

stole thousands of pounds' worth of goods from a shop who then'
– he put his forefinger on to the photograph – 'got abused and
disappeared. Thirty-five years ago, admittedly, but it doesn't make
it any less real, as his mother's suicide proved yesterday. The wounds
are still very raw.'

'Shit.'

'And, like I said, it adds some credibility to your preposterous
conspiracy theory. Just kidding,' he finished quickly, seeing her
expression change.

'Where do we take it from here, then?'

'I'm not certain.'

'I am,' Blackstone said forcefully. 'And it's just the kind of thing
a civilian investigator is paid to do. Three hundred a day, did you
say?' She supped the last of her coffee. 'Number crunching is always
a good start.'

'OK, boss.'

She pushed the photograph back to Henry and said, 'Poor lad,'
at which moment her mobile phone rang. 'Rik Dean,' she mouthed
to Henry, then answered it and listened as Rik asked her where she
was. 'Having a brew with Civilian Investigator Christie . . . dining
room at the training school . . . OK.' She glanced at Henry while
listening intently to what Rik was saying, responding occasionally.
'So that's happening now? You want us to attend? Yep, OK, boss.'

Finally, she terminated the call.

Henry didn't like the look on her face.

'That was your brother-in-law. Ricky boy.'

'I gathered.'

'He wants us to get over to Blackpool now.'

'Why?'

'The post-mortem's being done on Trish Benemy.'

Henry nodded. 'As expected.'

'Thing is, it's not suicide. It's murder.'

TEN

'Well, well, well, as I live and breathe,' the man said. He was holding up a pair of smoke-ravaged lungs in front of him, the blood from them dripping into a stainless-steel bowl in a sink. He was dressed in pathologist garb from head to toe, including a skull cap, face mask and wellington-type boots. The lungs he was holding had just been removed from the body on the slab, the torso wide open, displaying no internal organs whatsoever as the heart, liver, kidneys and stomach had also been removed and laid out on the dissecting table as though being prepared for a meal. The lungs had already been sliced open and the man was just holding them up for further inspection. He had looked over his shoulder as Henry and Blackstone entered the mortuary at Blackpool Victoria Hospital, both in scrubs and fitting their medical face masks in place of their personal ones. 'As I live and breathe,' the man said again, 'if it isn't that there Henry Christie.'

Even under the camouflage of his protective clothing, Henry recognized Professor Baines, the head Home Office pathologist for the North West region, whom Henry had first encountered for the very first time in the same public mortuary thirty-five years before. And since then Baines had become a 'sort of' friend to Henry. Baines had performed many post-mortems for Henry's cases and the two men had got to know each other well. Baines was also always interested in Henry's often entertaining love life.

'And if it isn't Professor Baines,' Henry said, recognizing the voice rather than the person underneath the gown.

'As you're no longer officially a police officer, I'm assuming this little lady is in charge of the investigation and you're just tagging along?'

From the corner of his eye, Henry saw the change in Blackstone's demeanour at the 'little lady' remark and he thought that Baines might be lucky if he made it out of the mortuary without having anything chopped off.

'I'm Detective Sergeant Blackstone . . . and I assume you're the quack,' she countered frostily.

Baines's ears rose half an inch as he smiled under the mask. 'Touché.'

'What have you got for us?' Blackstone went on, all business. She walked ahead of Henry past the mortuary slab to where Baines was still holding the dripping lungs aloft.

Henry followed but stopped momentarily at the empty body shell of Trish Benemy. He'd been to many PMs since his early days as a cop and knew they could be brutal affairs. Some pathologists treated dead bodies as lumps of meat, with disrespect and detachment, which Henry hated. He had even called a couple of them out on their attitudes, which had not endeared him to the police hierarchy, but despite having had the occasional flea in his ear, ironically about showing due deference to the pathologists concerned, Henry was ferociously on the side of the dead and realized that he and people like pathologists and undertakers had a huge responsibility towards their subjects. Baines was always fairly light-hearted in his approach, but Henry knew he took his work very seriously and had the utmost respect for the dead.

Henry gave a little sigh of sadness and went over to where Baines carefully laid out Trish's lungs.

'The police report stated this woman had been found with a plastic bag pulled over her head,' Baines was saying. 'And that she is suspected of having committed suicide.'

'Correct,' Blackstone confirmed.

Baines nodded. 'Her lungs have been decimated by a lifetime of heavy smoking,' he said, 'hence their colour – black. And there are cancerous growths in the lower right lobe.'

Baines prised open the right lung and pointed at several spots and said, 'Cancer. Untreated, it would have led to her death some way down the line – two years maybe. But she died of asphyxiation and putting a bag over her head would definitely have smothered her. I've performed post-mortems on many people who have committed suicide in this manner. Mainly women, I might add.'

'Why women?' Henry asked.

'Not sure, but it seems a more common method for a woman to take her own life . . . and this lady did die of asphyxiation by smothering – but not because of a plastic bag. I would suggest she was smothered by a pillow or a cushion. Her larynx, oesophagus and the bronchial tracts that make up her lungs have tiny fibres in them consistent with having inhaled them from something used to smother her, such as a pillow or cushion.'

'There was a fluffy cushion next to her,' Henry said.

'Then I suggest you seize it for evidence, Henry, my boy, because something like that has been held over her mouth and nose and she has inhaled some of the loose fibres from its surface as she struggled to stay alive.'

All three turned to look at Trish Benemy's cadaver.

'She was murdered and whoever did it tried to make it look like a suicide,' Baines said.

Henry and Blackstone returned to the bedsit in which Trish's body had been discovered. This time, Blackstone had no problem walking along the corridor to the room with Henry. It had been abandoned intact by the police who had immediately assumed suicide rather than murder, rather than the other way around, which was the standard operating procedure – *Think murder!* – but as Henry looked around the room, he guessed, hoped, there was no harm done in terms of evidence gathering.

On the floor beside the settee was the cushion Henry recalled having seen. It was pink and fluffy and looked to match the fibres Baines had tweezered out of Trish's respiratory system. A forensic comparison would be required, but in his heart Henry knew there would be a match.

Baines had also mentioned the smell of alcohol and had taken blood samples. He believed she would have been quite drunk and therefore easily overpowered, being such a lightly built person. Two empty gin bottles were on the floor.

'Thoughts, Henry?'

'Initially, having read the suicide note: despair, drink, suicide. Now: despair, drink, murder – but there's nothing to suggest her murder had any connection with Tommy at all. I imagine when we start looking into her lifestyle, that'll probably lead us pretty quickly to a killer, although we need to keep an open mind. I'd guess, looking round this dump, that she was in a very bad place in her head, and probably hung around with town-centre drunks.'

He was desperately trying to reconnect with his murder scene mojo, which had served him well on so many murders in the past – but he knew it was rusty. 'But, that said, she'd been searching daily for her long-lost son for more years than any parent should have to, apparently without discovering any answers. She never gave up, showed a depth of resolve that most of us, even in those circumstances, might never have within us. She tried and failed – or did she?'

'What do you mean?'

'Well, boringly, the old adage "find out how a person lived, find out why they died" must apply here.'

'So how did she live?'

Henry shrugged. 'Don't yet know. Maybe she *was* just a town-centre drunk; maybe she mixed with other drunks who are not above suffocating a person to death for a few quid. But she also kept up hope for Tommy. Her life will be scrutinized once an investigation gets underway, but the suicide note troubles me slightly.'

'Why?'

'It's only just struck me. It's incomplete . . . it's just three-quarters of a page; the bottom section is missing, ripped off, so it's unsigned, which is unusual. So maybe there is more to this . . . I don't know,' he said inadequately. 'Other than she's dead and I'm in some way connected to it. No matter what, even if this isn't linked to Tommy, the least I can do, with that photo of him from Clanfield's flat, is to get some closure for her, while assisting on the investigation into her death, too.'

'Well, I wouldn't bank on that,' Blackstone said. 'We're the Cold Case Unit, not the Murder Squad.'

And on those words, Blackstone's phone rang. Rik Dean.

She looked at the screen and then at Henry, and before answering, said, 'Are we taking bets?'

She walked out of the room into the corridor and spoke to Rik out of earshot of Henry. She came back a few minutes later, pretending to throw her phone down. But didn't.

'Told you!'

'What's happening?'

'He's bringing a team in, wants us to brief the SIO, then wave bye-bye. We're not on it,' she said. 'We've to wait until he arrives, tell him what we know, then head back to the office.'

'Well, let's just roll with that punch, eh?' Henry suggested.
'You know what? I get kicked aside all the piggin' time!'

It was a chilly day, a cool breeze coming in from the Irish Sea over
the Ribble Estuary, as Henry and Blackstone took a seat at an
outdoor picnic table at the Beach Café on the seafront at St Annes,
the resort a little further south than Blackpool – more genteel but
still on its way, sadly, to becoming a ghost town.

The café had reopened recently following lockdown. It was one
of Henry's favourite spots. It served good food and was a great
place for a meet and a chat, especially with someone like Blackstone
who was on edge and needed to chill.

They looked at each other across the table, hunched over yet
another coffee.

'Brrr,' she shivered.

'Tell me about your night in a dark corridor,' he said to her.

Obviously, he was no shrink but he thought he needed to get to
the bottom of this as far as possible – for his own sanity as well as
hers – because he could see how much it was holding her back.

He had seen the outer scars; she'd alluded to the inner ones, but
there hadn't really been any meat put on the bones. Purely from a
selfish point of view, Henry felt he had to know as much about the
incident as possible and she had to know he knew. Otherwise, this
fledgling relationship was going to get nowhere in the next six
months.

That was his take, anyway. Whatever lay ahead for him and
Blackstone as running partners, not just what was going on here
and now, needed them to be comfortable with each other, and that
comfort had to come from knowledge.

Blackstone seemed to sense it. 'Do I detect some amateur psycho-
babble shit coming up? Because if that's the case . . .' She left the
final words unsaid.

'That's what I like – an open mind.'

She tutted.

'Look, Debbie . . . I want you to know I've been down some
pretty dark holes in the last forty-odd years. I've had a nervous
breakdown. I've been chased by black dogs many times. I've had
to shoot people, yes. I've been hammered so many times I've lost
count; I've also been sidelined by the job more times than I care

to mention. Believe it or not, I wasn't the most popular cop on the block.'

'Honestly? I'd never have guessed.'

'I know, hard to imagine.' He smiled. 'I've lost my wife, then my fiancée; I've lost good friends . . .' He gulped and went silent, turned his head and stared across the sand dunes.

'Don't tell me – you had counselling for everything? CBT?'

'I've had my fair share,' he confessed. 'And, honestly, it never really did me much good.' He shrugged. 'I just learned how to deal with things myself. Compartmentalizing stuff so that in the course of time those little rooms are so far at the back of your brain it gets forgotten on a day-to-day basis, unless some arsehole chucks you the key!'

'Oh, great master, what do I do, then?' she mocked him, shook her head and scowled.

'How should I know?'

'So why the boo-hoo lecture? All that syrup and "woe is me"?'

'God, you really are hard work.'

'Whatev—'

'Petulant, abrasive, self-centred, arrogant, nasty – and definitely scarred,' Henry responded, reeling off her character defects.

She started at him, aghast. 'You swallowed a thesaurus?'

'But I do know something else.'

'That would be? Astound me with your vocabulary.'

'The world and this job owe you nothing, Debbie. Fuck all. It's all down to you and what you make of it. If you're not cut out for its harsh realities, then get the fuck out of it. You won't be missed; that I can assure you.'

'Sometimes I just want to work behind a till, or stocking shelves.'

'I'm not decrying those ambitions . . . but you are better, *much* better than that.'

'Even though I'm a twat?'

'I never said that . . . not sure it's in the thesaurus,' he said. 'Thing is, those qualities are part of what it takes to be a good detective, and what I've seen over the last couple of days is that you are a bloody good detective.'

Across the table from him, her tattooed eyebrows furrowed deeply.

'And if you keep going, one day all this shit will fall back into place for you. You have what it takes, but even I can see you somehow *must* deal with the acid thing.'

'Bit more than just an "acid thing",' she corrected him.

He held up his hands to pacify her.

'It screwed my life up, Henry,' she said with heart-rending bitterness. 'Made me hate myself, made me go into hiding, go on the defensive, come out attacking every time.'

She pinched the bridge of her nose, then her right hand snaked into the inside pocket of her denim jacket and she extracted her wallet. She took out a piece of A5-sized paper that had been folded to fit inside, unfolded it and pushed it across to him. It was a photograph.

'Me. As I was,' she said simply.

Henry flattened it out. Blackstone in uniform with short, bobbed, brunette hair, neat, tidy, immaculate. She looked very, very pretty, almost childlike.

'Pretty fit, eh? What d'you say, Henry?'

'Always had a thing for a lass in uniform – and yes, fit.' He grinned lopsidedly at her, then looked closely at the photo. Back then, whenever it was, the only adornment her face had was a couple of studs in her ear lobes. He glanced up at her current look with the numerous nose, eye, lip, ear and eyebrow rings.

She was getting another piece of paper out of her wallet – another photograph which she unfolded and smoothed out and pushed across to Henry who placed it alongside the first one.

This was a selfie, taken in a full-length mirror.

Blackstone's current look: dressed in only a sports bra and a pair of large black knickers. Her hair was spiked red, piercings abounded, including one in her belly button. A snake tattoo curved all the way around her torso, coloured with emerald scales and ruby eyes. It was truly stunning.

'I've had my nipples pierced too,' she added helpfully.

Henry said nothing, just compared the photographs, his eyes dancing from one to the other and back again.

He saw the caustic fingers of the acid burn in the selfie but also her sad eyes, the self-loathing in them.

'My boyfriend ditched me. He couldn't even look at me.'

Henry leaned back and pushed the photographs back to her. She re-folded them and slid them back into her wallet.

'Ever since it happened, I've been running away from myself. I hate what I've become. *I hate me.*'

Having instigated this, Henry started to feel he was out of his depth. He said, 'It wasn't your fault.'

'I know that. You can tell me that till you're blue in the face. Doesn't help.'

'And no one was ever caught for it?'

'Nope.'

'Tell you what,' Henry said, suddenly having an idea. 'Let's help each other out here and see if our paths cross at some point.'

'How exactly is that going to help?'

'You scratch my back, I'll scratch yours.'

'Again, I ask . . .'

'Well, I clearly have unresolved issues and so do you, so why don't we help each other? As I see it, it doesn't really matter that we aren't officially on any specific murder investigations. In fact, it helps us out a bit, gives us a bit of freedom to come and go. We're detectives, aren't we? Let's go and detect things that are bugging the life out of us both.'

'I think you'll find that I'm a detective and you're a civilian investigator.'

Henry shook his head in irritation. 'Be that as it may . . . but before we move on to rid Gotham City of all known crims, there is one more thing I need to tell you.'

He saw her draw away in mock horror.

'And I say this as purely a neutral observer, no axe to grind or agenda to pursue.'

'Shit – it gets worse.'

'Thing is, you are still fit and, above all, you are still beautiful, and don't you ever forget it.'

She blinked at him many times, nonplussed. Her mouth opened and she swallowed as she looked at him, completely shocked by this statement. A flush of red crept up from her scar and around her neck.

Then she laughed it off. 'I'm still not going to shag you, old guy.'

'Debbie, I'd never get past those gatekeeper knickers.'

They finished their coffees and put together their game plan, the first part of which was to visit the place where Blackstone had been splashed with acid. On the way, Henry asked her what set of circumstances had led up to her going to that location in the first place.

ELEVEN

DS Deborah Blackstone slammed the cell door on the prisoner after pushing him right into the cell itself, assisted by a gaoler and a custody sergeant. The prisoner stumbled to the back of the cell, whirled around ferociously on his captors and came back at them like a wounded tiger, although he was far from wounded.

He was furious because he'd just been interviewed for a serious assault and had smugly sat there for almost two hours, at first saying, 'No comment' and then, as the evidence against him mounted, vehemently denying the allegation – which was that he had held a man's forearm down on a kerb and jumped on it, breaking it badly. It was the culmination of a gruesome attack, one of those difficult ones to prove – one of those so common on the streets of Blackpool, committed by people only in town for a day and a night, then going back to their homes, often in the far reaches of the British Isles.

Blackstone had been relentless in her pursuit of this particular offender. Not because of the severity of the assault, but because an innocent gay man had been the target. She had spent many hours trawling through CCTV images, sifting through ANPR (Automated Number Plate Recognition) images and results, public transport records, submitting blood samples, interviewing night-club bouncers and circulating grainy photographs until she identified the man, a body builder from Glasgow.

She had enjoyed the pursuit, the digging, following leads; she was no analyst, but it suited her to sift through anything that might be evidence, even though some of her colleagues regarded her as a bit too bonkers. It was only an assault, but her response had been that if anyone, resident or visitor to the resort, was attacked, then the cops had a duty to chase the offender(s) and, if possible, bring them to justice.

Interviewing him had also been a pleasure.

Pushing gently as she questioned him, seeing the look in his eyes change as he realized that evidence against him really did exist, was stacking up irresistibly and crushing him against a brick wall so that he had nowhere to run.

That was the point at which he became aggressive in the interview room and had to be physically restrained and thrown back into his cell, where he had been deposited, it had to be said, with as much force as possible.

Blackstone swished the palms of her hands together and exhaled as she grinned at the gaoler and the custody sergeant. She then rearranged her bobbed, brunette hair back into place – she was fanatical about such things – and began the walk back to the custody office. The gaoler went on ahead, leaving Blackstone and the sergeant side by side, their steps slowing in synch as their shoulders touched gently – accidentally, it might have seemed to an observer. Actually, it was quite deliberate and each of them experienced a surge of static from the contact as their relationship was in the very fledgling stage.

'I'm off at ten,' the sergeant whispered.

'I know,' Blackstone said.

Both were talking with their lips closed, like ventriloquists.

'Can you hang about until then?' he asked.

'I have things I can be doing,' she said.

'How does a tryst at the Tram and Tower sound?'

'Sounds like a plan.'

By which time they had reached the turning into the custody office and Blackstone, in an effort to fool anyone who might suspect this liaison, continued talking as if partway through a conversation. 'So, I'm looking at a night in the cells for this guy, no bail, court tomorrow . . . oh, hi, boss,' she said, spotting the patrol inspector behind the custody desk, looking through the binder containing all the records of everyone in the traps – fourteen of them. A fairly quiet night in the sausage factory.

The inspector looked round as the two came into view.

Her name was Julie Clarke.

'Hi, Debs. Where are we up to with the guy from Glasgow? I just heard you talking to Dave about him' – Dave Allbridge was the name of the custody sergeant.

'Yeah, he's had his chance to confess. Bracey,' Blackstone said, referring to one of the DCs up in the CID office, 'is inputting the charges as we speak. No bail as there's every chance he wouldn't turn up for court or he will intimidate witnesses. Hope that's OK with you, boss?' Blackstone was more than happy to refer to anyone who outranked her as 'boss', uniform or otherwise.

'Absolutely fine,' Clarke said. As patrol inspector, it was her responsibility to review all the prisoners in custody and ensure the investigative process was carried out as swiftly as possible, which often meant chasing up detectives who wanted to 'play the game'. But with almost thirty years' service, Clarke was rarely hoodwinked. Also, by getting Blackstone's prisoner charged, there was one less body to worry about in the cells because he would now become the total responsibility of the custody sergeant until the court appearance. 'Looks like a job well done,' she complimented Blackstone.

'Cheers, boss.'

Blackstone was feeling quietly proud of herself. It had taken a lot of time and effort to track the guy down.

Clarke closed the binder and, with a nod to Blackstone and Allbridge, left the office.

Both officers watched her leave.

Allbridge said, 'Think she knows about us?'

'Wouldn't surprise me. Not much gets past her.'

'Hmm – she's one of the good ones,' Allbridge said.

'She is.'

'So,' Allbridge said, checking the wall clock. It was just after eight p.m. 'What're you doing for the next two hours?'

'Paperwork, though I might have a quick stroll up the Golden Mile.'

'Well, fancy that! Your pet project?'

'Just fancy.'

She gave him a wink and jabbed the tip of her tongue out of the corner of her mouth, spun on her heels and left the custody office, giving her arse an extra sashay for Allbridge's benefit because she knew he'd be leering at her. She didn't mind one bit because he was one horny cop, and she was happy to have him lusting after her. She fully intended to fuck his brains out later.

After checking with the detective she'd told to fix up the charge forms, she decided to go and mooch around the arcades. Grabbing her personal radio, she set off out, exiting the police station via the door on the mezzanine level across from the magistrates' court.

She trotted down the steps on to Bonny Street, then walked around to the promenade which was still packed with day trippers. Ear-splitting music and the reek of candyfloss and frying burgers came from the arcades and cafés.

Blackstone would miss this instant connection with the town centre when the police station moved out of the resort; building had just commenced on the new one. She understood the need. The present station, built in the mid-1970s, was no longer fit for purpose and there was no space in town for a new one.

Unfortunately, the move would mean she wouldn't get the chance to indulge in her 'pet project', as Allbridge had teased her.

Although missing persons cases were not really the remit of the CID unless they were related to serious offences, they were something that was part of the very fabric of Blackpool. Hundreds of people, mainly kids, surged into the resort every year having gone missing from their homes right across the UK. Even local kids could easily disappear into the heaving morass that was Blackpool, where anyone could get lost and become just another face among millions.

Most eventually turned up. Some unscathed, others having suffered horrific abuse that was often never uncovered; there were others who never, ever surfaced again. Those who might have been spotted in the resort but were never caught and never to be seen again, plunging their relatives into a lifetime of angst. Blackpool, despite its bright lights, had a very dark underbelly that few ever saw: organized crime that included the drugs trade and prostitution, yes, but also the ability to suck in the unwary, usually spit them out, but occasionally not.

Blackstone felt some responsibility for the children.

It was just 'a thing' – something she found difficult to explain – but she knew that if she could intervene and do something good for youngsters who were wayward and lost (in so many ways), and needed help, even if they didn't see it that way, it was better than nothing.

So over her time as a detective sergeant (she had been promoted in from Lancaster) at Blackpool, she had made it a bit of a mission during any downtime she might have (which wasn't much, admittedly) to get to know the 'community' of the Golden Mile, where the kids gravitated to, and try to make a difference.

Every day she checked missing-from-home reports and, if possible, spent a little time on foot.

Over the course of several months, Blackstone became as familiar a face on the Golden Mile as the local foot patrol officers and PCSOs. She got to know business people – shady and legit – stall holders, balloon sellers even; also the regular kids and the homeless, of which there were too many. She even managed to set up an old hotel undergoing renovations as a place for homeless people to get a night's sleep out of the rain, though funding for such projects was always problematic and temporary.

That night, as she strolled through the arcades, she got a lot of nods from the people she knew, plus lots of cautious glances from the local children who knew she was a cop – cautious because although she was there mainly for welfare, she didn't tolerate lawbreakers. In her 'mooches', she had ended up with some very good prisoners all under the age of fifteen.

She stopped to chat with a 'regular' homeless guy and then a couple of local teenagers she'd previously locked up for 'rolling' a drunk. They were obviously on the prowl again, so she gave them the hard word and the 'I'm watching you' gesture.

They slunk off into the night like scalded cats.

There seemed to be nothing out of the ordinary going on, although Blackstone knew that what she was seeing on her stroll was just the tip of the iceberg. She began to head back to the police station, wanting to be there when the Glasgow guy was charged with grievous bodily harm and his bail refused. She was anticipating seeing the expression on his face and knew that if she got everything right, he wouldn't be seeing the outside of a cell for a long time.

She was almost back at the station, turning off the prom on to New Bonny Street by the Coral Island amusement complex, when one of the supervisors rushed out, looking all around her until her eyes locked on Blackstone who had spotted the young woman, seen she was stressed and, easily guided by her finely tuned cop radar, was already walking urgently towards her. Blackstone knew the woman – her name was Judith.

'Debbie, I need your help,' she cried in a panic. 'There's been an abduction or a kidnapping or something not good . . . I don't know.'

She quickly led Blackstone into the arcade and to an office at the back in which a young girl, maybe twelve years old, sat in a chair with her head bowed over, long, straggly hair hanging down. Another member of staff was standing close by, keeping an eye on her.

The girl looked up as the two women entered. Tears and snot were smeared down her face. Blackstone immediately noticed the almost non-existent skirt, cut-off T-shirt exposing her thin white belly and the myriad of self-inflicted tattoos on her arms.

Even before knowing anything else, she would have laid bets that the girl was a runaway.

'Hi, I'm Detective Sergeant Blackstone from Blackpool police station. What's happened, love?' Blackstone bounced on to her haunches to bring her down to eye level. Tenderly, she tucked back the strands of the girl's unkempt hair that were plastered all over her face in the slime. It looked as if it hadn't been washed for days.

'My mate, my mate,' she babbled. 'They got her, she's been picked up, dragged off . . . three white guys in a van.' She was close to hyperventilation, sucking in air.

'OK, just try and keep calm, and tell me slowly what happened,' Blackstone said in her best soothing voice. She was good at this.

'No!' The girl grabbed Blackstone's arm fiercely. 'You need to find her now. They're gonna rape her.'

'How d'you know that?'

'I do, cos I do . . . cos . . .' Her voice began to falter. 'Cos we've been wi' 'em and we thought they were OK, but then they started messing and we did a runner.'

'When was this?'

'Yesterday . . . an' we seen 'em today . . . fuckin' prowlin' in their van an' they spotted us and called us over an' chatted to us through t'window and said they were sorry, but then the side door opened an' the third guy tried to drag us both in, but I got free an' ran like fuck! They drove off wi' Kelly. She were screamin', like, an' I just ran for me life, in here, an' I was screamin' too.'

'OK – what's your name, love?'

'Ruby Weatherall.'

'And where did this happen?'

'Just . . . just out there.' She pointed in the direction of New Bonny Street.

'Which way?'

'T'wards town.'

'Right . . . you think you'd know the van again?'

'Maybe . . . it were small an' black an' had a sliding door,' Ruby said.

Blackstone glanced at the Coral Island employee. 'I'll take it from here, thanks, Judith. Well done.'

'No problem.'

Blackstone focused on Ruby. 'Right, what we're going to do is this, love: we're going to the police station, which is just around the corner, we're going to jump into my car and then we're going to comb the streets and see if we can spot the van and Kelly, and I'll get all the other police officers out there to do the same thing, OK?'

Ruby nodded.

'We jog to the cop shop, OK? And you keep talking to me all the time, yeah?'

Ruby nodded again.

Blackstone said, 'Let's go. Time matters.'

Blackstone was in her car – a dull ten-year-old Ford Focus – within minutes, Ruby sitting alongside, slowly scouring the streets while pumping the girl for information – anything that would help to find her friend. At the same time she had an ear to the radio, listening as patrols were deployed around the resort based on her information, so she was concentrating on several things at once.

'Where are you from, Ruby?'

'Huddersfield.'

'I take it you're missing from home?'

'Suppose I am,' she said sullenly.

'DS Blackstone from Inspector Clarke, receiving?'

'Go ahead, boss.'

'Are you thinking this is genuine?'

'Yes, ma'am.'

'Roger that.'

'How long have you been in Blackpool?'

'Uh, two weeks, I guess.'

'Where have you been staying?'

No response from Ruby.

'I asked where you've been staying.'

'Uh . . . wi' them guys.'

'Who are they?'

'Dunno . . . just first names is all I know . . . David an' someone else.'

'What the hell were you thinking?'

She shrugged, obviously feeling under pressure.

Blackstone had so many questions. 'Did they molest you, touch you?'

'Not at first.'

'So what happened first, love?' Blackstone was finding it hard to be too empathetic at that moment.

'They had us nicking an' dropping packages off, like.'

'Nicking what?'

'Y'know – shoplifting.'

'Shoplifting?'

'Yeah . . . designer goods . . . and they looked after us.'

'What sort of goods?'

'Perfume 'n' stuff . . . trainers, dresses, like . . . but not super-market shit if you know what I mean? At first it were good. They gave us booze and we 'ad fun. Then it got creepy. Hands up me skirt, on me cunt, y'know?'

Blackstone shivered at the word. Its usage had become much more common of late, especially on social media, but it didn't mean she liked it. In her eyes, it would never be an acceptable word to bandy about.

'Where did you stay with these people, Ruby?'

'Fuck should I know? No idea where I even am, 'cept in Blackpool . . . but if I see the place, I might recognize it . . . and the van.'

'Describe the van again.'

'Just a small black van with a sliding door . . . like a painter might have . . . there were buckets in it.'

'And the house you stayed in? Where was it? What was it like?'

'Wasn't a house . . . it were like a hotel – but being done up. A fuckin' wreck of a place.'

'Being refurbished, you mean?'

Ruby shrugged her slim shoulders. 'Suppose.'

Every available patrol was working the streets now, plus a static traffic car on a checkpoint on the M55, the main artery into and out of Blackpool.

'Inspector Clarke to DS Blackstone, receiving?'

'Yes, boss.'

'Your location and the description of the suspect vehicle again, please.'

'Currently Talbot Square . . . and it's a small black van, make unknown, registration unknown, with a sliding side door, like a work van of some sort. Two white males in the front, a third white male, probably out of sight in the back of the van. Best I can do.'

Then Clarke said, 'Urgent – I'm following a similar vehicle, Church Street towards Devonshire Square . . . three vehicles between me and it, which I'm struggling to pass because I'm in my own car, no blues and twos.'

Comms cut in: 'Patrols to make.'

Three mobiles piped up, responding from different locations.

Then: 'Inspector Clarke to patrols, vehicle has run a red light across Whitegate Drive . . . I'm stuck in traffic both ways.'

'They seem to be going out of town, if that's the van,' Blackstone said to Ruby. The temptation was to make that way herself – the conditioning of a cop: rush to everything. But she held back. Plenty of patrols were on their way now, and if it wasn't the right van, then valuable time would be wasted on a wild goose chase. She stayed cruising streets just off the town centre, that maze between Talbot Road and Warbreck Road in the North Shore area, continually asking questions of this witness and possibly victim, who seemed to be more and more reluctant to divulge information as time went by.

'Recognize this street?' Blackstone asked.

'They're all the same.'

'But do you think it could be around here? The hotel that's being refurbished?'

'Maybe . . .'

Blackstone was under no illusions. Many of the streets behind the prom had a similar look and were a maze, and at any one time there could be twenty hotels in different stages of being done up. Needle/haystack came to mind. Under her breath, she swore with frustration.

She listened to the voices of patrols as they converged on the area where Inspector Clarke had seen the van fitting the description. She turned on to Dickinson Road, down to Gynn Square roundabout.

She was intending to loop around and head back towards the town when Ruby suddenly sat upright and pointed north along Queen's Promenade.

'It might be up there!' she said excitedly.

Blackstone didn't question it but circumnavigated the roundabout and kept going north towards Bispham. The road inclined upwards. On the left were cliffs overlooking the beach; on the right, a string of hotels of varying sizes.

'Could be one of these,' she said to Blackstone, leaning across to get a look, making the detective wince at the young girl's body odour. She needed a bloody good shower.

Blackstone slowed to a crawl. Ruby peered across.

Then: 'That one! I'm sure it is.'

It was a very large hotel right on the front at the junction of Knowle Avenue, surrounded by a high metal fence of the type used to secure building sites. Blackstone slewed across the road and stopped.

Indeed, it was a hotel undergoing refurbishment.

'How did you get in and out?'

'Round the back, all the time. That's why I was confused, I think. Only saw this side of it the once.'

'Is there a gap in the fencing at the back?'

Ruby nodded.

Blackstone turned into Knowle Avenue and stopped. The fencing around the hotel continued here and then around the back of the premises.

'You stay here, OK? Do not move.'

'What're you doing?'

'Going for a gander.'

TWELVE

'This one,' Blackstone said to Henry Christie. She pointed across the road to the Park Lane Hotel. Henry shot across into the large car park at the front of the hotel, which was deserted. Even from the car they could see *Closed* signs and various COVID notices on the doors and windows of the premises.

'This is such a shame,' Henry said, feeling empathy with all hotel owners. 'Looks like a pretty nice hotel, actually.'

He saw Blackstone shiver. 'Didn't look like this the last time I was here,' she said and wrapped her arms around her as if she was cuddling herself.

'Never been back, ever?' Henry asked.

She shook her head.

'Let's go see, eh . . . talk me through it.'

The Park Lane Hotel, back then known as the Belmont, had been refurbished to a high standard, Blackstone noted, as, both masked, she and Henry walked up the steps from his car to the front door and rang the bell. A conservatory ran the full length of the front of the building, an ideal place to sit, eat and watch life go by, but now all the cane chairs and tables were stacked high.

'It was just a shell,' she said to Henry. 'Virtually completely gutted. I left the girl, Ruby, in my car with strict instructions to stay put and walked down the alley behind the hotel with my penlight torch, like the little girl I was. I made my way along the fence which was, I dunno, maybe eight feet high, made of mesh but backed with metal plates so you couldn't really see through, other than where the panels interlinked each other. Then I found two of the panels weren't connected or chained, so I pushed my way through into the back yard of the hotel. Loads of building materials stacked up, bricks, all sorts of shit. A small JCB-type digger thing, concrete mixers . . .'

She stopped and looked at Henry, who rang the bell.

Henry said, 'And a van?'

'How did you . . .?'

'Know? I'm just good at finishing people's sentences.' His ears rose as he smiled behind his face mask.

Despite reliving a terrifying past, Blackstone smiled too, but made sure her ears didn't move so as not to give her away. Smiling wasn't something she did easily these days.

'Yeah, a van . . .'

'We were eighty per cent booked up,' the hotel proprietor said as he led them through the hotel. He was called Risdon, late fifties, and came across as very avuncular, just the right kind of person to be running a hotel – *not*, Henry fleetingly thought, *like me*. Henry had never seen himself as having the right sort of personality to run The Tawny Owl. Too grumpy, too short-tempered by half. His secret ambition might have been to marry a landlady and that would have suited him fine. Instead, he ended up running the place. 'This was to be our first season since the refurbishment. Took the best part of four years to do because when I bought the place, the previous owners had let it rot to ruin, basically. If we don't open up very soon, I'm going to go to the wall,' Risdon finished.

'It's been a tough year, no doubt,' Henry commiserated. 'It's been . . . What's that thing everybody now says?'

'Unprecedented,' Blackstone said with a wink, finishing his sentence.

'Yeah – unprecedented,' Risdon said, ushering them through a foyer and up a flight of steps to a landing, through a set of fire doors to emerge at a long, first-floor corridor, stretching the whole length of the hotel, off which were bedrooms front and rear. It was nicely painted in beige with cheap, pleasant art on the walls. 'What's your interest?' he asked.

'Sometime during the refurbishment, a police officer stumbled across something happening in the hotel,' Henry explained, keeping it simple by adding, 'Intruders.'

'Oh, right . . . I think there were a few.'

'The officer was assaulted, the intruder escaped. It's a while ago, but something's come up and we're just doing some follow-up enquiries.' Henry kept it vague.

Risdon looked puzzled. 'I wonder why I don't know anything about it. When exactly was it?'

Henry looked at Blackstone, who reeled off the date. Risdon made some mental calculations. 'Ahh . . . the penny drops . . . that was in the very early days of the refurb. I was still running my hotel up in Cartmel and I left the gutting of the place and other basic stuff like plumbing and electrics to my builder, who did a great job, I have to say. I only came down here after all that was done.'

'Who was your builder?' Henry asked.

'Hindle's. Really good they were.'

'Blackpool based?'

'Yeah – quite an old established company.'

Henry stopped for a moment as he computed the name, trying to discover if it meant something to him.

Blackstone noticed. 'What is it?'

'Nothing, nothing.'

To Risdon, Blackstone said, 'Are we OK to have mooch around ourselves?'

'Sure, help yourself. No guests to disturb. I'll be down in reception . . . coffee's going on if I can tempt you?'

'Good plan,' Henry said.

Henry leaned on the window ledge. It was a nice room, as modern as could be within the old fabric of the existing building which, however good the refurb, meant slightly squeaky, uneven floors, but it was good enough to match any of the budget chain hotels out there that Henry had had the misfortune to stay in over the years, although – and he felt just a bit smug on this point – they were not a patch on the rooms at Th'Owl.

Blackstone leaned on the door jamb so that they were standing opposite each other, the double bed between them.

'This could well have been the room . . . I don't know. I didn't quite make it this far.'

As they were now standing further apart than two metres, they had removed their masks, although adherence to the social distancing rule had pretty much gone between the two of them.

'So,' Henry said. 'Van?'

Blackstone blinked rapidly as she recalled finding the gap in the fence, contorting through it with her torch between her teeth, to find a black van with a sliding side door which was unlocked.

She had peered in. It was basic – nothing to see with the pathetic beam of the torch, other than builder's materials. She pressed the flat of her hand on the bonnet lid: still warm.

And now, standing there across the room from Henry, she found she had to take a deep breath, that her throat, even four years later, had constricted and her heart was attempting to burrow its way out of her chest.

Beyond Henry, she could see the grey of the Irish Sea.

'I made a rookie mistake.'

Henry licked his lips.

'I acted too soon.'

'In what way?'

'All patrols were on the other side of town searching for the van the inspector had seen. Radio traffic was intense. I mean, a suspected snatching, kidnap, whatever. And my adrenaline was gushing like I was coming,' she said. Henry raised his eyebrows at the comparison. 'Then I heard a scream from inside the hotel. Girl screams. Horrific. Terror screams.'

Blackstone was in a trance as she spoke quietly.

'Nevertheless, I should have waited. I should have called it in – but, y'know? Fuck! Would it have made any difference to have taken the vehicle number, then shouted up where I was, even though I didn't know the name of the hotel, and then proceeded with caution? Nope. Raging bull, china shop. I heard that scream and it did something to me, something primal.' She clutched a fist to her heart. 'Then bam! I was gone . . . like a rookie, as I said.'

She had raced to a door covered with hardboard panels, yanked at them and they'd come off, and she'd stepped inside an unlit building. There was the smell of freshly planed timber – that stuck with her – and she found herself on a corridor on the ground floor.

Another scream – somewhere in the distance on an upper floor.

That drove her on to find a set of stairs, which she sprinted up. She came out on the first floor, all bare boards, freshly skimmed walls, doors either side, mostly boarded up and no lighting . . . other than from the door at the far end on the right-hand side. She saw shadows. She heard male voices. Then another scream and the sound of a slap and sobbing and a crashing noise. Underfoot, she remembered, the floorboards were bare, uneven.

'Even at that point I was petrified,' she told Henry. 'I knew I was going to find something deeply unpleasant going on . . . I didn't know how I was going to handle it, just that I had to.'

'It's what cops do,' Henry said, 'even in the world of today, which is something a lot of people don't understand. They go forward when other people run for their lives.'

'I moved down the corridor and, to be honest, I made a noise. Up to that point, I'd had my radio turned down, but I turned it up and then they knew I was coming. I was reckless . . . trying to protect a kid . . . number one in the reckless charts,' she said.

'Hmm, yeah, really reckless,' Henry agreed. 'Putting yourself in the firing line.'

'Whatever.' She wanted to smile but couldn't. 'Just before I reached the doorway' – she tapped the doorframe in which she was standing – 'someone stepped out – a guy, I think . . . a shadow, a silhouette, no features. Believe me, I tried to see who it was.' She paused. 'And his hand jerked towards me. He had some sort of container in it and I felt a splash across my neck and on my thin blouse at my chest.' She placed the flat of her hand on the place. 'My first thought was that he'd chucked water at me, or turpentine – a lot of it, y'know? I staggered back, more from shock than anything. And it was really cold and then itchy and then, fuck, Henry, it set my skin on fire. I was the one screaming then, clawing at my blouse and my neck, my skin. I went down on my knees and then, whack! Some bastard cracked me across the back of my head, and that's all I remember until I was on a stretcher between two paramedics being sluiced with painkillers and chucked into an ambulance, and Inspector Clarke was holding my hand, stroking it, saying everything would be OK.'

THIRTEEN

'What happened to the girls, Ruby and Kelly?' Henry asked.

The hotel owner, Risdon, had filtered wonderful coffee for them, got a couple of chairs out and let them sit in the conservatory at the front of the hotel to drink it while he went about his business.

'Never seen again. Ruby must have done a runner from my car, I suppose, and as for the other one, Kelly – who I presume was in the room, and I presume was being assaulted or whatever – no idea. As far as I know, missing-from-home reports from all over West Yorkshire were checked, but nothing was found. They might not even have been called Ruby and Kelly. It's common for mispers to change their ID, and easy.'

'And you? What happened to you?' Henry asked.

'Ta-dah!' she said, opening her arms in a gesture of *Here I am*. Then she sighed and seemed to withdraw into herself. 'Six months off sick . . . not long enough really, but I had to come back to work or get my pay cut to half-salary.'

'That old chestnut . . . bastards.'

'I had a nervous breakdown . . . shaved my actual head, basically changed myself as a person because I couldn't come to terms with what I saw in a mirror. Got dumped by my a-hole of a boyfriend, and at work I got dumped, too . . . first on to some half-baked special projects group full of waifs, strays and the sick, lame and lazy . . .'

Henry swallowed. 'Been there, done that.'

'Well, I couldn't handle that lot; ended up in the control room and couldn't handle that pressure either – members of the public ruin this job, always calling in, moaning about crap . . . then the Intel Unit and now the CCU for my sins, which are aplenty. Powers-that-be seem to think I'm better off dealing with the long dead, and I've done OK with it, though I think I'm a nightmare to work with.'

'You're a good detective,' Henry said. 'I'd tell you if you weren't, whether you're my sergeant or not.'

She shrugged modestly. 'I took up kung fu, for goodness' sake – I'm a blue belt now. And I did that Mini up off my own bat – from books and YouTube videos; found it gathering rust in a garage. Now, that *was* therapeutic.'

'It's a great job,' Henry complimented her. 'Seats are a bit tight for me, though.'

The conversation stalled as each pondered things. Henry's face screwed up as he thought through everything Blackstone had told him, then said, 'Looks like my saviour was your saviour, too.'

'Julie Clarke?'

'I woke up with my head on her lap.'

'Same here, pretty much. I owe her.'

'Would it be worth chatting to her, see if she remembers anything more . . . I'm thinking about your incident rather than mine, or maybe both.'

'She's retired now.'

'Oh, OK. Any idea where she is, what she's up to?'

'Funnily enough I do.'

'But before we talk to her,' Henry said, 'can I ask you one thing?'

Blackstone looked at him warily. 'Go on.'

'Do you want revenge?'

She thought about that for a long time, then answered, 'No, I don't. I want my life back.'

After thanking Risdon, they jumped into Henry's Audi, and Blackstone directed him to the town centre, slouching back as she did.

'Nice motor,' she said, letting her fingertips brush the dashboard. 'All mod cons, I see.'

'I've only just learned that I can actually ask the hi-fi for a particular song and it'll play it. Most other stuff remains a mystery – satnav, GPS, all that kind of stuff . . . I just like driving it.'

'Bit fancier than my Mini,' she said and directed Henry to Granville Street, where he parked up. They got out and walked along a row of shops until they came to a door which led up to a small complex of offices for different businesses over the shops.

Blackstone looked down the list of names on the intercom and pressed the button next to *Blackpool Children's Charity*.

A tinny but friendly female voice sounded over the intercom. 'BCC – can I help you?'

Blackstone introduced herself and Henry, and asked if Julie Clarke was available for a chat. They were immediately allowed in and told to go up the steps and along the corridor to the office at the far end – the door of which was opened as they approached.

Julie Clarke greeted them with a huge smile of welcome, giving Blackstone a tender hug and shaking hands with Henry before also pulling him towards her for a hug, all against COVID guidelines.

'Wow,' she said, gently pushing him away and giving him a once-over.

Despite himself, he stepped back and said, 'Wow!' too.

When Henry had first encountered her, his head being cradled in her lap in a grotty back alley, he had been in his mid-twenties and she had just turned twenty. Back then, she had been very attractive and now, unlike himself, he thought she still was. It felt patronizing to think she'd 'aged well', but there wasn't a better way of describing it. Now in her mid-fifties, she was still slim and quite stunning.

'Come in, come in – welcome to my humble abode,' she said and ushered the two detectives in like a mother hen. She took them through an outer office where a young girl was working at a desk, into a slightly larger main office which was hers. 'Tea? Coffee?' she asked, beckoning them to sit on a suite of comfortable chairs set to one side as an informal meeting area.

'I'm fine, thanks,' Blackstone said. She was coffee'd out.

'I'm OK, too,' Henry said.

Clarke took a seat and leaned towards Blackstone, concern in her eyes. 'How are you, Debbie?' obviously asking about the acid incident and its aftermath.

'I'm not too bad. All the better for working with this old fogey,' she said and jerked a thumb at Henry.

'And how are you, Henry?' Then she looked puzzled. 'But you retired, didn't you?'

'Civilian investigator now. I was tempted back. The lure of the hunt, I guess.'

'That's good.'

'But what of you, Julie?' Henry gestured around the office.

'Well, I retired, of course. Most of my service was around the Fylde coast in and out of uniform, a lot of roles relating to vulnerable children – even the patrol inspector role is a lot about kids. It just seemed right that when I finished, I kept involved, so I set up this charity, helping kids on the streets, kids from broken homes – that kind of thing.'

'That's amazing – such valuable work,' Henry said genuinely. He'd had no such vocation in mind when he retired; mostly his thoughts were about sun-drenched beaches, drinking cold beer and not doing anything much for society.

'I'm impressed, too,' Blackstone said.

'There's no money in it and COVID has meant we have really struggled, but so has every other charity from the really big ones down.' She smiled. Formalities over, catch-up done, she asked, 'So, what brings you guys here?'

The pair exchanged a glance and Blackstone nodded at Henry.

'Two things, really, Julie. First of all, I presume you recall me being assaulted in that back alley way back when?'

'I'll say. The shoplifter, little lad who went missing, supposedly, and never got prosecuted? You were badly injured.'

'And if it hadn't been for you . . .'

She waved the compliment away with a modest gesture.

'Anyway . . . the lad's mother, who, apparently, every day since his disappearance, has searched for him, was found dead yesterday . . . she'd been murdered.'

'Oh my God,' Clarke said. 'Has the killer been caught?'

'No, but we arrested a guy for rape yesterday, unconnected with the woman's murder, and in his flat we found a photograph . . . this one.' Henry took out his phone, with which he had taken a snap of the photograph of the boy he believed was Tommy Benemy being sexually assaulted. He found the file and then hesitated. Blackstone shot him a stunned look, wondering what he was doing. 'Erm, this is a tough one to look at and I apologize,' he warned Clarke.

'I've seen some terrible things in my time, Henry.' She took the phone and looked, emitting a little gasp of shock. She licked her lips. 'What about it?'

'You see the tattoo on the lad's forearm, the square with a triangle on top? Looks like a house?'

She nodded.

'Tommy Benemy had one just like that, and I think the lad in this photo is Tommy.'

'Really? That's awful.' She handed the phone back.

'I was wondering if you remembered anything more about the incident in the alley. Obviously, I found Tommy handing over his stash of perfume to another, older youth and then I got whacked. I wondered if you could remember anything more about it. I know memory's a funny thing at best.'

Clarke shook her head. 'No . . . I have thought a lot about it since, but there was no one else around when I found you . . . Sorry.'

'What about Tommy's fate?' Blackstone asked.

Henry said, 'I kept in touch with his mum for years after and every so often I re-checked the MFH file on him. I remember you put in the occasional entry on the log regarding information received from anonymous sources that he had been seen in Manchester.'

'Vaguely remember that,' Clarke said. 'We did one or two appeals for him on the press and local TV, but nothing ever came from that. I did send officers to Manchester to make enquiries a couple of times, but they came to nothing.'

'Fair enough,' Henry said. 'Oh, does the "house" tattoo mean anything to you at all?'

'Should it?'

'Just wondered if you'd seen something similar on other kids?'

'No, I didn't,' Clarke said. 'So what are you going to do with the rapist you have in custody – and that photograph?'

'Question the shit out of him,' Blackstone said vehemently. 'With the rape accusation hanging over him, his back's against the wall.'

'Let's hope so,' Clarke said. She eyed Blackstone. 'You said you wanted to ask me two things?'

'Thing is,' Henry said, 'because both of us have, shall we say, "unresolved issues", we decided to look into each other's unsolved cases, if you will. Me – the fact I got my head kicked in and no one was locked up . . .'

'And me,' Blackstone said, picking it up, 'because I got a vat of acid poured over me and a whack on the head, and no one got prosecuted for that either.'

'So you're here unofficially?'

'Both unsolved, serious cases, so not really,' Blackstone said. 'I suppose it's the same question for you, Julie – do you remember anything more about the night I was assaulted? Anything that could help us now – because we're on a bit of a roll here.'

Clarke sighed deeply. 'Not really. Wish I did have something. I do think about it a lot, actually, like your incident, Henry.'

'How did you actually find Debbie that night?' Henry asked. He looked at Blackstone. 'You said you heard screams from inside the hotel and you ran into the place without radioing in your position.' He looked back at Clarke, his forehead creased.

'Just luck. Saw her car which was parked up at the side of the hotel . . . The Belmont, was it?'

'Was the car empty?'

Clarke nodded. 'There was no one in the car . . . then I went looking and found you inside, in that corridor, unconscious.'

'Did you notice the black van in the back yard of the hotel?' Henry asked her.

'No, no van and no one else in the hotel. Whoever had thrown acid at you and knocked you out had gone. I'm sorry I wasn't on the scene quicker.'

'Can't be helped . . . I'm just thankful you did show up – otherwise that acid would have done even more damage to me . . . as it is, it just did "lasting damage".' She grinned crookedly and rolled her eyes.

There was an awkward silence, broken when Henry said, 'You worked the mean streets of Blackpool for a long time, at the cutting edge from PC to inspector . . . Did you ever come across any suggestion that someone was running an organized gang – y'know, targeting and using kids, maybe abusing them too, to steal to order? I seem to recall we had a bit of a chat about it back then.'

'Kids are always stealing to order – that's what they often do,' Clarke said thoughtfully. 'But organized as such? Not to any great extent – nothing that I came across other than kids getting together and stealing. Now, if you're talking about organized shoplifting teams coming in from out of town, that was – *is* – happening all the time.'

'What about kids being preyed on in an organized way?'

'Same answer, Henry – as you'll know from your time in CID. Kids get preyed on. It's Blackpool, for goodness' sake. They get sucked into unsavoury things, but mostly it's just individuals who are doing it – occasionally like-minded groups, I suppose – and just occasionally a kid meets a killer, as you know. But if you're suggesting something more, I don't think so. Just doesn't ring true.'

They thanked her. She accompanied them out of the office and back down to street level, passing the other businesses with offices in the complex.

At the door they bade her goodbye and walked to Henry's car, both deep in thought until finally, as Blackstone dropped heavily into the passenger seat of the Audi, she said, 'Not moved us any further forward, but nice to catch up with her.'

'Yep, she's keeping well, but you're right: we don't seem to have learned anything more about our demons.'

'*My* demons,' she corrected him. 'You've compartmentalized yours.'

Henry twisted squarely to look at her. 'Actually, I'd hate to be one of your demons right now, Debbie . . . I've a feeling one or more of 'em are going to get their arses toasted. Anyhow, what say we go and see how Clanfield is going on in Preston cells? See if we can get an interview slot with him?'

'Good plan,' she said. She had her phone in her hand. 'I'm going to play Candy Crush, if that's all right? Chills me out, keeps me quiet.'

'What's Candy Crush?' Henry had heard of it, but it really meant nothing to him.

'A game of skill and passion. Just drive, OK?'

Henry set off, cutting on to Church Street and driving away from the town centre to the junction with Devonshire Square where he intended to turn right on to Whitegate Drive and make towards Preston.

As he made the turn across the busy junction, something jarred his mind, but he couldn't say for sure exactly what.

'I'm on level two thousand, six hundred and thirty-one,' Blackstone announced.

'I don't know what you mean, but I'm in awe of you,' Henry replied.

A few minutes later, they reached Marton Circle, the large roundabout where the M55 ended. Henry drove straight across, keeping on the direct road to Preston.

Henry hadn't spoken up to that point, letting Blackstone

concentrate on her game, but then he said, 'Call me a suspicious old bastard if you will.'

Blackstone looked up from her phone. 'You're a suspicious old bastard.'

'And not one to give a dog a bad name.'

'But . . .'

'I don't have many hobbies,' he admitted. He was driving, not looking at her, but knew she was scrutinizing him.

'Sad old bastard,' she said.

'But I quite like reading about old court cases, and when I say old, I mean old. You know, Victorian ones and the like. Some can be quite juicy and lurid.'

'Lovely. Is this going anywhere?'

'Just me mulling.'

Blackstone tutted. 'Look, you've distracted me now and I've lost a life, so you'd better say something or I'll punch you.'

'OK. One I read recently: police – in Cardiff, I think – visited a house and found prostitutes in bed with men in every room, including a drunken prostitute on the sofa downstairs. They arrested the house owner who was sentenced to six months' hard labour for keeping a brothel.'

'Still goes on, except the hard labour bit. Now it's widescreen TVs, Jacuzzis and comfy beds. Your point being?'

'I love a good coincidence . . . because coincidences are clues, which in itself has nothing to do with the coincidence I'm referring to, because it's all a bit vague.'

'As are you.'

'Probably . . . anyway . . . the guy who ended up doing hard labour for keeping a brothel was actually a salvationist dedicated to saving fallen women. Touch of irony, there.'

Blackstone just shook her head.

'Just thinking out loud,' he said, then let it go because he knew he'd planted a seed. He changed the subject. 'How about phoning ahead to Preston CID – let them know we're coming?'

The two DCs who had interviewed Clanfield the day before had been working on him all day, and by the time Henry and Blackstone landed, they were busily compiling the remand court file. The fast-tracked DNA results had come through and matched the sample from the offence, and Melanie Wooton herself had identified the necklace found in Clanfield's flat as hers. Clanfield was genuinely stitched up and would probably not set foot outside a cell for fourteen years.

The detectives were in the CID office, ties off, shirt sleeves rolled up, deep into paperwork. It was obvious they worked together regularly as a team.

Henry liked the aura they emanated. Cool professionalism, good humour. In synch with each other. A bond. Henry bet they got results.

When Blackstone walked into the CID office just ahead of Henry, both DCs stood up and gave her a genuine round of applause.

Henry watched her reaction: taken aback, embarrassed, pleased. She took a bow.

'Really, really well done, Sarge,' one of the DCs said. His name was Eddows. 'You can drop jobs like this on our laps anytime you want.'

'Thank you, guys, appreciated. Where are you up to with him?'

'Charged with rape, bail refused, court in the a.m. with a request for a three-day lie down,' the other DC said. His name was Cattle. The 'three-day lie down' referred to a seventy-two-hour extension of Clanfield's custody to police cells for further questioning, authorized by magistrates.

'Have you mentioned to him the photographs we found in his possession yet?' Blackstone asked.

'Not had the chance,' Cattle said. 'Mainly because he admitted two more rapes that we had to look into.'

'Local?' Henry asked.

'Manchester.'

'Wow!' Blackstone exclaimed.

'We get the feeling there may be more,' Eddows said.

'A serial rapist,' Blackstone said.

'So just at the moment the photos are running second place, plus his hard drives are still being examined by the techies, so when that's all done, we'll lay it all in front of him.'

'Can we speak to him?' Henry asked.

'Not under caution – off the record, just a bit of intelligence gathering,' Blackstone added for clarity.

The two detectives shared a concerned look.

Eddows said, 'About what?'

'One of the photographs is of particular interest to us.'

'Which one?'

Henry showed him the photograph on his phone and was open about why he wanted to ask Clanfield about it.

And Eddows was open with him. 'As you can imagine, we don't want anything to happen which allows this guy to squirm off the hook, so it has to be totally above board, yeah? Proper custody record entry, names, signatures, reason for interview – everything.'

'Understood,' Blackstone said.

'And one of us in the room,' Eddows added.

'No problem with that.'

Clanfield was retrieved from his cell by a gaoler and placed in an interview room where he waited for the officers.

Henry had to hide a smirk when he saw the state of the prisoner's face a day after he'd been punched out by Blackstone. It was a bent, twisted, dirtily bruised mess, deep purple-black patches under both eyes, now turning mustard yellow. Even the disposable mask he was wearing could not hide the injuries.

Eddows hovered by the door.

Henry and Blackstone, face masks on, settled themselves opposite Clanfield, who glared at them. His face was obviously causing him severe pain.

'So how are you, Mr COVID man?' Blackstone asked.

'What is this about?' he asked suspiciously.

'We'd like to ask you some questions – off the record for the moment.'

'Fuck's that supposed to mean?'

'That whatever you say to us is off the record for the moment. If we need to change that, we'll caution you, turn the tape on, start from the beginning and with your solicitor present.'

'What, then?'

Henry took out a hard copy of the photograph but kept his palm over it to obscure it.

He let Blackstone do the talking. 'You've been found in possession of thousands of photographs of an obscene nature, all involving young children and teenagers. Your computer is being checked as we speak and no doubt many more obscene images will be found, even if you think you might have deleted them. You will be questioned under caution about those when the time comes.'

Clanfield folded his arms, tried to look impassive.

Underneath the veneer, Henry guessed the man would be very afraid. At least, that is what he hoped.

'So you have to know that, generally speaking, you're goosed, my COVID friend who spits at women. Bearing this in mind,' Blackstone said, 'I want you to look at one particular photograph and help us by telling us about it.'

'Why would I do that? Not as if I'm going to get anything from cooperating with you.'

'Well, let's see, shall we?' Henry said.

He pushed the photograph across the expanse of the table. Henry watched Clanfield's facial and body language reaction as his hand came away to reveal the image, and spotted the sudden change in Clanfield's face.

A tic.

A flicker.

A blink.

Henry would even swear Clanfield's nostrils flared under the face mask.

The gulp: Clanfield's Adam's apple rising and falling.

Then back to normal, all over in a second.

He knew something about it. Something more than it just being a photograph in his collection.

Clanfield shrugged. 'Don't even remember this one,' he said blandly, 'because, as you know' – he leaned forward on his elbow conspiratorially – 'I've got thousands of them, most with my jizz on them.'

Blackstone said, 'You really are a disgusting monster, aren't you?'

'Pretty much.'

'Anyway – this photograph,' she said, trying to maintain her calm. 'Tell me about it, because you do know something, don't you?'

'Just part of a beloved collection.'

'Where did it come from?'

He shrugged. Bored now.

'Who is this lad in the photo?' Henry asked.

'How should I know?'

'Is that you behind him?'

'Yeah, right, I wish. Don't think so.'

'Your face showed me that you know exactly who he is,' Henry said.

'I'm wearing a mask, so you can't see my face, dick.'

'I can see enough of it. The photo,' Henry said, tapping it. Clanfield glanced at it. 'It's old, older than me – so how should I know? It's just kiddie porn. Put that phrase into any internet search and see what you get: tons of stuff like this.'

Henry leaned slightly forward and placed the tip of his forefinger on the arm of the young lad on the photo and tapped the 'house' tattoo. 'That tattoo – what does it mean?'

'How should I know?' Clanfield's eyes were wary now.

'Roll up your right sleeve,' Henry said.

'Why?'

'Just do it, Ellis, or I'll pin you down and do it myself.'

Blackstone looked sharply at Henry, who sensed that DC Eddows had stood upright.

'No,' Clanfield said.

Henry's eyes became fierce. 'If I have to ask again, Ellis, I'll get really angry . . . remember, no video on here, no tape running, no solicitor, just us in a soundproof room.'

Henry and the prisoner locked eyes across the tops of their face masks. Then Clanfield's closed in defeat, before reopening.

Slowly, he pulled his shirt sleeve up to reveal his right forearm on which was the exact same tattoo as on the photograph: a square, a triangle, a slash diagonally across the square.

Henry heard Blackstone breathe in sharply.

'Where did you get it?' Henry asked. 'And who did it for you?'

'I don't remember. Long time ago, when I was a kid – just fooling around.'

'Who did it for you?' Henry asked again.

'I have no fucking idea.' He had become resolute.

'You can see it exactly matches the one on the boy's arm, can't you?' Blackstone said.

'And millions of people have "ACAB" on their knuckles, don't they? I wonder why?' he said with a sneer. 'It's just a coincidence.'

Henry and Blackstone exchanged a fleeting eye-to-eye look on that last word, *coincidence*.

'So a square with a triangle on it with a line going through it

diagonally, rising from left to right, is a coincidence?' Blackstone
demanded.

'Clearly . . . and, like I said, that photo looks well old, well
before my time.'

Henry sighed inwardly. Clanfield had a point. If this photograph
was of Tommy Benemy, it could be thirty-five years old; the man
opposite was only twenty-four – almost a generation apart.

Nevertheless, Henry said, 'You're lying. Who put this tatt on you?'

'Can't remember,' Clanfield said with a hint of 'come and get
me' in his voice.

'He's right, in terms of timeline – he and the photo are well out of
synch. Could be a real coincidence . . . for once.' Blackstone sighed.

She and Henry were back in the CID office sitting either side of
DC Eddows's desk. The two local detectives had nipped out to catch
a bite to eat, leaving the CCU ones in the office, sifting through
paperwork and speculating.

Henry was looking at the form on which Clanfield's antecedents
had been recorded, plus the descriptive form which listed the prisoner's tattoos.

Henry said, 'Nah.'

'You just got blindsided by coincidences,' Blackstone said.

'Didn't you find it very, very odd?'

'Yeah, I did . . . an odd coincidence, but that's all.' She was
also looking through the paperwork associated with Clanfield. A
lot of it was tedious, form-filling, tick-box stuff, and from what
she could see, the two local jacks had done a brilliant job of
amassing everything about Clanfield they could lay their hands
on. 'Just a coincidence,' she was muttering absentmindedly under
her breath. 'Just a one in a million . . .' Then she stopped talking
suddenly and said, 'Oh my fucking God!' which, even for her,
Henry thought, was a tad strong.

'Well,' Henry said conceitedly, 'we go on about the word that should
not be said' – and he whispered it – '*coincidences* – but they really
do exist, and in my world they exist to trap criminals.'

'Don't rub it in,' Blackstone responded crossly. Then she frowned
and looked at him. 'You're a canny one, in't ya? Did you have a
feeling about it, or something?'

'Not really.'

'I mean, I sort of wondered about it at the time.'

'Wondered what?'

'Why you said we'd only found one photograph in Clanfield's possession when you showed her the one with Tommy in, when we knew there was easily over a thousand.' She was referring to their short chat with Julie Clarke, former cop, now charity worker. 'Why didn't you tell her we'd found so many?'

Henry scratched his head Stan Laurel style. 'Um, not sure.'

'Bollocks! Instinct?'

He shrugged modestly. 'I suppose it's because she's an ex-cop – and when someone's an ex-cop, it means they're not a cop anymore, and as such they don't automatically have a right to know anything more than I'm willing to share with them. I'm just suspicious of everyone and don't trust anyone.'

'But you're an ex-cop,' Blackstone ribbed him.

'Christie, Henry Christie, Civilian Investigator,' he corrected her.

They were still in the CID office in Preston but had moved across to an unoccupied desk in the corner of the room when Eddows and Cattle returned from their short refreshment break.

And they were looking at the paperwork Blackstone had unearthed in relation to Clanfield that had made her exclaim rudely: a missing-from-home file from eleven years ago.

Ellis Clanfield, as a thirteen-year-old lad, had been reported missing by his parents from his home in Preston. He had been missing for over six weeks during the summer until he'd been found by a police patrol in Blackpool, having been chased from a shop in the town with a plastic bag full of expensive aftershave. He was quickly returned to his home in Preston, but according to the log that accompanied the report, he refused to say where he had been, what he had been doing and who he had been with.

The log itself – which had been kept in Preston comms then – listed all the updates, information and intelligence as to the missing person's whereabouts and began with the suspicion that Ellis had gone to Blackpool, and the main point of contact there was Inspector Julie Clarke. Following Clanfield's arrest for the shoplifting, he was cautioned for it, as it was a first offence, and the caution was administered as per force protocol by an officer of the rank of inspector or above.

That officer was Inspector Clarke.

'None of this really means anything,' Henry admitted.

'No, you're right, it's all tosh,' Blackstone agreed.

As is usual with MFH reports, a recent photograph is requested from the family. The photo is returned at the completion of the enquiry but will usually have been photocopied and the copy retained on the file. This was the case with Clanfield's MFH file. The photograph was a family one which showed the young Clanfield standing there sullenly, being forced to have it taken, dressed in a T-shirt and jogging bottoms with his hands thrust deep into his pockets; obviously, the photograph was taken prior to him having gone missing.

'Looks a shifty little shit, even then,' Henry said, inspecting the photograph. 'Funny how you can read people by just looking at them.'

'He was – and looking at the dates of when he was missing, he then went on to commit the rape we just arrested him for.'

Henry, who was ready to admit his eyes were not as good as they once were, lifted the photograph up close to his nose to focus on it better. As Clanfield's hands were in his pockets and he was wearing a T-shirt, Henry could see that his right arm did not have any marks or tattoos on it. He pointed this out to Blackstone.

'I wonder if he got the tatt when he was in Blackpool?' she speculated, then rocked forward on her chair. 'One way of finding out – see if I can find the actual caution file from the archives. There should be descriptives in it and, being a caution, the paperwork would probably have stayed local in Blackpool.'

'What about asking Julie Clarke if she remembers him?' Henry suggested.

'I have an even better plan,' Blackstone said. 'Why not do that, yeah, but look her in the eye while asking her and see if she squirms?'

Which meant another trip to Blackpool, making the pair of them feel as though they were attached to some sort of elastic band.

It wasn't such a long journey and twenty-five minutes later they were using the doorbell to Clarke's children's charity's office on Granville Street. There was no response this time and Blackstone said, 'Maybe we should have rung ahead?'

'Nah,' Henry said, 'always catch people on the hop if you can – but we were coming to Blackpool anyway, so it's not a wasted journey.' He checked his watch, then looked at Blackstone. 'What say we see if we can find that caution file, then let's call it a day?' He was feeling jaded. 'That said, maybe we should give Clarke a ring now anyway? We have her mobile number. At least it might give us a feel for things, even if we're not looking her in the eye.'

'Hi, sorry to bother you again, Julie . . . this is Debbie Blackstone; me and Henry Christie called earlier.'

Blackstone glanced at Henry who was driving. She was holding her phone upright in front of her and had it on speakerphone so both could hear the conversation.

'No problem. What can I help you with?' Clarke sounded relaxed.

'You recall we spoke about a man we had in custody for rape?'

She said she did.

'Well, we were just doing some background checks on him, and it turns out that you and he crossed paths about eleven years ago.'

'Really?'

'Yeah, amazing what a small world it is. Anyhow, he went missing from his home in Preston and turned up a few weeks later in Blackpool – got picked up for shoplifting and you cautioned him.'

'As I did many juveniles. Do you have a name that might jog my memory?'

'Ellis Clanfield. He'd be thirteen and he'd been missing from Preston for about six weeks.'

There was a pause. Blackstone assumed Clarke was thinking. She looked at Henry and winked.

Then Clarke said, 'Doesn't ring any bells.'

'If it helps, he was stealing aftershave.'

'No – nothing.'

'OK, thanks.'

'Before you go, what's happening with this man?'

'Court in the morning, remand in custody and then we'll really have time to get into his ribs,' Blackstone said enthusiastically.

'Right, OK . . . sorry I can't help.' Clarke hung up.

Blackstone ended the call at her end too, then sat pensively in the passenger seat.

'You didn't mention the tattoo,' Henry said.

'She didn't need to know,' Blackstone said. 'She's an ex-cop.'

'You're learning.'

'Feels a bit uncomfortable, though.'

'It's just a path we have to take. If it's a dead end, which I hope it will be, nothing's lost. No accusations made. No falling out.'

Once again driving through Blackpool, this time heading back to the new police station from which Blackstone said she needed to collect the keys for the archive warehouse, Henry reached the junction where Church Street met Whitegate Drive at Devonshire Square. He hit a queue of traffic at the lights. It was a busy time, approaching rush hour, so there was a build-up.

Blackstone swore. 'Now I get what you were saying in that convoluted way of yours, which I obviously put down to dementia!' she blurted out and twisted to face him.

'You've lost me.' She had smashed into his train of thought which, admittedly, had reached the equivalent of Crewe Station – many lines, some running parallel, some crossing others, others coming to a thumping halt in the sidings.

'Your daft rant about Victorian crime reporting,' she clarified.

'What about it?'

'Now I know what you meant. The salvationist saving fallen women.'

'What did I mean?' Henry was only half paying attention because his thought-train had left the station and was now going intercity at full lick.

'Poacher turned gamekeeper . . . no, got that wrong: gamekeeper turned poacher! A proverb turned on its head.'

Henry acknowledged her brilliance, but as he was about to pass the lights on Whitegate Drive, they turned red on him and he shot through.

'What're you doing, Henry?' Blackstone said, searching for the inner door handle to cling on to, missing it with her fingers and being thrown sideways by centrifugal force as Henry went left at the lights instead of right, just making it through. He put his foot down, then slammed on the brakes and veered into the top of Granville Street again.

He was shaking his head and tutting.

He said, 'The tattoo – the box with a triangle on top of it, what does it look like?'

'Duh – a house drawn by a kid, or by me.'

'Bear with me.'

He shot down the street and instead of finding somewhere legal to park, he stopped on the double yellow lines outside the building that housed Julie Clarke's office on the first floor above a row of shops.

'I could be wrong,' he admitted. 'Often am.' He got out and dashed to the door, next to which was a panel of intercom buttons for the businesses up on the first floor. He ran his finger down the business names next to the buttons.

Blackstone leaned across the driver's seat, watching him.

Henry then spun 180 degrees and looked at a display of all the business names behind a Perspex sheet screwed to the opposite side of the doorway.

Then he breathed out and beckoned to Blackstone. 'Come and have a look at this.'

FOURTEEN

They went their separate ways when they got back to Hutton Hall, Henry heading off back to Kendleton, Blackstone going for the docks.

Both were exhausted, and despite what they thought they'd learned, they decided to call it a day and begin the next one, refreshed, at Preston Magistrates' Court where they wanted to witness Clanfield being remanded to police cells. After that, they would beg, borrow and steal any opportunity they could to interview him on the record – although they also knew that detectives from all over the North West would be queueing up to get into his ribs.

In spite of the distance he had to travel, Henry was looking forward to the journey alone for two reasons.

First, he was on the way home to spend time with Diane and Ginny at The Tawny Owl, and maybe there was a way he might be able to douse some of the simmering issues between the two women in his life; second, he was driving a good, fast car and could listen to high-quality, surround-sound audio on the hi-fi system; he was going to sit through something he hadn't listened to in a while, the Rolling Stones' album *Sticky Fingers*.

As he settled into the car he said, 'Sticky Fingers, please,' and the first track was selected: 'Brown Sugar'.

They left headquarters at the same time, Henry peeling left out of the gate to make his way to the motorway, Blackstone going straight on to the A59 in her Mini.

She was ahead of him and flipped him a fond finger over her shoulder. Henry waved back and grinned. One thing he hadn't expected was to be paired up with someone as completely outrageous as Blackstone, although he already had a soft spot for her and could see what a bloody good detective she was. So, so vulnerable – but hard-edged with it.

One thing was for certain – she was a real, volatile mix.

Within a couple of minutes, Blackstone was calling him.

'Is that my new partner?' she asked.

'It is,' Henry said on his hands-free.

'Clanfield's mum just got back to me about the tattoo – and guess what? Like we thought, he didn't have the tattoo when he went missing but had it when he got back from his adventures. She remembers having a barney with him about it – after which he hit her in the face for the first time. Something to talk to him about tomorrow.'

'What a nice lad he was.'

'Who grew into an evil young man. Anyways, see you in the morning, old guy.'

'Yeah, have a good one,' Henry said and ended the call. The music had paused while he was on the phone and picked up on track two, 'Sway'.

The tattoo had really become something of interest now, having been on Tommy's forearm and now Clanfield's, and clearly it had some significance that he and Blackstone were now getting to the bottom of. Possibly a gang thing, Henry guessed, although it was an image that spanned thirty-odd years. A long time.

And whether what Henry had driven back to Granville Street in Blackpool to show Blackstone was just another coincidence (and he was trying to be generous enough to believe that, away from criminal investigations, such innocent things were possible), what had suddenly occurred to him at the traffic lights in Blackpool had felt serious enough for him to do an 'about-face' and drive back to the door of the children's charity and look at the list of businesses which also occupied some of the offices on the first floor – one of which was Hindle's Builders.

'Hindle's Builders,' Henry thought aloud.

The building company that had gutted the Belmont Hotel and renovated it to become the swish, swanky Park Lane Hotel on the North Shore seafront.

Henry had recalled fleetingly seeing the name as he and Blackstone had left Julie Clarke's office, and alongside that name was the company logo which was a square with a triangle on top with a line slashed diagonally across the middle of the square to rise at a slight angle, obviously designed simply to represent a house or a building. Simple, but effective. Nothing special, but designed in such a way that it took only a small leap of the imagination to link it – possibly – to the tattoos on the arms of two individuals, many years apart, both of whom had been missing persons in Blackpool at some time in their lives and both of whom had been caught stealing a lot of perfume.

Blackstone had uttered her usual expletive as she looked at the logo and its possible significance fell into place for her.

Henry had stared hard at the image as they stood in the doorway. Again, something stirred in his memory but he couldn't quite pin it down. He'd seen this before somewhere, many years ago, other than on Tommy's arm, but try as he might, it wouldn't come back to him.

'Something worth following up?' Henry asked her.

'Absolutely,' Blackstone agreed.

'Tomorrow,' Henry said. 'There's nothing spoiling tonight.'

Reluctantly, she agreed. There was no one in any of the offices anyway – at least no one was responding to her thumb on any of the intercom buzzers. She took a photo of the logo with her phone and said, 'I'll do a bit of research tonight, you know, while you're being wined and dined and I'm on pizza.'

'You're welcome to come and stay if you want,' Henry offered. 'All our rooms are vacant, but there would be every chance of catching COVID from the natives up there. You just don't know where they've been.'

'I'm sure Diane would love me turning up – another addition to your harem. Not.'

'I like to think of it as my COVID bubble . . . and actually, I think she would like to see you. It's been a long recuperation for her and any new face is a treat . . . and I'm always looking to add to the harem – sorry, bubble – as you say.'

'I'll take a rain check and just hunker down with my computer and maybe do a few laps of the docks to get a sweat up.'

Henry gunned it up the motorway, taking what he thought were calculated risks with the speed, touching an easy ninety occasionally, but hovering just below eighty mostly. By the time he pulled up outside Th'Owl, the last strains of the final track, 'Moonlight Mile', were playing out heartbreakingly, and Diane was on the front steps waiting for him. She hated the Rolling Stones with a vengeance, but Henry, old romantic fool that he was, thought the song was the perfect accompaniment to his arrival home and he climbed out, clasping his palms to his heart, serenading Diane with the chorus as if he was an Italian opera singer, but without the voice.

Blackstone left her Mini in the secure underground car park, which was the basement of the converted warehouse where her apartment was located, a block called Edward Mansions, although none of the apartments could really be called mansions. The two-bedroomed flat she had bought on the top floor was one of the larger ones. She rode up in the lift and entered her living space, now glad to close the door on the world, although conversely she'd had a good day working with Henry who, quietly, had proved to be something of a revelation to her – ish.

She stripped off, took a tepid shower, ensuring the water more or less missed the burns, though at the end of the shower she turned it to cold and angled her body so the jets cascaded on to the burned area, cooling it. Even after four years, it stung terribly all night, all day, despite aloe vera lotion and painkillers; generally, she managed to get through most days without taking analgesics, but night-time was usually a problem in terms of comfort in bed, and she almost always took something to help her sleep. On a good night she could manage four hours straight, but mostly it was in fits and starts.

After dabbing herself dry and treating the burns, she changed into loose clothing. She planned to do a few circuits of the docks before bed, but for the moment, she put a Sloppy Giuseppe in the oven, fired up her laptop and began to dig.

Within minutes she'd found something of interest.

'Henry – you near a computer?'

'I'm near a bar if that's of any use?'

'No – get to a computer now, then call me back.'

Henry ended the call with a thumb-press of annoyance if there was such a thing.

He really was near a bar – behind the main one at The Tawny Owl where he'd been pressganged into service to help serve drinks that evening because a member of staff had been forced to self-isolate. All customers were required to register their details on entering and were shown to tables from where they placed their orders with the waiting staff, and the food or drink was then brought to them. Impractical but necessary to keep people from clustering around the bar as they used to in the good old days.

Because the usual barman was the one with COVID symptoms, Henry had stepped into his shoes and was enjoying pulling a pint. Diane was also helping with waiting duties and enjoying it, especially as she was allowed to flirt outrageously with the boss who, in turn, knew he could get away with making lewd remarks at the staff. Well, just her.

His phone had rung just as he'd finished pulling a pint of perfect Guinness, shamrock and all in the froth.

Blackstone's message was curt, straight to the point.

'Gonna have to leave it with you for a while,' he told the other barman, who nodded.

He went into the private accommodation area and settled himself on the sofa with his laptop and logged in. There was already an email in his inbox from Blackstone (her email address began D.B.BURNEDFLESH) which Henry opened. There were two links for him to follow.

The first took him to a website on which fairly basic company details and accounts could be accessed for free, such as names and addresses of directors, turnovers, profit and loss. More detailed information could be seen on payment of a fee. The link took him to Hindle's Builders (Blackpool & Fylde Coast) Ltd, which, to Henry's untrained eye, looked to have a fairly healthy turnover in the low millions and with little debt. The business had been established in 1984.

He clicked on the page that listed the company officials.

Two directors were listed, the first being David Hindle. It gave his date of birth, and his place of residence was listed as the office address in Granville Street, Blackpool. He had been a director since the company was established.

The next one listed, who had been a director since 2016, was Julie Clarke.

Although seeing this jarred Henry, he wasn't completely sure if that meant anything.

His mobile rang: Blackstone.

'You looking at this shit?' she demanded.

'Looking at company accounts at the moment.'

'See what I see?'

'I assume so, but I'm wondering what it might mean, if anything.'

'But interesting,' she insisted. 'C'mon.'

'Definitely.'

'Now have a look at the next link I sent you – it's the company website.' She hung up.

Henry did so and entered the company website. On each page, in the top right-hand corner was the company logo, which made Henry wince. Surely gang tatts didn't look like the *Play School* house, he thought, recalling the popular tots' TV show from the 1970s.

There was a potted history of the company, from its origins as a one-man band doing any job that came along, via a few notable milestones, to its present-day work of predominantly renovating hotels and office buildings, building new ones too; the blurb proudly cooed about the company's work in doing its bit to transform Blackpool and the Fylde.

The major current project was the refurbishment of a huge country hotel near Kirkham, turning it into a swish hotel and wedding venue with a pool and extensive leisure facilities.

It looked impressive.

Then Henry blinked and went back to the start of the article where David Hindle, company director, proudly boasted about his first ever full renovation of a small hotel in Blackpool town centre.

It was called the Dolphin Hotel and was on Abingdon Street.

Henry returned to the bar and helped out until closing time. He then spent half an hour cleaning up before deciding he'd had enough, helped himself to two double whiskies and went to join Diane who was sitting outside, knackered from her stint as a waitress. Her wounds took everything out of her, but she knew she had to keep moving, pushing herself in order to get better.

Henry gave her one of the whiskies, kissed her on the cheek and sat close beside her on the bench.

He watched her profile as she sipped the spirit, briefly recalling how close he had been to losing her after she'd taken two bullets from a ruthless gunman. It had been touch-and-go for many hours, but the surgeons at Royal Lancaster Infirmary had been awesome and now, well into the pandemic, Henry had been one of the loudest Thursday-evening 'clappers' for the NHS.

Henry said, 'Ginny mentioned that you and she have had a conflab.'

'We have.'

'Air cleared?'

'Boundaries defined,' she said. 'It's been tough for her losing her mum, then me stepping into the breach. I get it, but I told her not to worry: I won't be trying to step into Alison's shoes as well, not least because I have a job to go to once I'm better and I'll be out for most of the day – and because I don't really live here. I have a flat of my own.'

'You're planning to go back to work, then?' Henry hadn't been certain what her plans were.

'I am. I need to.'

He nodded, understanding, but then said, 'Your flat? You're going back to it? You don't have to. I love having you around here, you know.'

'I appreciate what you've done for me and I don't want to appear ungrateful, but I'm not sure yet . . . depends on us, doesn't it?'

'Suppose so . . . but just so you know, I love you.'

She sipped her whisky, didn't respond to that declaration – which slightly worried Henry, but then said, 'I think Ginny's as worried about you as she is about me encroaching on her world, you know.'

'In what way?'

'She doesn't want you to get hurt – by me, or anyone.'

'Are you planning on hurting me?'

'Far from it.'

'That's good to know.'

'I did tell her something that I probably should have kept under wraps, but it seemed to put her mind at ease.'

'And that was?'

'I told her I was in love with you.'

It was gone midnight. Although Henry had access to some of the best champagne money could buy and could have had it for 'free', he thought it would be better to make a profit on it, so it stayed in the cellar. So he did the old-fashioned thing and took Diane by the hand, led her to the bedroom and tried his best to make long, slow love to her. The excitement coursing through his veins meant that long and slow became short and fast, but it still had the desired effect.

'That was nice, thank you,' Diane said huskily as Henry gently slid off her, put his arm around her shoulders and pulled her tightly to him.

Had either of them smoked, that would have been the ideal time to light up, share a cigarette and blow smoke rings up to the ceiling.

Instead, Henry shattered the moment by asking, 'Mind if I ask you about child abuse?'

Blackstone found it impossible to sleep even on the lounger she'd set out on her balcony, on which she'd spent many nights before. Usually, the chill helped to settle her, but not that night. Things were not helped by the noise of the boy racers charging up and down Mariner's Way on the opposite side of the dock, engines screaming, voices screaming, sounds booming across the water, as they went unchecked by the cops. It was a constant problem.

Finally, she gave up, grabbed her car keys, purse and phone, went down to the basement garage and fired up the Cooper. She drove out with tyres squealing and around to Mariner's Way, expecting some form of harassment from the illegal racers, and wasn't surprised to find a souped-up Subaru Impreza right on her tail with a few lads on board. She wasn't intimidated by them, gave them the finger and turned into the McDonald's drive-through. All of a sudden, only a burger would do.

The Subaru kept on going with a scream of the engine, a blast of 'La Cucaracha' and a loud cheer from its occupants.

She joined the short, after-midnight queue, and when she glanced in her rear-view mirror, she saw the shape of a big black Range Rover up close behind. Adjusting the mirror, she could just see two men in the front seats, but couldn't make out their features.

She dismissed them from her mind as she called her order into the intercom, then drove up to the serving window, reached out for her bag of goodies, and slowly drove around the perimeter of the restaurant back on to Mariner's Way. Only then did she realize the occupants of the Range Rover had not ordered any food and were still close behind her when she turned out on to the road, intending to loop back around the port to her apartment.

She went straight across the small roundabout into Pedders Way, taking it easy but still aware the Range Rover was close behind and now getting a queasy feeling about its presence.

A bad feeling confirmed by a bang and a tup as the front of the big car shunted into the back of the Mini.

Deliberately.

And again, jerking her roughly forward with the crash, then slamming back in her seat as the five-point harness seatbelt grabbed her.

Then another bang. This time harder. She heard the lion-like roar of the Range Rover's big engine.

Smack!

Suddenly, she *was* scared. She put her foot down on the accelerator and the sprightly, finely tuned 1275cc engine responded instantly and put distance between the two vehicles, but not for more than a moment because the immense, modern and responsive engine of the big four-wheel drive surged forward like a lion pouncing on its prey – a weak, but agile gazelle, maybe – and even before Blackstone reached the swing bridge over the lock, she had been struck again, the back wheels of the Mini lifting off the ground. Blackstone tipped forward, but knew that because the Cooper was front-wheel drive, there was still power on the road even though she was up in the air. She applied full throttle as her back wheels crashed down, and despite almost slewing out of control, she raced ahead of the Range Rover across the bridge and cried, 'C'mon, babe!' to her car.

As she reached the other side of the bridge, the Range Rover was looming ominously again, but Blackstone put her foot down, causing her engine to screech as she raced past the backs of the converted warehouses in which she lived.

She was already thinking ahead: a game plan.

She knew exactly where she was going to turn and outsmart the fast but less agile beast on her tail, but she had to get there first.

She'd already dismissed going home.

It took the automatic garage gates too long to open and she would have been trapped at them. That was a no-go.

She weaved from side to side, relying on the grip of her wide racing tyres and then, at one point where she had veered across to the right, she timed it to the millisecond and yanked the steering wheel down to the left. She wasn't sure, but she thought both offside wheels, back and front, rose off the tarmac as she swerved a sharp left into the entrance of the large car park at the rear of the cinema complex, knowing the Range Rover had little chance of following her so quickly.

And indeed she caught sight of the vehicle slamming on and slithering to a halt past the opening and hurriedly going into reverse – giving Blackstone the crucial seconds she needed to put distance between her and her pursuer.

She cut diagonally across the car park, down by the side of the cinema building against the one-way system, and then shot out through the opposite entrance before the Range Rover had even managed to manoeuvre into the car park entrance.

'Wanker!' she shouted triumphantly as she sped on to Parkway, leaving the dock area completely, right on to Watery Lane up towards Preston with no sign of the Range Rover on her tail.

She was heading for the sanctuary of the cop shop.

Diane had sat upright, but Henry stayed laid out, plumping up a pillow for his head. He was looking up at her, angling his face as she frowned.

'I mean,' he said, 'you spent a lot of years protecting kids before you moved on to CID and then FMIT. If I'm honest, that was only something I dealt with when it hit me in the face – murders and suchlike. It's never been my day-to-day life.'

'I know . . . but what you're saying about organized abuse . . . well, yeah, some abuse is organized, for sure, but most I don't think is in the way you're insinuating – planned, controlled . . . but there are always rumours, of course, that the establishment is involved.'

'Like the government thing?'

'Yeah – which came to nothing in the end. Yes, there is trafficking and there is prostitution and girls sold or passed into slavery – that happens, we know it does. It is rife, almost unstoppable, and you take any little victories you can find – but generally it's an imported problem. That said, there's the Rotherham thing, the Rochdale thing and others where girls – mainly – were systematically abused, and the cops knew about it and didn't thoroughly investigate. But here, while I'm not saying it doesn't exist, I haven't heard the rumours so much or come across evidence of it to the degree you're on about. But the people behind it are very secretive and probably powerful and dangerous . . .'

Henry's mobile rang, interrupting Diane's musings.

He rolled sideways and picked it up off the bedside cabinet. 'Debbie again,' he said.

'Well, this'd better be good,' Diane warned him. 'Strange women calling you at this time of night!'

Henry answered, 'Can't you sleep or something?'

'Oh, sorry, Henry, so sorry to disturb you.' Blackstone's voice was shaky.

Henry sat upright. 'What is it?'

'Someone just tried to kill me by running me off the road and I'm too terrified to go back home. I'm at Preston nick and eating a Big Mac.'

FIFTEEN

A traffic cop in a liveried car escorted Blackstone from Preston nick up to junction 34 of the M6 and, happy she hadn't been followed, he came off the motorway, looped around, came back on and headed south; meanwhile, Blackstone also left the motorway at the same junction – Lancaster north – and took the eastbound A683, following Henry's instructions on how to get to Kendleton. On reaching the village of Caton, she took a right and found herself driving through narrow lanes, presently picking up a sign for Kendleton and descending the steep road into the village, crossing the stream and drawing into the car park of The Tawny Owl.

Henry was standing on the front patio in a baggy T-shirt and shorts, with old-guy slippers on his feet.

'So, this is your pad?' Blackstone said admiringly.

'Partly,' he said. 'Come in.'

He led her through to the owner's accommodation where Diane, wrapped in a fluffy dressing gown, said a cautious hello. The two women knew each other but only in passing. They had heard much about each other and would have met properly in FMIT if Diane hadn't been wounded before she could even get her feet under the table.

Diane, though, had probably heard more about Blackstone than vice versa. Mainly whispers, rumour and innuendo, and most of it, as was still often the case in police culture concerning women, negative. She'd heard words bandied about like 'feisty', 'OTT', 'emotional', and 'fucking hard work', and taken them with a pinch of salt. Had Blackstone been a man, the adjectives would have been more complimentary, although 'weak' men were also derided within the macho culture.

'Can I get you anything?' Diane asked as Blackstone dropped like an exhausted rock on to the sofa.

'I could murder a vodka tonic if I'm honest.'

'Coming up.' She glanced at Henry who asked for Scotch.

As Diane went out to the bar, Henry sat down opposite Blackstone in an armchair.

'Look, mate, I really don't want to intrude, but thanks for the offer. Home didn't seem safe.'

'You're welcome; now tell me what happened.'

When she'd finished – now with a very large, chilled vodka in hand – Henry asked, 'You're sure it wasn't a boy racer?'

'Boy racers don't have big, eff-off Range Rovers, Henry. These guys were intent on . . . I don't know . . . forcing me off the road and God knows what. I'm surprised there isn't more damage to the back of my little car.'

'And you didn't get the reg number?'

'I was kinda busy, y'know, avoiding death.'

'Yeah, of course. Do you think there's a connection to what we're – haphazardly – looking into?'

'You're the one always blithering on about coincidences: you tell me.'

'Fair enough . . . no point taking chances, is there?'

'I was going to inform Rik Dean, just to keep him in the picture, but I guess I'll do it in the morning; I've left a message for him and asked him to come and see us at Preston nick first thing if he can.'

'That's good . . . and he can let us know what his plans are for running a murder enquiry into Trish Benemy's death. He might want us on the team.'

'Maybe. Whatever . . . we'll have a good long chat with him,' she said and necked the vodka with a long swig and a satisfied, 'Ahh.'

'Are you OK now?' Henry asked her.

'I need a bed, unless you want me to crash out on this.' She stroked the sofa.

'There's a guest room down the hall,' Diane said. 'Better than being up alone in the hotel. I've sorted some towels for you.'

'You're very kind,' Blackstone said sincerely to Diane. To Henry, she said, 'And you're not so bad yourself.'

Henry and Blackstone checked in with Rik Dean at seven a.m. in the CID office at Preston. He confirmed he was going to instigate a full-scale murder investigation into Trish's death and that both of them would be part of the team, which made Blackstone shudder with delight.

'The briefing's at ten in Blackpool . . . but I know you guys won't be able to attend that, so make it across when you can. I've got enough to kick off a few detectives doing some groundwork. You need to interview Ellis Clanfield first of all, don't you?'

'There's a long queue of folk who want to do the same,' Blackstone said. 'Detectives from GMP are due to land sometime this morning after his remand hearing, but we'll sneak in ahead of them, all being well.'

'Good stuff,' Rik said. To Henry, he asked, 'How's it all going, being a civvie?'

'It'll do. Obviously, I miss the power of rank.'

Rik left, and the pair then set about putting an interview strategy together for when they began questioning Clanfield, who would have a solicitor present this time.

By eight thirty, they were happy with their plan and had a little time to kill before Clanfield appeared at court. Blackstone decided she needed a change of clothing even though she had showered at The Tawny Owl. Henry offered to take her to her flat in his car.

'You don't have to. I'm a big girl now.'

'I know I don't have to, and I know you are . . . but going off the fact someone tried to run you off the road last night not very far from where you live, I think it might be a sensible thing for me to tag along.'

'Back-up, you mean? From a sixty-odd-year-old bloke?'

Henry stared at her until she relented. 'OK, OK.'

It was less than a ten-minute drive and Blackstone used the remote fob on her key chain to open the basement garage for Henry to park underneath the warehouse.

On the top floor, they stepped out of the lift and walked along the short hallway to her apartment. She was just ahead of Henry and stopped abruptly, causing Henry to stumble into her. He had to grab her shoulders to prevent himself from barging her over, and in so doing saw what had brought her to a sudden halt.

Her apartment door was open.

There were jemmy marks around the lock, which had been prised open, causing quite a lot of wood-splitting damage to the substantial frame and door.

Blackstone spun to Henry. 'Shit,' she said, her face very close to his. 'I've been screwed.' She looked at him, terrified, unsure how to proceed.

'Let's do it,' he said.

She turned back and went to the door. Henry was fairly sure he could hear her heartbeat.

She toed it open, not touching anything with her fingers, and cautiously stepped across the threshold and walked down the short hallway to the living room which had been well and truly – maliciously – ransacked. The sofa had been slashed and overturned, the TV smashed, every ornament broken on the floor, every painting ripped from the wall and destroyed.

Henry looked at the devastation over her shoulder.

'Bastards,' Blackstone hissed in fury. Then, 'Oh, shit.'

She spun round to Henry, who saw dismay on her face. 'What?' he said.

'When I went out, I'd been on my laptop, Googling, and I was also logged remotely into the force computer network. I left the computer open, unlocked. I only expected to be away for ten minutes while I got a burger.'

'And?'

'Laptop's gone.'

It was easy enough to sort: with just one call, the IT department changed her password and security clearance. It was also easy enough to check if whoever had stolen the laptop had gone surfing on the Lancon intranet, but there didn't seem to be any activity beyond what she had logged on to. However, she told the IT department to contact her if anyone tried to use her details again.

The computer had also been open on Google and would have shown her search history, which included delving into the accounts of Hindle's Builders.

'If the break in is connected to what we're investigating, they'll now be aware of it,' Henry said unnecessarily.

They were back in his car en route to the police station after nipping to the McDonald's on the docks to see if they could access any security footage from when Blackstone had driven through followed by the Range Rover. The staff were hesitant about handing anything over because of data protection laws. Fuming, Blackstone said she'd be back with a warrant.

Henry parked at the police station and they walked down to the magistrates' court on Ringway and made a cheeky bid to see a magistrate who gladly signed a warrant for release of the CCTV footage.

They hung around the court, expecting that Clanfield – being an overnight prisoner – would be one of the first to be brought up before the magistrates. They sat at the back of the appropriate courtroom chatting quietly, with Henry quite concerned about Blackstone's state of mind. Edgy at the best of times, as Henry had learned over the last three days, her experiences the previous night and that morning were obviously weighing heavily on her.

'You should take time off,' Henry suggested. 'Sort your flat out.'

She shook her head vehemently. 'It's all locked up now and it'll still be there when I get home.' The police had turned out an on-call joiner who had done a good job on her front door which was now heavily padlocked and probably as impenetrable as Fort Knox. A crime scene investigator was scheduled to arrive at four that afternoon, giving her a window to interview Clanfield if all went according to plan.

Even so, Henry could sense the effect the invasion of her home was having on her. She was jittery, unfocused, angry and scared – all those things people who'd been burgled felt. Henry knew this was the sort of crime that was currently out of favour in terms of being properly investigated by the police, although they would not openly admit it. They had been side-tracked into dealing with other types of activity such as internet hate crime which meant little to most members of the public. Most people, he knew, wanted good, efficient, empathetic, reassuring cops to turn up on their doorsteps when they needed them and be a shoulder to cry on. Few members of the public got that these days.

Henry sighed resignedly. 'OK, whatever.' He sat back and watched the court proceedings, now very stilted and slightly unreal because of COVID. The public were not now allowed access and press numbers were restricted; in fact, no one from the press was there that morning. Everyone had to wear a face mask, although because the distance between the solicitors' tables and the magistrates' bench was over two metres, they were allowed to address the bench without masks.

Henry glanced sideways as a woman he thought he recognized – in spite of a face mask – entered the court and deposited her briefcase on the defence solicitor's table. When she removed her mask, he was certain he knew her, not least because he'd done more than his share of verbal jousting with her over the years.

'That's Hortense Thorogood,' Henry whispered to Blackstone.

'I know! What's she doing here? She's well off her beat.'

Blackstone also knew Thorogood from her time as a detective in Blackpool. She was notorious for defending suspects. She was devious and quick-witted, had the ear of some gullible magistrates and occasionally used her sexuality and appearance – she was a stunning, statuesque woman – for gain. Henry knew people like her were all part of the rich tapestry of justice, but she made his flesh creep and blood boil all in one cauldron.

And then Henry's heart almost failed when the Crown Prosecution Service solicitor walked in, dropped all his papers on the floor when his briefcase flipped open and had to scrabble around on his hands and knees to collect them before taking his place alongside Thorogood, who was wearing a smile of contempt right across her handsome face.

'Jesus, a schoolboy,' Blackstone said. 'David and Goliath. We're fucked before we even start if she's here for Clanfield.'

'Do you know the CPS guy?' Henry asked.

'Never seen him before, but I'm not picking up good vibrations on this one.'

'Nor me.' Henry had never seen him before either, but he too was already expecting the worst, particularly when he saw Thorogood's supercilious expression as she watched her counterpart try to sort out his mixed-up files.

The clerk to the court strolled in from a side door and took his position at the desk in front of the bench below the magistrates, facing the court.

'All rise,' he said wearily. Henry knew this clerk, and whatever the magistrates might think, it was he who controlled proceedings.

Three magistrates shuffled in from a door behind the bench, all wearing face masks, and sat down two metres apart from each other.

The clerk announced, 'First case, your worships, a remand-in-custody application . . . Ellis Clanfield . . .' He rang a secret buzzer.

Henry heard a door being opened somewhere down below the dock, which was separated from the court by a high Perspex screen.

'Actually, I'm surprised he's appearing in person,' Henry muttered, 'with this COVID shit going on.'

But there was a very good reason for the magistrates to see him. Clanfield was now wearing a smart suit and had been cleaned up, but his face was still a very damaged mess from Blackstone's retaliatory punch.

Henry made a quick guess. 'Thorogood's going to use the broken nose, cite police brutality, say that he's been threatened, intimidated and, I'll bet, interviewed unlawfully, and that he will gladly respond to any police request for him to attend the station; she'll flower it up, stick it to the beaks and they'll crumble, I know they will.'

Henry was beginning to feel even more concerned about this.

And the ultra-smoothie that she was, Thorogood twisted the magistrates around her little finger and rode roughshod over the CPS solicitor who flailed like a drowning man. After only a few moments' of consideration, Clanfield was a free man.

'Fuck that!' Blackstone shot to her feet. 'What the hell are you playing at?' she screamed at the bench. Her move had been telegraphed, but Henry didn't react quickly enough to grab her and stop her from jumping up. 'That man is a fucking rapist and you're going to let him walk free? This is an absolute joke, you set of snowflakes!'

Henry managed to get to his feet at that point and twisted himself round so he half stood in front of her.

'Debbie, shut it,' he hissed through his teeth.

But, having none of it, she tried to jump up to see over him, gesticulating with a finger, 'You useless set of twa—'

Henry clamped his hand over her mouth to prevent the last word from coming out and with his other hand he tried to restrain her. 'Calm down,' he said and turned his head to the magistrates, all of whom were looking on askance. The CPS solicitor stood open-mouthed, while Thorogood had a wicked grin on her face as her submission to the bench was effectively given the final seal of approval by Blackstone's outburst. There was nothing better than a cop losing it in court.

'Officer!' the clerk of the court said firmly. 'You are in contempt of court.' He turned to the magistrates.

Henry quickly said to Blackstone, 'Apologize now or you'll be reflecting on this from a cell.'

'Fuck 'em!'

Henry clamped his hand back over her mouth and could feel the burning rage within her. It was like putting his hand on a boiling pan.

The chief magistrate – one Henry had interacted with many times over the years – adjusted his glasses. 'Officer, we find you in contempt of court and order that you are taken down to the cells below to reflect on your outburst. If, by the end of the day, you come to apologize to the bench, we will accept this. If you cannot do that, you will spend a night in police cells and will be fined a hundred pounds. Do I make myself clear?'

Henry spoke for her. 'Yes, your worship.'

The clerk signalled for a court usher who approached Blackstone. 'Come with me, please.'

She squirmed angrily out of Henry's grip with very special glares for the magistrates and the defence solicitor and the wimpish CPS solicitor. Then, with her shoulders drooping, she meekly followed the usher.

Henry shot the magistrates and solicitors an apologetic glance and made his way down to the cells.

At least Blackstone hadn't been thrown into a cell. She was sitting forlornly in the usher's office below the court with her head in her hands.

As Henry made his way from the bottom of the stairs, he upped his pace because he saw Rik Dean burst in through the secure outer door and storm across ahead of Henry. Rik had a fully formed raging storm on his face and didn't look as though he was going to take any prisoners. Henry knew he had to intercept.

He began to jog. Rik noticed him and gave him a glower which warned him to stay back.

But Henry was having none of it. He and Rik Dean went too far back, were too intertwined in so many ways to be constrained by niceties. Henry grabbed his arm just a few feet from the office door.

'Fuck off, Henry.' Rik shrugged himself out of the grasp. Both men were acutely aware they were being observed by the people around, which included police officers, private security personnel and court officials.

'Come – speak,' Henry cajoled him, taking a gentle grip of Rik's arm again. He could see fury in his friend's face. 'Come on.' In spite of himself, Rik relented and allowed himself to be escorted to a dark corner.

'Don't be too harsh on her,' Henry said.

'Oh, boo-hoo, has she had a bad day?'

'Yes: as you know, someone tried to kill her and she's had her flat burgled, and on top of that a rapist has somehow been released from court.'

'Shit happens, Henry. In the space of about one minute, she's brought the whole force into disrepute, for God's sake.'

'I know, and she'll beg the court's forgiveness.'

Rik's angry eyes played over Henry's face like a bagatelle as he considered Henry's plea. 'She better had. But whatever, it won't stop here. I'll make sure she's carpeted in front of the chief, and for the time being at least, she's on restricted duties in the office until I decide what to do with her. She's too unhinged to let loose!'

Henry nodded.

'You make sure that apology happens, Henry.'

Rik stormed out of the holding area. Henry watched him leave, then went back to the usher's office to see Hortense Thorogood being escorted to the secure interview room in which, presumably, she was going to have a private consultation with her client, Clanfield.

Henry changed tack and went for another intercept. Thorogood saw his approach and her expression of smugness altered to one of apprehension.

Henry stepped in front of her, very aware she was the same height as him, and shot a look at the usher who was showing her to the interview room. The usher backed off.

'I'm here to speak to my client before he's released.'

'He's a rapist and you know it. I hope you're proud of yourself. It might be just a game to you, Hortense, but I am livid.'

'Just doing my job, Henry.'

'Good on you . . . and anyway, how come Blackpool's premier hotshot scum-protecting brief is over in Preston defending low life like Ellis Clanfield?'

There was a shimmer of something in Thorogood's eyes that Henry did not quite understand, but it was gone in a flash to be replaced by the usual contempt for people on the other side of the game. 'I wasn't defending him, Henry, simply ensuring his rights were protected, that's all . . . which is what I did and the lady cop didn't like it. So sad.'

'But why are you over here?' Henry wanted to know.

'Because I'm good at my job. Now, if you'll excuse me.' She shouldered her way into the interview room, giving Henry a whiff of very expensive perfume.

He gave up, walked over to the usher's office and sat next to Blackstone, still with her head in her hands.

Without raising her eyes, she could obviously tell it was Henry.

'Say nothing. Please say nothing,' she said to the tiled floor.

'Sorry, but I need to: you're a jackass.'

'I don't even know what one of them is.'

'Use your imagination.'

He saw her nod.

'So what now?' she asked.

'Well, you're in detention at work, so I suggest you grovel to the magistrates, then either go into the CCU office and play Candy Crush for the rest of the day, or go home and sort your shit out.'

'My shit?'

'Yep – whatever your shit might be.'

'And what does all that mean?'

'You're off the investigation either way. You'll probably get a dressing-down from the chief and you'll need to keep your head down for a while.'

'They can't do that!'

'You have pissed on your chips, love,' Henry said. 'You lost it in the magistrates' court. You were lucky there were no reporters in there at the time, or you'd be hung out to dry in the *Lancashire Post* tonight and the whole force would look unprofessional.'

At the office door, the young and ineffective CPS solicitor appeared, a little breathless. 'The court is in recess for twenty minutes. The chief magistrate has said if you wish to speak to him in private now, you can. Otherwise, you'll be here all day.'

Blackstone nodded and stood up.

'You want me to come?' Henry offered.

'I'll fight my own battles.'

* * *

Blackstone decided to call it quits and go home to get her head together while sorting out her apartment and organizing repairs to her Mini Cooper where the Range Rover had shunted her from behind.

In the CCU office, Henry watched her get her things together like a kid who'd been expelled from school. When she'd got her bag sorted – including taking her work laptop with her – she stood up and looked at him.

'Lost it, didn't I?'

'And then some.'

'I'm so fragile.' She sighed.

'I think the word you're looking for is volatile.'

She nodded. 'Volatile. I'll have that.'

Henry kicked his heels listlessly for a few hours. All his enthusiasm had drained from him like sluice gates opening as he'd watched Blackstone leave the office with her tail between her legs. In theory, he probably should have gone across to Blackpool to parade in front of whoever was running the Trish Benemy murder.

But he had a serious case of CBA.

Can't be arsed.

Instead, he hovered at his desk, which at least gave him time to take stock of how much had happened over the last three days.

As was his wont, he got a sheet of A4 paper from the printer and began to jot a few things down, not in any sort of order.

The arrest of Ellis Clanfield for rape.

Finding the photograph of a kid who could've been Tommy Benemy.

The visit to Julie Clarke and watching her squirm a bit, which might mean nothing.

Clanfield's tattoo. House. Similar to Tommy's. Got it when he was in Blackpool!!

Similar to the Hindle logo?

Trish's murder. Desperate woman. But what about the suicide note?

Was she meddling? Did she find some truth?

Reliance on making Clanfield crack under interview.

Hortense Thorogood? From Blackpool. Why?

Not much happening in brain here.
Blackstone's incidents. Similarity to mine – i.e. the presence
    of Clarke.
Fuck knows. Speak to Clanfield again, maybe?

His sigh was long and deep.

He rocked back in his chair, which creaked worryingly, either from old age or his weight, and let his mind run on a little.

Way back to 1985. Such a long time ago.

Chasing a very lithe Tommy Benemy through the streets of Blackpool, finding him in the alley, then not much else – a bang on the head and years of not being able to discover the whereabouts of Tommy, who, if Henry was being honest, was probably dead.

That was something that gave Henry an overwhelming feeling of worthlessness: not having found Tommy for Trish. When kids went missing and were murdered, the two events were usually close timewise, but Tommy had allegedly been spotted in Manchester from time to time, according to the file and to Clarke who had taken the anonymous calls. If this was true, then it looked as if Tommy had either gone on to make a life for himself or met his maker in Manchester, neither of which sat easily with Henry.

Henry wracked his mind over the incident in the alley that had put him in hospital. Tommy sharing or handing over his spoils to another older lad . . . Henry had been able to ID Tommy from the mugshot book; if he'd seen a photograph of the other lad in the photo album, he felt sure he would have been able to identify him too, but his face wasn't in there, which intimated he didn't have any previous convictions, certainly in the Blackpool area. Henry pondered this, reliving the incident, seeing the other lad turn to him and glance over his shoulder at the person who undoubtedly hit Henry over the head. Henry wished it was one of those moments in a film where one character looks into the eyes of another and sees a reflection of someone else approaching. But it wasn't. He had never looked anyone in the eye and seen someone else, ever.

His mobile phone rang: Blackstone.

'Debs,' Henry said.

'I've had a home visit from your mate, Ricky boy.'

'Not too unpleasant, I hope.'

'It was for him. I played the wounded female card.' She paused.

'Nah, I didn't really. I was too busy sweeping up the broken screen of my TV for that.'

'What did he have to say?'

'That I was a naughty, naughty girl and deserved to be spanked.'

'No surprise there.'

'It really is what he said, but not in quite such a sexist way; however, he told me he'd spoken to the court clerk who said the magistrates were happy with my apology.'

'You never told me what you said.'

'I told them I was a naughty, naughty girl and that—'

'OK, I get it,' Henry interrupted her.

'Anyway, Rik then spoke to the chief constable who isn't interested in bollocking me, so Rik's visit was *the* bollocking, and if I want, I'm good to go. Got my gun and badge back. Officially off the bench.'

'That's brilliant.'

'But I'm going to chill tonight, surrounded by broken things. What say we meet up in Blackpool in the morning and tag along with Trish's murder investigation?'

'OK.'

'Oh, and . . .' She hesitated.

'What?'

'Nothing. Just . . . thanks . . . you know?'

'I know. See you.'

'Wouldn't want to be you.'

The call ended, but immediately Henry's mobile rang again, this time number withheld. Fearing it was a nuisance caller, he almost cut it off, but decided to answer.

'Am I speaking to Henry Christie?'

Henry instantly recognized the sultry female voice. 'What can I do for you, Hortense?' He was on the defensive straight away.

'Firstly,' Hortense Thorogood, solicitor, said, 'I would like to thank you for your complimentary remarks about me and my profession.' From sultry, the voice became chilly.

'Pleasure.' Henry was now wondering if this call was the precursor to a complaint about his behaviour which, even if it went nowhere, would probably end his tenure as a civilian investigator.

'You're right – I do defend scum, but usually they are illiterate toe-rags from the streets who, guilty or otherwise, need some

weight behind them to deal with a justice system that will fuck
'em royally if it gets the chance.'

Henry kept his thoughts to himself. In his experience, it was the
victims who were royally fucked over. 'And secondly?'

'I didn't defend Clanfield. I just made sure he was able to contest
what is usually a done deal. In fact, if you delve into my record,
I've never actually defended anyone charged with rape or other
serious sexual offences. I hate them.'

'But you've just put a rapist back on the street,' Henry protested.

'Admittedly, but I was asked to step in and couldn't really refuse.
It is my job, after all.'

'But you're based in Blackpool, not Preston.'

'Like I said, I was asked.'

Henry swallowed. His notes were still in front of him, but he got
hold of a pad of Post-it notes and scribbled *Clanfield* on it.

The solicitor went on, 'I have not made this call, Henry – OK?
Do you understand? In fact, I'm using a burner phone that one of
my clients gave to me, and once I've used it, the SIM will be
snapped in two and the phone dropped down a drain.'

Henry kept silent.

'You may think I'm a shit, and I assure you, the feeling's mutual,
but I'm not happy about what I did today for reasons you will never
discover . . . but what I'm about to say breaches all client/solicitor
confidentiality. I'm going to tell you who hired me to deal with
Clanfield's remand hearing . . . but I haven't told you, OK? I need
your word on that, Henry, because these are very scary people, and
if it ever came out I told you, I'm pretty sure my tits would be
toast.'

'You can trust me,' Henry said. His pen hovered over the sticky
notes.

'I know I can. Now I'm saying this only once and you do with
it whatever you will.'

'Got it.' Henry scribbled down the time.

Thorogood said, 'David Hindle.'

The line went dead.

SIXTEEN

The thing about Henry Christie was that when he'd been a 'real' cop, whatever rank he was at – and he'd reached (what he cynically called) the less than heady heights of detective superintendent before retirement – he had always been one to lead from the front. There were stages in his career when he could, probably should, have taken things more easily, become a desk-jockey and delegated more stuff, but that had never been him, especially when he was part of or leading investigations into serious offences. He revelled in being involved with the front line, coming face to face with criminals and pitting himself against them.

Which is why, following the 'anonymous' phone call from Hortense Thorogood, he stared at the names scribbled on the sticky note – *Clanfield* and *David Hindle* – with an arrow from one to the other, and felt his anus twitch, expanding and contracting as though it was keeping the beat to a rock 'n' roll song – that 'thing' his arsehole did when he became truly excited and knew he was on to something.

'David Hindle,' he whispered to himself, then underlined and encircled it in pen.

Then he stood up and said to no one, because the CCU office was empty, 'I may be Christie, Henry Christie, Civilian Investigator, but that doesn't mean I can't go out and ruffle feathers.'

He banged on the door, hard, repeatedly. Bent down to the letterbox and peered up the stairs beyond, then put his lips to the open slot and shouted, 'Ellis Clanfield, open up. This is the police.' He let the flap shut with a clatter and said, 'Sort of.'

Then he bent low again, opened the letterbox and continued to peer up towards Clanfield's flat.

He had no idea whether or not this was a good idea, but because Clanfield's flat in Preston was the closest port of call of the several he planned to make, that was why he was now knocking even harder because he was pretty sure the guy was in and he wanted to put the awkward question to him: what is your relationship with David Hindle?

He shouted again.

This time he heard some movement, and with his eyes to the letterbox he saw a pair of feet step on to the small landing at the top of the stairs.

'What do you want? I'm a free man. I'm going to show up for interview, so stop harassing me,' Clanfield called down.

'Let me in, let's chat,' Henry said.

'No way.'

'It's a condition of your release that you allow the police in to see if you are at home,' Henry bluffed.

'I don't remember that.'

'You were too excited being allowed out. Now come on, show yourself properly and let me talk to you.'

'You know I'm here, so fuck off.'

'Ellis, I'd hate to start thinking you have something to hide.'

'Hold on.'

Blackstone finally managed to bring some semblance of normality to her day. A CSI had been, done a fairly perfunctory sweep of the apartment and said he was certain whoever trashed her place had been wearing gloves. He held out little hope of a result.

By then she was past caring.

All she wanted was to return to her version of normal.

When everything was tidied up, she went down to the garage to have another look at the damage to her car – which looked worse than before: the boot was staved in and the rear bumper twisted. It almost made her weep, but she knew a guy who did body repairs and managed to book the Mini in for the following week. Then she phoned up for a pizza and killed a bit of time strolling around the dock until the delivery guy arrived.

She tipped him, then retreated to her flat where she intended to hole up for the evening; she'd previously nipped out to a nearby supermarket and bought herself a new TV which was big enough not to have to squint at but small enough for her to carry. It would suffice until the insurance claim was settled and she could replace the smashed-up one with a huge new one.

Her intention was: feet up, drink wine, watch a crap film and journey into herself to come to terms with the fact she was, as Henry put it, a jackass.

She'd been called worse.

With the new TV set up and ready to go, she opened the pizza, which was far too big for one; she would do her best with it, though, because the act of stuffing herself made her feel a whole lot better.

However, two large slices into the New Yorker, she decided she'd had enough. She closed the box lid and switched the TV off because the film she wanted to watch wasn't on until later. Something about Armageddon, which seemed just about right for her mood.

Suddenly, she was bored.

Until her courtroom outburst, the last three days had been the best three consecutive days of her life for a very long time.

More by accident than design, she had to admit.

She had been dreading having Henry Christie foisted on her, but he'd been a revelation of sorts, not least because he stood his ground against her onslaughts, gave as good as he got and didn't suffer her nonsense. He had taken her as he found her but had also, in some strange way, made her look at herself properly for once and come to realize that she didn't have to be the image she projected.

It was complicated, she knew.

She didn't see him as a saviour – that's definitely not what he was – but maybe someone who, for the first time in a while, she could rub along with and not feel the need to intimidate or bully just because she felt crap about herself; she was always either on the defensive or the attack – never seemed to have a nice equilibrium to her.

'Enough introspection!' she chided herself.

That said, although she had been forgiven by others for her unprofessional outburst in court, she was struggling to forgive herself. She'd allowed her thin veneer to slip and she didn't like what she saw underneath it.

She went into the bathroom – the intruders had broken the mirror over the washbasin. Standing in front of it, she removed her T-shirt and regarded herself critically in the cracked image which cut across like the zigzag of forked lightning.

And she smiled.

Because she didn't detest what she saw.

She was different, yes. Not the twee, pretty woman she used to

be with nicely bobbed, trimmed hair, but a scarred version of that
person with whacky hair, piercings, tattoos – although she didn't
really have pierced nipples as she'd claimed to Henry.

She smirked at that, visualizing his face.

'Like I said, enough introspection for the moment. There's a long
way to go yet before we get into here' – she tapped her forehead
– 'but I think we're en route.'

She slid the T-shirt back on, returned to the lounge and plugged
in her work laptop. She rubbed her hands and said, 'Now, where
was I?'

Henry's impatience grew as he waited for Clanfield to come to the
door. He wasn't rushing – not that he was obliged to, but the delay
made Henry suspicious.

Finally, the door opened.

Clanfield stood there in a ragged rugby shirt and equally tatty
shorts. 'What?'

'What are you up to?' Henry asked: too many years as an over-
suspicious cop made him pose that one.

'Nowt.'

'Who have you got up there?'

'No one.'

Henry looked into his shifty eyes which tried to avoid contact.
'Really?'

'Yeah, fuckin' really.'

'You won't mind if I have a glance, then?'

Clanfield instantly became jittery. Henry saw the mouth twitch,
but most of all he saw panic in his eyes.

'Help yourself,' Clanfield said. He stepped aside to let Henry
pass in the confined space of the tiny vestibule at the foot of the
stairs. Then he gave Henry an almighty shove, pushing him into
the steps. Henry's right arm shot out to stop himself crashing down,
while at the same time he tried to grab Clanfield with his left and
missed – because the guy was out of the front door like a greyhound
out of the traps.

As Henry pivoted, he lost balance and plonked squarely down
on the third step with a bump and saw Clanfield's back as he legged
it across the street.

But Henry's expression, which started off as one of huge

annoyance with himself for being hoodwinked by Clanfield and then changed to anger at seeing him flee, became one of complete horror – all in the space of perhaps three seconds.

Horror because when Clanfield reached the middle of the street, he was mown down by a huge, speeding, black Range Rover that crashed into the man's hip, slammed him down to the ground, went right over him with bone-chilling crunches as the wheels crushed his head. As Henry still looked on, dumbfounded, the vehicle screeched to a halt, then reversed back over Clanfield's body as though going over a badly constructed speed bump – and then pulled up.

Henry shot to his feet and ran out of Clanfield's front door to the edge of the pavement where he stopped, teetering as though on the edge of a precipice, his arms windmilling, completely stunned by what he'd just witnessed.

A terrible accident, he'd thought at first as his mind whirred.

Clanfield running across the road without looking.

Served him right.

The car careering down the street too fast. Shit happens.

But then – no! Not a terrible accident.

A deliberate act, proven by the reverse over the – probably – already dead body of the fleeing man, if his crushed head was anything to go by.

And he was dead, almost instantly. Henry saw the devastatingly flattened head, unrecognisable as a human being.

And then Henry's mind processed the black Range Rover.

And he thought of Debbie Blackstone. And a black Range Rover out to run her off the road.

Henry was in a whirl as the front and rear nearside doors opened and two men jumped out of the car.

They were wearing face masks.

Both were holding handguns, pointed at Henry.

'In the car,' one of them ordered him.

Henry didn't move. Considered running.

Didn't.

His hesitation seemed to anger them. The one who'd dropped out of the front seat stepped over and jabbed him hard under the ribs with the barrel of the gun, grabbed his right arm, dragged him over to the car, shoved him through the open door, face down, over the back seat, and held the gun to his head. The other man went through Henry's pockets quickly, found his car keys and phone, took them, and both men bundled him into the back seat.

'Get his car, ditch the phone,' one of them said – Henry wasn't sure which, as he was forced into the centre of the seat while one of them got in alongside him and crushed him against another person who was sitting by the opposite door.

The back door slammed as Henry squirmed and tried to lurch forward between the seats but was clubbed across the side of his head with something that hurt and stunned him.

The Range Rover set off, mounting Clanfield's body again.

It was only then that Henry, his vision swimming, turned to the other person by the opposite door who, up to that moment, had been in shadow, but now angled forwards and brought their face into the light.

'Now that was a happy coincidence,' the person said.

Julie Clarke was holding a snub-nosed revolver pointing at Henry's guts and wearing a terrifying smile, but he only saw her for a moment because the man next to him pulled a thick hessian bag over his head and tightened a drawstring around his neck.

Where Blackstone had been in the cyber world was logged remotely into the constabulary's computer system. That was before she'd set out for a Big Mac and got somewhat diverted by an angry Range Rover. She had actually been looking at various aspects of the comms room log from the night four years ago when she'd had an acid shower, the night that had surely changed her forever, although she knew she'd been lucky in one respect – that the acid had missed her face and hit her on the underside of her chin and below.

If she'd had a face full, she knew she would not have been able to handle it at all.

She would still be in hiding.

Or dead, hanging from a noose.

She shook off that feeling and continued to look at the logs of the incident that began when she'd been approached by the member of staff from the amusement arcade and taken to see a distraught young girl whose friend had supposedly been dragged into a car by three men and driven away.

That, through a series of events, had resulted in the acid attack.

'In a hotel being done up by Hindle's Builders,' she mumbled to herself.

That thought took her on another trajectory, leaving the comms log behind and delving once more into the Hindle's Builders company website.

The story of a local lad made good. 'From little acorns and all that shit,' Blackstone said to herself.

She then managed to track down a long article in a local business publication from a couple of months earlier in 2020 when David Hindle, the managing director, was interviewed in some depth. In it, he seemed to bare all. In a frank interview, he admitted he'd had a troubled youth in that he'd gone through the care system following some (alleged) abuse from his parents. At some point, he had been fostered long-term by a good couple in the Stoke area and taken on their surname – Hindle – although the article did not say what his birth name was. However, he'd done poorly at school, been a runaway on several occasions (although Blackstone could find no police reports on this) but had been good at practical things and knuckled down to study building, joinery and associated trades and crafts in the 1980s before setting up a business restoring decrepit hotels in Blackpool and old farmhouses on the Fylde coast.

Definitely a success from an underprivileged background.

There were some photos of Hindle standing proudly in front of some of his projects. The most recent one was of him outside a very big old country house near Preston which he intended to turn into a posh hotel . . . there was also a black-and-white photograph of him standing in front of one of his first ever projects, the renovation of a small hotel on Abingdon Street in Blackpool in 1986.

Blackstone looked at this one for a long time, willing something to come to mind, something Henry Christie had spoken about. It didn't.

Finally, she gave up thinking . . . it was hurting her head, and she returned to the comms log for the night of the acid attack.

And there was something here that didn't seem to add up either, another thing she couldn't quite put her finger on.

Maybe it was time for a stroll around the docks to clear her mind.

It was just over a mile and a half to circumnavigate the Albert Edward Dock, once the thriving commercial heartbeat of Preston – now, not so much. No big ships, just a small marina and the water, seemingly constantly polluted by green algae which gave it an unappealing tinge.

Blackstone had only made it from her apartment to the dock side when her mobile phone rang. Rik Dean. 'Evening, boss.'

'Where are you now?' he snapped.

She told him.

'Where's Henry?'

'Don't know. Not seen or spoken to him for a while . . . I assume he's gone home.'

'OK.' Rik sounded harassed.

'Is there a problem, boss?'

'Ellis Clanfield has been mown down by a hit-and-run driver on the street outside his flat.'

'Really? How is he?'

'Very, very dead. Looks like he was run over a few times, back and forth if you will. Made a real soupy mess. I'm not at the scene yet – traffic are covering – but I'm en route.'

'Crikey!'

'Since you're off the bench and it's looking like this could be a murder, I'd like you to come up and take a look as you are involved with the guy.'

'I'm on my way.'

Almost before she had finished saying those words, Rik said, 'And find Henry, OK?'

As she hurried back, she phoned Henry's mobile but got the metallic female voice saying, 'The person at this number is unable to take your call, please leave a message after the tone.' Blackstone did: a terse, 'Call me, old guy.'

Then she called him again, just in case. It still reverted to voicemail.

'Fuck you up to, Christie?' she said. 'Or have you just gone home and shut up shop for the night?'

She had to look up the number of The Tawny Owl on the internet via her phone. Two numbers were listed, a landline and a mobile.

Blackstone phoned the landline.

'Hello, this is Ginny at The Tawny Owl, can I help you?'

'Ginny, it's Debbie Blackstone – I crashed at Th'Owl last night?'

'Oh, yeah, hiya, Debbie. Are you OK?'

'I'm fine now . . . Is there any chance of speaking to Henry? I can't seem to get through on his mobile number.'

'Erm, he isn't here . . . well, not that I know of, and I haven't spoken to or seen him all day.'

'Any chance of speaking to Diane if she's knocking around?'

'Sure. Hold on.'

By this time, Blackstone was at the door of her Mini in the basement garage.

'Hiya, Debbie, it's Diane.'

'Hiya, love, sorry to trouble you. Any idea where Henry is, or how I can best contact him? I've tried his mobile – no deal.'

'I haven't heard from him . . . I thought he'd be with you.'

'Uh, no, long story . . . So you've no idea where he is?'

'No,' Diane said cautiously. 'Do I need to be worried?'

'About Henry? Nah, don't think so.'

They said goodbye. Blackstone got into the Mini and screamed her way up to Preston.

The street outside Clanfield's flat had been sealed off with cordon tape, and an evidence tent had been erected over his body. Blackstone had to park almost a quarter of a mile away and jog the remaining distance. She shouldered through a crowd of gaping onlookers, most of whom were not wearing face masks, and then flashed her warrant card so the bobby on duty at the cordon tape lifted it for her to duck under.

She weaved her way through an overload of cop cars, uniforms and detectives, most, she guessed, probably having descended on to the scene for its gruesome content rather than to add value to an investigation; and the sight of a young uniformed cop throwing up into a grate by the kerb seemed to prove this assumption.

A pale-looking Rik Dean emerged from the tent.

He looked at Blackstone and blew out his cheeks.

'You really don't have to,' he warned her.

'I should.'

'Be my guest.'

She was in and out in a matter of seconds. 'Fuckin' hell,' she said to Rik. 'You can hardly tell it was a human being!'

Blackstone glanced across the street to the open door and the stairs leading up to Clanfield's flat. 'Anyone checked the place, yet?'

'Just a cursory glance. We're waiting for the circus to arrive.'

Circus meaning CSI, forensics, search teams.

'Mind if I . . .?' Blackstone gestured towards the flat.

'Gloves and mask and don't touch anything,' Rik told her.

She was already pulling on a pair of latex gloves. 'Any witnesses yet?' she asked.

Rik shook his head.

Blackstone went through the door and trod carefully up the steps, bearing in mind this could easily be an extension of the crime scene until it was found to be otherwise. The flat, obviously, was exactly as she remembered it – a grot-bag hovel for a grot-bag of a man who had just met a more than grotty end. Blackstone wished she felt a bit sorrier for him, but she didn't, although she would fight tooth and nail to be on the squad to catch his killer.

She moved across the flat, touching nothing, able to hear pretty clearly what was going on down the street as more police vehicles arrived and voices barked instructions. There wasn't much space in the flat – no room to swing a cat, she thought. The bedroom in which she'd found the necklace belonging to Melanie Wooton, his rape victim; the living area with the sofa; the kitchen sink with a cupboard underneath it. There was a half-eaten pizza, now cold, on the coffee table. Off to one side was a door to the shower which she glanced into and screwed up her nose: even through the face mask it stank.

So, nothing to see; not that she'd expected anything.

She went to the door, looked down the steps to the pavement and pulled off the gloves. As she placed her foot on the first step, she stopped mid-stride, stock-still, listening, frowning, certain she'd heard something.

A murmur or a whimper.

Then nothing. The foot went on the step.

And the sound came again.

Blackstone backed up, listening hard, trying to pinpoint the source of the sound. She re-entered the living room, standing just over the threshold, another of those times she wished she had ears that swivelled – and she heard the noise again.

Then she rushed across the room, going down on one knee by the cupboard under the sink and yanked it open.

*   *   *

'He literally snatched her on his way home from court,' Blackstone said to Rik Dean. It was two hours later, the evening was getting on, and they were at Preston police station. Blackstone was managing to keep it together but teetered on rage. 'Opportunistic bastard,' she added through her clenched teeth. 'The little lass just happened to be walking down his street and he caught her and bundled her up his stairs, just like that!' She clicked her fingers, made Rik jump. 'She was overpowered, trussed up within seconds, punched in the face, tied and gagged with tape, then further taped to a radiator while he went out and bought a pizza.'

Even as she was saying it, Blackstone was reliving the recent, vivid memory of opening the under-sink cupboard to see the tiny, terrified figure of an eleven-year-old girl in school uniform who had been crammed into the small space with her hands behind her back, secured by parcel tape, ankles too, and a length of it over her mouth – and the look in her eyes.

Blackstone had eased her gently out, carefully removed the tape and then, because she had to, she held the little, sobbing lass tenderly in her arms, telling her she was OK now.

She had reunited her with her mother – who was just on the verge of calling the police to report her daughter missing – at Preston police station and had been able to get a good statement from the girl when her mum had eventually managed to calm her down.

'But he didn't assault her sexually in any way?' Rik asked.

'No. That was next on the agenda after the pizza. He'd come back with the food, released her from the radiator and sat her down on the floor at his feet, stroking her hair, while he ate the pizza – the git,' Blackstone said.

'So what stopped him?' Rik asked.

'A knock on the door and somebody shouting up through the letterbox. The girl said that sent him into a panic, saying – and I quote – "The fucking pigs are at the door." The lass didn't know what he meant by "pigs". That was when he shoved her under the sink and threatened to slit her throat if she moved or made a sound.'

'I'm surprised he didn't anyway,' Rik commented.

'Me too.'

'So – who was at the door, Debbie?'

'I've checked with comms and there are no logs or record of

anyone going to the address. Comms has asked over the radio since
and it's a negative.'

'Could it have been Henry?'

Blackstone shook her head. 'I don't know, but it wouldn't surprise
me, although I don't know why he would have been there.'
Blackstone took the opportunity for a dig. 'Now you know why I
was so incensed at Clanfield being released from court.'

'I get it, but you were still wrong to act the way you did.'

'Will I get an apology from the magistrates for their huge
mistake?'

Rik looked at her as if she'd lost it again. 'Don't even go there.'

'So not a cat in hell's chance?'

'Nope! Anyway, what do you think? Someone comes to Clanfield's
door, either is or isn't a cop, Clanfield panics, shoves the girl under
the sink and then ends up under the wheels of a black car.'

'A black car? I didn't know that . . . How?'

'The traffic man says there's black paint on Clanfield's trousers,'
Rik explained.

'Any witnesses yet?'

'No . . . but from what the girl says, do you really think it was
a cop at the door?'

'According to the girl, Clanfield shouted down to whoever it was,
something about him being a free man now, but she was too frightened to take it all in properly, other than the "pig" reference. So he
sticks her under the sink, goes down to answer, and we don't really
know what happened then, other than he was run over and the next
person on the scene was another driver who just about managed not
to run over his body again.'

Rik's mouth twisted. 'I get the feeling we need to speak to Henry
sharpish, don't you?'

At which moment Blackstone's mobile rang. It was Diane
Daniels.

SEVENTEEN

'Debbie, have you heard from Henry yet?' Diane asked tentatively.

'Not a sausage. Have you . . . well, obviously not.'

'No, but the thing is, you might not know, the phone signal up here in Kendleton varies from appalling to very appalling, although Henry does assure me it has got better . . . Anyway, a message has just landed on my voicemail from him.'

'Oh, right, that's good.'

Diane did not reply.

'That's not good?'

'Even though it's only just arrived, it's timed two hours ago.'

Blackstone swallowed dryly.

'He said he was going to be late back home . . . he was going to "ruffle some feathers" – his exact words.' As Diane spoke, her own words were becoming distinctly shaky.

'He didn't say whose feathers?'

'No, just that he'd see me later and call on the way home.'

'OK, Diane, leave it with me. I'm sure there's nothing to worry about, love. I'll get back to you as soon as we've tracked him down. He's probably in the office with the phones off the hook.' She ended the call and looked at Rik Dean who'd eavesdropped every word. They eyed each other uncertainly. Blackstone dialled the CCU office number and, while it rang out, said to Rik, 'Maybe he *is* back at the office?'

There was no reply. The call went on to the office voicemail.

'Worth a try.' She hung up.

'What do you reckon?'

Blackstone opened her hands and shrugged. 'No idea.'

'Like you say, maybe it's nothing. Henry just doing his thing,' Rik said hopefully. 'Like he always did and clearly still does.'

'I do know he spent most of the afternoon slobbing about in the office . . . I wonder if there's something on his computer search history that would give us a clue?'

'Worth checking, I suppose,' Rik said less than hopefully.

Blackstone jogged to her car and gunned it all the way back to Hutton Hall. Before going into the office, she did a fast sweep around all the car parks on which Henry might have parked up to see if his Audi was around, but she couldn't spot it.

Then she parked as close as possible to the FMIT building, went into the CCU office and sat at Henry's empty desk. His computer was on and when she shook the mouse the screen came to life but – and she realized she hadn't quite thought this through – she did not have Henry's password. As she sat there pondering this predicament, her mobile rang.

'Hi, boss,' she said to Rik Dean.

'Anything?'

'Nope . . . just realized I can't access his computer. I'll need the on-call IT bod to help, whoever that may be. Comms will know.'

'OK.'

There was a pause. Blackstone sensed something. 'You OK, boss?'

'Look, I just got a call from the Telephone Unit. I asked them to track Henry's phone.'

'And?' Blackstone could almost visualize Rik Dean standing wherever he was with his phone clasped to his ear and his other hand clamped to the top of his head.

'They've managed to do it.'

'That's good, then.'

'Meh! Not so much,' he said. 'They can tell he made a call somewhere between headquarters and Preston.'

'That would be the one he made to Diane that went to voicemail.'

'Yeah, probably . . . and they've also managed to pinpoint a pulse from the phone which puts him within five metres of where I'm standing now.'

'Which is where?'

'Outside Clanfield's front door. So it definitely looks as if he came here to see Clanfield.'

'That's brilliant! So where is he now? In a pub?'

'Well, that's just it, Debbie . . . that was the last pulse. Since then nothing, other than the exact time that pulse was sent from his phone, which seems to indicate that Henry was here at the exact time Clanfield was run down. Like I said, though, that's the very last thing from his phone. I've sent a few cops to nosy around the streets to see if they can spot Henry's car, but there is no trace of it around here.'

'Henry and his car have gone missing then, for sure?'

'Look, Debbie – I'm trying not to overreact to this, but my gut tells me this is crappy information.'

'Well, I *am* going to overreact because my gut tells me the same, boss, and I'm very worried.'

The call ended.

Blackstone rocked back and forth in Henry's chair. As she tilted forward, she saw a sticky note under the desk which had obviously wafted down. She heeled the chair backwards and picked it up. The writing was spidery but legible, as was the little sketch on the bottom of the note.

There was a time: 1649.

There were two names – *Clanfield* and *David Hindle* with an arrow from one to the other and a double circle around *Clanfield*.

The sketch was of something she had come to know well in the last few days – the square with a pointed roof and a diagonal slash across the square.

She swore. She knew Henry had spent virtually no time on this chair or at this desk since he'd started on Monday morning; it had all been go, go, go, non-stop. Which meant he'd had no time to write anything or jot stuff down, so what she was looking at was the only thing he could have written and must have been done that afternoon. Then she looked at the jotter next to the phone and opened it to see Henry had been scribbling down some notes maybe to free up his creative process. She scanned through them, then her eyes returned to the sticky note.

Why was there a time on a Post-it note?

Something drilled into all cops from day one, real bread-and-butter stuff, was always *Make a note of the time*; it was something she did almost without thinking about now, even when she received a call in the office.

Had Henry taken a phone call?

Had he received a call while sitting here doodling his meandering thoughts? And did that call spur him out of his creaky chair and send him to Clanfield's address?

Blackstone read that name again – David Hindle – then jumped over to her desk and logged into her computer. She'd done some digging into Hindle at home; maybe she needed to dig deeper?

Blackstone ran out of the FMIT building to her Mini. She fired up the engine after slotting her phone into its cradle. She sped off, screeching to a halt at the horrendously slow-opening main gate, revving impatiently because it didn't rise anywhere near fast enough for her. She almost caught the roof on the bottom edge of the gate when she shot out on to the road, then accelerated up the A59 before looping under the bridge to head back to Preston.

She was on the phone to Rik Dean.

'He wasn't convicted up here,' she said breathlessly. 'That's why he's never been on our radar. As a lad, he ended up in the care system and he committed his one and only recorded crime in Staffordshire.'

'Who the hell are you talking about?'

'David Hindle.'

'Who?'

'Look, boss, just go with this. Thing is, he wasn't called Hindle when he was a kid – at least not to start with; it was a name he took from foster parents . . . I found it all, but it's very old stuff,' Blackstone said hurriedly.

She was now speeding towards the city, swerving the Mini through and past other traffic.

'Thing is, his original name, his *birth* name was Clarke . . .'

She waited for it to register with Rik Dean.

It didn't.

So she almost shouted, 'As in Julie Clarke? Yeah? Ex-policewoman, inspector, now charity worker?'

'Gotta be a coincidence.'

'Now *you* sound like Henry Christie, boss. And maybe it is, maybe it isn't . . . but the offence he was convicted for, and he was only twelve, was abducting a young lass off the street, sexually abusing her and dripping sulphuric acid into her face and watching her burn. *Fuck off, dickhead!*' she screamed as a guy in a swanky Jag cut her up at a set of lights. 'Not you, boss . . . Jeez, I need a blue light for this car. Can I have one?'

'No. Keep talking.'

'I think Clarke and Hindle are siblings,' she said. 'David and Julie, but I haven't had time to dig that deep. It took me long enough to find that shit about Hindle. Be interesting to know *her* background before joining the cops.'

'I'll get someone from Intel on to that now,' Rik said.

'Cheers.'

She crossed the bridge over the River Ribble south of Preston, then forked left to take the road through Preston docks, virtually past her apartment.

'What's your thinking, Debs?' Rik asked.

'That me and Henry have lucked into something big that's been going on for a lot of years right under our noses – by instinct and mistake, obviously, but I think we've upset some really nervous, jittery and dangerous people.'

'What's the "something"?'

'Haven't a clue, boss, but I think it involves missing kids and organized criminality, if that doesn't sound too dramatic. And it involves people who are more than happy to kill.' She took a breath. 'Anyway, first things first.'

'Find Henry?'

'And if I do find him and he's in a bloody pub, I'll knock his bleedin' lights out.'

'What's your plan?'

'Head to the coast and go and knock on a few doors on spec, give 'em a surprise.'

'Now *you* sound like Henry Christie!'

'And all the better for it. Gotta go!' she said, ended the call and dialled 999 because that was the only sure way she knew of contacting the police directly.

The call was answered on the sixth ring. 'Police emergency.'

Blackstone quickly told the operator who she was and asked for someone to call her back immediately so as not to clog up the emergency line. A comms room despatcher was back on to her within a minute. Blackstone gave him instructions to look up the keyholder details for the offices of Blackpool Children's Charity and Hindle's Builders on Granville Street, Blackpool. ASAP.

When she outlined the urgency of the call, he said he would do it straight away.

The problem with Blackstone's request was that keyholder lists for properties were not always up to date and even non-existent for many places. It relied on the property owner to keep police records up to date, but not many did, which often caused problems when police attended a burglary at a property and they couldn't get hold of anyone to turn out.

Nevertheless, she drove hard and fast along the A583, ignoring the average-speed cameras dotted along the route, realizing she would have to plead an emergency if she ended up with a fixed penalty notice through the letterbox. She already had six points on her licence and any more would put her in danger of disqualification.

A call came in on her phone.

It was comms responding to her request with just two mobile phone numbers for keyholders, which was a start, but no actual physical address for either, which was a bummer but the way of the world. She told the operator to text both numbers to her, then she had a bit of a brainstorm.

'Do me another favour, will you? Look up Blackpool Children's Charity on the internet. See if you can get the address of a Julie Clarke from that.'

Blackstone knew that accessing details of registered charities was usually simple enough because it was a legal requirement for them to post all financial dealings to the Charity Commission, which then shared them publicly online.

She hung up and waited for the response as she hurtled towards Blackpool while counting up the extra penalty points she was surely accruing and fervently hoping she was heading in the right direction, in more ways than one.

A minute or so later, the comms operator was on the phone again. 'The charity is actually registered to that office in Granville Street – no other addresses listed.'

'Whose names are listed as officers of the charity?'

'Julie Clarke – at that address.'

She thanked him and hung up, then swerved on to a garage forecourt, stopped and banged both hands on the steering wheel in frustration.

Her mobile phone rang again.

*   *   *

'I knew something would turn up,' Rik Dean said, 'but it's not good,' he added bleakly.

'What is it?' Blackstone asked, afraid she didn't really want to know.

'CCTV footage from a house further down the street from Clanfield's flat. The occupant arrived home, saw the police activity and checked his security camera, which was inside his house, looking out; it gives an oblique view along the street . . . it's on an SD card but I've got a copy of it on my phone – just the crucial minutes.'

'Send it to me, boss.'

Moments later, Blackstone's phone pinged as the incoming message from Rik Dean landed. She tapped her screen to open up what he'd sent.

The camera must have been in an upstairs room, positioned to get a view along the street, which she recognized as the one on which Clanfield's front door was located, but the angle was such that she couldn't actually see the door itself, nor anyone at the door.

A black Range Rover crept into view at the top of the street and stopped. A beast on the prowl.

From the left of the screen, Clanfield burst into view, exiting the front door of his flat, Blackstone assumed, into the road, looking over his shoulder, and the Range Rover shot forward and was on him, ploughing him down, running over him and then reversing. The splurge of blood and brain from his flattened head was horribly visible.

Blackstone could hardly believe her eyes.

Then, from the same direction as Clanfield, Henry Christie came into view, dashing to the edge of the footpath, almost losing his balance, his arms flailing as he seemed to teeter.

Blackstone watched as two masked men jumped out of the car, both clearly armed with handguns, and overpowered Henry quickly. They dragged him to the car, pinned him down, searched him and bundled him into the back seat. One of the men, a slightly built guy, did not get in, but jogged away out of sight – was he going for Henry's car? – and the Range Rover set off with Henry as a prisoner, running over Clanfield's prostrate, mangled body *again*.

She paused the image, rewound it a little way and used her finger and thumb to enlarge it.

The front registration plate of the car had been deliberately obliterated, but she could see what seemed to be some damage to the front bumper. It was hard to make out for certain because as the image was made bigger, the grainier it became, but there seemed to be a dent in it, which, in her soul, she knew would perfectly match the damage caused to the rear of her Mini Cooper. She peered closely at the driver, but he seemed to be wearing a face mask.

She let the video run on and the vehicle zoomed out of shot. Maybe there were three people, including the abducted Henry, in the back seat, but they too were hard to make out properly.

Her phone rang. Rik Dean said, 'Have you watched it?'

'Yep.' She gulped. 'This is bad.'

'What the hell have you two got your noses stuck into?' Rik demanded rhetorically. He'd asked a similar question before, but that was before he knew that his colleague, close friend and brother-in-law had been snatched off the street at gunpoint following a brutal murder. 'These guys are armed. I've already got two armed response vehicles cruising the area. I just hope we won't need them.'

Blackstone felt she was about to explode, that a time bomb was masquerading inside her chest as her heart and there was nothing she could do to disarm it. She also wanted to bang her head against a brick wall to knock some down-to-earth cop sense into her brain.

She had tried the two mobile numbers that comms had texted to her, those of Clarke and Hindle, but both were unanswered and went to voicemail. She had left an urgent message on both, coupled with a hint of threat.

But now, quite simply, she did not know what to do or where to go.

Henry had been taken at gunpoint and his car had also disappeared. She had no idea where he was, how to find him, how to rescue him. Suddenly, she felt useless.

'C'mon, c'mon, work through this,' she intoned to herself, still fist-pounding the steering wheel. 'They've got Henry, they've got his car . . . Jesus! *The car!*'

For some unaccountable reason, Blackstone was now driving back along the A583 towards Preston, away from Blackpool. She didn't know why she'd spun around, hardly even recalled doing it, but realized she must have done so at Marton Circle.

Her mind was a blur and she knew she had to get a grip to be of any use to Henry.

At that moment, she had reached the outskirts of Kirkham on her left-hand side, a town about halfway between Blackpool and Preston.

His car! Henry's car, for goodness' sake.

Gripping the wheel with her right hand, she searched her phone for the numbers of the people who had most recently called her: Rik Dean and Diane Daniels.

She was about to press Diane's number when magically it came up on the screen: Diane was calling Blackstone.

Simultaneously, the first words the two women said were, 'His car!'

'You first,' Blackstone said to Diane.

'It's got a GPS tracker on it, came as standard with all the other bells and whistles,' Diane said. 'If nothing else, it tells you exactly where the car is, even if Henry isn't with it.'

Blackstone did an air punch and said, 'Yes! And how do we access that information?'

'I rooted out all of the bumf for the car and I'm logged on to the manufacturer's website now. I followed the links to the GPS company website, entered the correct codes and passwords, et cetera, and I'm now looking at the car's location on a map. It's stationary at the mom— No, it isn't,' she cried. 'It's moving . . . it's just started moving,' Diane said. 'And it's moving fast!'

'Where is it?' Blackstone asked. She was driving towards Preston, still not knowing if she was going in the right direction.

'Spen Lane, now New Hey Lane.'

'Those names mean nothing to me,' Blackstone admitted.

'Countryside, between Kirkham and Clifton,' Diane clarified. 'Wow – fast, sharp left into Moor Hall Lane . . . going really fast . . . now sharp right, Vicarage Lane, heading towards Blackpool Road.'

'I'm on Blackpool Road!' Debbie shouted. 'Just gone past Kirkham,' she said, trying to work out the geography in her head, hoping she was in the right area. This was a road she had travelled many times, and in the fairly recent past she had spent a bit of time on the back roads putting her Mini through its paces on the narrow lanes where, with its wonderful balance and grip, the car came into its own. But she hadn't actually known the names of the roads she'd hurtled along.

'Turning left out of Vicarage Lane on to Blackpool Road, heading towards Preston – now!' Diane said.

'And I'm right behind it,' Blackstone shouted. 'And it's definitely not Henry at the wheel.'

The white Audi convertible skidded out of the side road maybe thirty metres in front of Blackstone without even pausing at the junction. She had to slam on her brakes, but the sports car accelerated away towards Preston. Although the driver didn't look in her direction and the evening was now dark, she could tell from the build of the man at the wheel that it wasn't Henry. This was a man smaller in stature, slouched quite low down on the seat. It could have been the man from the CCTV footage who, Blackstone had assumed, had gone to get Henry's car after Henry had been bundled into the Range Rover.

The car slithered as he put his foot down, and Blackstone almost thought he was going to lose control, but he kept it going. Although she ground her gears into second to start picking up the speed she'd lost by braking, the Audi was soon well ahead of her and she knew she had no chance of keeping up with it in a straight line. It was a very fast car.

'I'm with him, Diane,' Blackstone said into her phone. 'Can you stay with the tracker? I need to speak to Rik Dean and I don't have my PR with me. I'll have to use my phone.'

'Got it – stay safe,' Diane said, immediately understanding the situation. The line went dead.

Blackstone, cursing that she didn't have a personal radio, steered with her right hand and had to dab at the screen of the mobile phone with her left hand to get to Rik's number, while still concentrating on keeping up with the Audi which soared away from her.

'Debbie – what's happening?' Rik answered immediately.

Ahead was a set of traffic lights at which the Audi bore left – ignoring the red – off the main road and into the village of Clifton, which gave Blackstone some hope, as she too ran the red light on to the narrow, twisty main street of the village, on both sides of which were many parked cars, making it even tighter.

At least now she had both hands on the wheel as she sped through the village and made up some ground on Henry's car.

Blackstone's mobile phone was quickly patched by comms into the force radio system and her transmissions were now being broadcast across the Preston and Blackpool areas so patrols could hear what she was saying as her car screamed through Clifton at sixty miles an hour in the twenty zone.

'He's gone through Clifton village and turned left, heading towards that nuclear place,' she said, knowing she needed to keep her voice calm and measured, rather than shouty. 'Don't know the name of road.'

The comms operator who had inherited this chase – and was now looking at a screen in front of her which showed a live map with the position of Blackstone's car from the signal transmitted by her phone, plus the positions of all the patrols converging on the area – took cool control of the pursuit.

The first thing she did was to caution Blackstone and ask her to comply with the force pursuit policy. Meaning, 'Back off.'

Blackstone gave a harsh chuckle and muttered, 'As if.'

It was a response the operator knew she would get, so she didn't push it for the moment because what was important was to keep tabs on the Audi; when other patrols were properly involved, she would give Blackstone the hard word to pull out of the chase.

'Suspect vehicle on Clifton Lane,' the operator said, filling in Blackstone's lack of street-name knowledge. 'Towards Westinghouse,' she said, 'the nuclear fuel processing plant. DS Blackstone is in her private vehicle in pursuit for the moment.'

Several patrols gave their positions and confirmed they were closing in, as did the police helicopter which had been scrambled from its base at Warton, close by. It would be with the pursuit within a couple of minutes at most.

As Blackstone's Mini left the environs of the village, the Audi was well ahead of her, and she struggled to keep it in view on the bends, but her hope was that the driver didn't even yet know he was being chased by the cops. With luck, that nugget would come as a surprise to him very shortly.

Then: 'He's done a right!' Blackstone said, knowing her voice was rising shrilly again.

The operator said, 'Patrols, that is on to Deepdale Lane.'

The lights of the vehicle disappeared as Blackstone skidded around the very sharp right-hand junction, feeling her two nearside wheels lifting off the ground.

The road twisted and dipped, with the nuclear processing plant on her left; once past it, there was a ninety-degree left-hander as the road became Darkinson Lane for a stretch and straightened out but passed over a narrow railway bridge and then almost immediately over an even narrower canal bridge. Blackstone saw the lights of the Audi up ahead as she skittered around this bend and put her foot to the floor of the Mini.

A patrol called up saying he was at the far end of this road with another and that they intended to block the junction, which would give the Audi driver nowhere to go, other than up a farm track.

Blackstone sped over the railway bridge, then into the dip prior to the next hump that was the canal bridge, not slowing down and hitting it at about fifty, which was much too fast and the little car took off, all four wheels leaving the road, then crashed down heavily and swerved wildly as she fought for control, and got it.

'We're in position, road is blocked,' the patrol called up.

In the distance – as she'd flown through the air – Blackstone had seen a glimpse of blue and red flashing lights in the moment before she hit the tarmac. And ahead she saw the force helicopter appear low in the sky as the powerful night spotlight came on and illuminated the Audi.

The guy was trapped.

Except that as he raced towards the roadblock, the driver suddenly anchored on and swerved into a ditch, leapt out and over a low hedge to run across what was once a field but had been scraped and cleared in preparation for a new distributor road that would connect the M55 to the north with the dockland area of Preston to the south.

As Blackstone reached the scene, the helicopter had already picked up the fleeing man in the beam of the spotlight as he ran, stumbled, picked himself up and ran again. He was just a dark shape, but Blackstone could make out he had a handgun as he twisted around, stopped, shaded his eyes with one hand and loosed off two wild shots at the helicopter.

Blackstone slewed to a halt in front of the two police cars – one of which was an ARV – that blocked the road, as a third one joined them – a dog patrol. Within moments, a huge German Shepherd had been deployed and was on the trail of the man who was still being remorselessly followed by the crew of the helicopter.

Blackstone swore, knowing that she could not get involved in this and that it was also wasting time. Quickly thinking the scenarios through, there was every chance that the man could be brought down by the dog, or get shot, or go to ground and escape, or he might decide to stage a siege . . . She knew he might even surrender immediately, but having taken several shots at the helicopter, she thought that unlikely. And even if he did throw down his gun and stick up his hands, time would be dragging on for Henry. And possibly running out.

She disconnected her mobile phone from the force radio system and called Diane as she did a reverse three-point turn in the narrow road – because she suddenly had an idea how to get to Henry quickly. Possibly.

Now facing the direction from which she'd come, Blackstone stuck her foot to the floor and the Mini picked up speed.

Diane answered immediately. 'Debs! What's happening?' she asked worriedly.

'The guy's ditched the car – literally – and he's on the run, but won't get far, there's a German Shepherd on his arse and cops with guns and mean dispositions . . . but I've come away from it. Listen, you said Henry's car— *Fuck!*' she groaned as the Mini took off again over the canal bridge and bounced down the other side, throwing her up into the roof and down again into her racing seat. 'Sorry . . . you said his car had just set off. Where exactly was it when it set off?'

EIGHTEEN

Even if he'd been thirty-five years younger, fitter, more courageous, Henry Christie was pretty sure he would still have been completely terrified by this experience.

First, to witness the deliberate, ultra-violent act that wiped Ellis Clanfield off the face of the earth and then be abducted off the street himself, bundled at gunpoint into the back of the offending vehicle, a hood put over his head.

Perhaps if he was thirty-five years younger, he might have been on his toes more and been able to do something about it.

But he wasn't and he hadn't.

And then to come face to face with Julie Clarke, which only confirmed his suspicions about her involvement in so many awful things over a long period of time.

'It was you, wasn't it?' Henry asked through the thick, harsh material of the hood.

No reply.

'All the time – you.'

Still nothing.

'You were the one behind me in the alley. You were the one who clobbered me, put me down. I saw it in that lad's eyes – saw your reflection,' he said, although he was doing a bit of embellishment. 'You must have hit me very hard.'

The guy sitting on Henry's right jabbed the barrel of his gun against Henry's head and warned him, 'Shut the fuck up or I'll blow your head off.'

It sounded corny, but also believable. Even so, Henry couldn't resist riling him a little and, dangerously, calling his bluff. 'What? In this car? Interior's far too nice for that, surely . . . oh, by the way, is this the car you chased Debbie Blackstone with? It's too nice for my blood and brains to decorate the interior, surely?' He knew he was babbling.

'Don't fucking tempt me.' The man tapped the muzzle hard against his head.

Then there was silence for a while and Henry briefly tried to work out the direction of travel, but gave up.

'Was that lad your boyfriend, Julie?' Henry probed. Frightened though he was, something inside him made him want to annoy criminals. 'He was just about the right age, wasn't he? Twenty, maybe? And what did poor little Tommy Benemy do to you? What happened to him, Julie? What was his fate? Because I'm bloody sure he didn't end up in Manchester, did he?'

Nothing.

'Can I keep asking questions? Hope you don't mind because I'm full of them, bursting for knowledge.'

Again, Clarke said nothing.

'I really do think you need to shut it,' the man said.

Henry ignored him. 'Funny how, even now, I can re-run things through my head from all those years ago. Not that I see things differently; just that I see the truth in what I saw – not what I wanted to believe back then. And Debbie Blackstone . . . some things don't necessarily add up there either, do they?'

For some reason that, or a culmination of what he was saying, brought a reaction from his captors.

This time it came from the side on which Julie Clarke was sitting, and although he couldn't see it coming because of the hood, he knew it must have been her who smashed him on the head with her small revolver, a blow which sent sparklers through his brain like fireworks on a dark night, making him swoon, although it didn't quite knock him out.

It did, however, make him realize it might be better to keep his mouth shut. At least for the time being.

He slumped forwards between the two people either side of him. His brain cleared quickly, but he thought it might be useful to keep up the pretence of being stunned in case there was any chance of doing a runner. He groaned and moaned, hoping he wasn't overdoing it.

Finally, the car slowed and stopped after a journey, Henry estimated, of about fifteen minutes at most.

He hadn't been able to keep track of it but he was sure they hadn't been on a motorway and, in fact, not long after being taken, despite the bang to the head, he was sure they were travelling on country roads as the car raced around tight bends before eventually slowing down almost to a stop and then taking a tight turn on to a track of some sort. He wondered if they were going to a farm.

After about a hundred metres of slow travel, the car stopped and the engine turned off.

He heard car doors open.

'Out,' he was ordered.

The man on his right dragged him along the seat and Henry stumbled as he misjudged the distance from the car to the ground.

They let him crash down on one knee, then heaved him back up to his feet.

He heard another car drive up and stop, recognized the sound of the engine or at least thought he did: it was his Audi and he'd come to love the noise it made in the few months he'd owned it.

Despite his predicament, underneath the hood, his lips quivered with a smile: *his Audi*.

But the smile was wiped off his face when his right arm was jacked painfully up his back between his shoulder blades and he was walked on tiptoe across gravelly ground and up some steps.

Henry spurted to life when he was pinned against a wall and felt his jacket being torn from him and then fingers grabbing his shirt and ripping it off, making him naked from the waist up. It was only then he decided to throw his weight around, even though he did it with blind hope because the hood was still over his head, the drawstring tight around his neck.

'Fuck you think you're doing?' he screamed, squirming and lashing out. He connected with someone, heard a man swear and say, 'You bastard!' But then he was thrown back against the wall and his shirt was fully pulled off him, as two men – he guessed – held him and then another punched him in the stomach. Hard. Driving all the breath out of him like a set of wheezy old bellows.

Then a hand went to his throat, his head was whacked twice against the wall and the fingers squeezed tightly around his windpipe until he gagged for breath.

'No hitting, OK?' he was warned gruffly.

Henry said nothing because that wasn't a promise he was going to make.

Unfortunately, the lack of response elicited another tightening of the fingers around his throat and another smack of his head on the wall.

'Understand?' the voice growled.

'Yuh,' Henry managed to gasp.

Things then began to get even worse for him.

He was pulled away from the wall and shoved along, and then a huge blow to the back of his head sank him to his knees. He reached out with his hands to break his fall, but his arms were kicked away and he went face down to the floor. This time he passed out properly.

He came sluggishly back to consciousness, struggling to comprehend his predicament. The hood had been removed and he was lying on his back, face up, but when he tried to move, he couldn't. His arms were trapped tight by his sides and his legs seemed to be strapped together. He could raise his head a few inches, although the pain shooting around his brain was intense.

But as his senses returned, he forced himself to raise his head to such an angle that he could see down his body and he realized he was laid out in some kind of trench, with boards either side of him. He had been tightly wrapped from just below his bare shoulders, right down to his ankles in something similar to cling film, a clear, plastic wrap that stuck to him and had been wound around him repeatedly, tight, completely constricting, like an Egyptian mummy in a sarcophagus. He realized that when he'd been unconscious, his captors must have removed the hood, rolled him in the film and laid him in this trench, or whatever it was – he could not quite work it out. He looked upwards as his senses continued to return and his vision cleared; he could see a vaulted roof high above him and realized he was actually in a building of some sort, and that he was lying between two floor joists. Maybe he was going to be covered by floorboards.

'Help me!' he said. Then shouted, 'Help!'

He started to struggle against the wrap, but it hugged tight and seemed to grip him remorselessly as he moved.

Eventually his efforts subsided as he became exhausted, and he gave up, knowing he had neither the strength nor technique to break free from the wrap. Instead, he focused to control his breathing, his heart rate and his fear, while listening hard.

He heard the scuffling of feet, low whispers, almost inaudible.

Finally, he said, 'OK, Julie, where are we?' His voice was croaky, his throat dry, and there was more than a note of trepidation in his tone.

And then he went still, because he was suddenly aware that someone was very close to him. He saw someone on their haunches looking over him – a man wearing a mask and holding something in his hands. Henry could not make out what it was at first.

Then a tiny clinking noise. Like tapping. Glass on glass.

Tap, tap.

Henry saw that the man was holding in one hand a small, brown glass medicine bottle and in the other a pipette. The man inserted the pipette into the bottle, used the plunger to draw out some of the liquid from the brown bottle, then tapped a drip off the end of the pipette.

The man held the pipette over Henry's right shoulder. Henry contorted his head as he tried to watch what was happening and saw a drop of clear liquid appear at the end of the slender tube, hang there a tantalizing moment and then drop on to his bare skin.

It was ice-cold, like a drop of water from a mountain stream.

But the chill only lasted a microsecond.

Then whatever it was started to itch ferociously, making Henry squirm. Again, that sensation lasted only a few seconds.

Because the drip then became a bubbling, burning fury, as if he'd been prodded with the tip of a hot, soldering iron.

He screamed instantly, writhed upwards, straining against the film he was wrapped in, and almost felt the strength to break free.

He knew that acid had been dripped on to him and, *Jesus, fuck, shit*, it hurt so much – like nothing he'd ever experienced before. The surprise of it and the process – the chill, the itch, then the incredible heat – took his breath away and he could still feel his skin fizzling, burning, then smouldering and reeking of his own burned flesh.

'What the hell! What the hell!' he uttered through his teeth, rocking against the film, but the only response he got from the man bending over him was raucous laughter.

Gritting his teeth, Henry watched the figure as he dipped the pipette back into the bottle, extracted the plunger, pulled it out and then tap-tap-tapped it on the neck of the bottle. Henry waited in terrible anticipation as the man moved the instrument across and held it above Henry's left shoulder. Henry's eyes grew wide, terrified, as once more a tiny blob of clear liquid formed at the end of the tube as the plunger was slowly depressed. This next chilled blob of acid dropped on to his shoulder, followed by the intense agony – like a nail being hammered home as the burning started again after the chill and itch.

And Henry screamed.

Henry hissed through his teeth at this new point of pain. Under the cling film, his fingers were bunched into tight fists and his toes were curled as he tried to deal with this intense, pinpointed torture.

'Bastards, bastards, bastards!' he said, grinding his teeth, the sound of which echoed through his cranium.

Then the man who had done this to Henry removed the mask that covered his face. He smirked as he said, 'Recognize me, Henry – the reflection in a woman's eyes?'

While still trying to deal with the intensifying pain from the acid drops on his shoulders, Henry tried to focus on the face of the man above him, sneering.

'Should I?' Henry snarled in reply to the question.

The man rocked back on his haunches and cocked his head smugly. 'Oh, come on, Henry, surely you know who I am?'

Henry squinted up at him. The face meant nothing. A man, maybe mid-fifties, jowled, grey-haired.

'Older, maybe not wiser,' the man said.

'Still nothing,' Henry said.

The man leaned over again, his face perhaps a foot away from Henry's. 'Last time I looked at you was thirty-five years ago.'

Henry squinted and blinked even more, still fighting the agony from the acid. It felt as if it was fizzing through him.

The man moved the pipette over Henry's left nipple and slowly depressed the plunger with his thumb.

Henry braced himself, still struggling to get free, but could not do anything against the wrap. He watched in horror again as a tiny blob of liquid formed at the end of the instrument and hung there, going nowhere.

Then it fell on to his delicate nipple. Cold. Then the itch.

Then agonizingly hot, and Henry screamed and his writhing became manic as the man stood up, watched and laughed uproariously as Henry's nipple fizzed.

Henry glared at him just as someone else stepped into his line of sight.

Julie Clarke came alongside the man who was torturing Henry and placed her arm around his shoulder. The man turned to her and kissed her fully on the lips – a long, slobbering snog that churned Henry's stomach. The man broke away from the kiss and said to Henry, 'Come on, you must know who I am now.'

'David Hindle,' Henry said as it all seemed to slot into place.

Henry peered at the face again. In his mind's eye, he still held – perfectly – the face of the young man who had been with Tommy Benemy all those years before. A face he had never knowingly seen since, and although this man may well have been that lad once, if Henry had passed him in the street, he would never have made the connection.

Henry looked at Julie Clarke. 'Boyfriend, I assume?'

She smiled indulgently. 'Brother.'

The couple looked lovingly at each other again. Their lips mashed together passionately, sickeningly. Then they broke apart.

Henry said, 'Give me another shot of the acid, please, because that's really sickening me. I mean, hell – your brother? You sick pair of fuckers.'

'You know, Henry,' Hindle said, 'I really enjoyed kicking the shit out of you and half strangling you.'

'If I hadn't stopped him, you'd have been dead,' Julie said.

'You want a medal for that? You're the one who put me down in the first place, aren't you?'

'Oh, yeah, those tiny girly truncheons could pack a punch if you used them properly,' she gloated. 'But I didn't want you dead, just unconscious so David could escape and I, of course, would be a heroine. Which I was.'

'But he still had to give me a good kicking?'

'Like I said, I enjoyed it. Couldn't resist.'

'And what about Tommy Benemy?'

'That cowering little shit? He never even gave you a kick, just watched on, petrified, crying, and then ran for his life, useless sod.'

'And what was his fate?' Henry asked.

'He was going to blab it all to you,' Clarke said. 'About us, about what we were doing; he'd have blown it all apart before our life's journey had even got started, and that was no good to us . . . despite my warning in his ear when you so generously let me take him home and search his house because you were working late.'

'You killed him,' Henry said flatly, suddenly not feeling the acid burn any more. Rage replaced pain.

The siblings shared a look, a smile.

Hindle said, 'Eventually.'

'In fact,' Clarke said, 'we did it shortly after we took that photograph you showed me. Incidentally, I knew Ellis Clanfield had thousands of them because he got them from us, so it was a big fat warning signal when you told me you'd only found that one. That meant you were on to something.'

'I wasn't really,' Henry admitted. 'I'm not that good.'

Clarke shrugged. 'All academic now.'

Henry's mind spun, trying to put all this together, but it didn't help his thought process that he'd been smacked on the skull recently with a gun, been unconscious, wrapped in cling film, had acid dripped on to his tit and was lying between two floor joists.

He was woozy, but still hunting and looking for any advantage.

He tried to take it all back to the beginning – at least as far back as when he came into the picture.

'What did you do with Tommy?'

'Very bad things,' Hindle said. 'Then killed him. A few drops of acid for fun, just to hear the screams, then a plastic bag over his head . . . while you watched on, darling.' He looked fondly at Clarke. Brotherly love.

Henry realized he was in the presence of two extremely deranged psychopaths and paedophiles. Somehow he had to keep them talking – keep them glorying in their triumphs, reliving them. He guessed it probably wasn't often they had a captive audience . . . or maybe he was wrong there.

'And Tommy's mum?'

Hindle shrugged sadly. 'Silly, silly bitch. By sheer chance, she crashed out one night in the doorway of the office in Granville Street after a cider bender, woke up, saw the business logo and came knocking, making stupid allegations and shouting and bawling about Tommy's tattoo.'

'Ah, the tattoo,' Henry said. 'What's all that about?'

Hindle pulled up his sleeve and showed Henry his inner forearm. Clarke did the same. Both had the 'house' tattoos: square box, triangle and a line slashed across the middle.

'Actually, it's based on the letter H,' Hindle said, 'so it's quite clever, isn't it? My initial and like a house – me being a builder and all that,' he said proudly. 'A badge of belonging, a badge of honour,' he added.

'Really?'

'Yeah – to my – *our* – exclusive club. All my babies get it, all of them.'

'And how many is that?'

Hindle glanced at Clarke and calculated, 'A hundred, perhaps? We don't really keep track.'

The number hit Henry like a gut punch. One hundred. And so fucking blasé about it.

Nevertheless, he kept them on track and, fighting his revulsion, said, 'You were telling me about Mrs Benemy.'

'Oh, yeah, I just followed her back to her shithole of a bedsit where I discovered that she'd actually been on the verge of committing suicide anyway. She'd already written the note to you, but when I got there, she was about to rip it up and go to the police again and make waves . . . I just assisted the suicide, shall we say?'

'Except we knew it was murder,' Henry countered, recalling how the bottom quarter of the suicide note Trish had written had been torn off – the first part of ripping it up. Now it made sense.

'You'd never have caught me. It would have been put down to some other town drunk – a bit like another close encounter you and I had years ago.'

'Which one would that be . . . ah, yes, I know . . . homeless guy in the hotel?' Henry said, taking a punt. That was another investigation early in his service where he'd been sidelined off the main enquiry and it all came to nothing – another unsolved murder, when the hypothesis, which was never veered from, was that the vagrant had been killed by other vagrants and set on fire. No one was ever convicted of that one. 'One of your first property development schemes, Abingdon Road. What had he done to you?'

'Stumbled on to what I was engaged in, made a run for it, so he had to be dealt with.'

'Murdered, set on fire . . . nice,' Henry said. 'What were you doing?'

'Lifting the floorboards.'

'What does that mean?'

'Burying the bodies.'

'What bodies?'

'Couple of kids, no one special.' Hindle shrugged. 'He'd obviously been holing up there for shelter, stumbled on us.'

Henry's eyes darted from one to the other.

Clarke shrugged her shoulders. 'Sometimes they had to go,' she said. She sounded reasonable, as if she was disposing of trash: one of those things that had to be done.

'What?' Henry said in numb disbelief. 'And here's me thinking you were just running a Fagin-like operation, getting kids to steal for you.'

'That too,' Hindle said. 'In fact, you know the term "county lines"? Yeah? We've been doing that shit for years and years. Nothing new under the sun.'

'Guess you're right – using kids, abusing kids,' Henry said. He looked at Clarke. 'You've been working with children all your life. Vulnerable, easy targets. Missing from home or just local kids on the streets of Blackpool. You targeted them, didn't you?'

'Of course I did. Ninety-nine per cent of the time I did the right thing by them . . . just used the occasional one who was useful to us.' She smiled at Hindle. 'Useful to you, dear.'

'Oh, come on,' he said. 'Not just me – many others, obviously. I mean' – he looked at Henry now – 'how on earth do you think I continually get permission to renovate properties in and around Blackpool and make millions from it?'

'Councillors,' Henry guessed as all parts of this five-hundred-piece jigsaw began to slot into place. Up to then, it had all been edges and corners, not the centre of the picture – and Blackstone had been so right, after all: a terrible conspiracy that spanned thirty-odd years.

'And cops,' Clarke added. 'You'd be surprised by the appetites of some high-ranking officers. Ravenous bastards!'

'And others,' Hindle added.

'The Leylands!' Henry gasped, guessing.

'An integral link in our little set-up, but they got careless with

it. Those two kids should have been under the floorboards like all
the others, not left out to rot; then we wouldn't have had to deal
with them so severely,' Clarke said.

'You gave them the tools to kill themselves,' Henry accused
her. Even then, his mind skimmed backwards, seeing her in the
old cell complex at Blackpool police station, leaning into Cressida
Leyland's cell as he walked down the corridor towards her, obviously giving Cressida the razor blade with which she then
committed suicide. Clarke had been brought in to search and look
after the female prisoner, and no doubt she'd also managed to
sneak down the male cell corridor and give Terry Leyland a length
of garden twine long enough for him to hang himself from the
door.

She nodded. 'Rumbled.'

'You must have been laughing your socks off at me at the post-
mortem of the homeless guy,' Henry said vehemently, feeling as if
he had been taken for an immature fool.

She snickered. 'You were being so nice – and we even flirted a
bit. I would've let you, you know.'

'Would have been like dancing with Mrs D,' Henry said.

'And I would have watched, obviously,' Hindle said creepily.

Henry didn't even want to think about that. Instead, and to keep
them talking, he said, 'By floorboards, I assume you mean under
the floors of the properties you've renovated?' Both smiled at him
and he knew he was right and they were proud of whatever they'd
achieved. 'How many? How many have you killed?'

'Hmm . . . like we said, about a hundred, give or take,' Hindle
said. 'But if it is one hundred, you'll be the one hundred and first,
Henry, and, like them, your body will never be discovered, nor your
car, come to that.'

Hindle looked at the pipette in his hand, then at Henry. He
bounced back down on to his haunches and said, 'Sulphuric acid
. . . lovely stuff, been a fan of it for years.' He twitched and his
face jerked. 'Do you know what kicked off my fascination?'

'Do tell,' Henry said. He was just about managing to control the
pain of the drips on his shoulders and nipple but was dreading more.

'Chemistry lessons. Back in the day before health and safety, it
was easy to sneak into the storeroom at the back of the chemistry
classroom where all the acids were kept, supposedly under lock and

key, and steal an undiluted bottle. I'd seen a lad drop some of the diluted stuff we used in class on to the back of his hand. Should've heard him scream! Then I thought I'd like to get the class bully, except with undiluted acid. I made it look like an accident, and somehow he spilled a whole bottle down his leg . . . he was in short trousers, too.' Hindle smiled at the memory. 'Scarred the little runt for life.'

'You like hurting people, then?' Henry observed. Suddenly, the trio of pinpricks of acid on his skin came alive again all at once and seared his skin in unison. He grimaced and squirmed against the wrap holding him down. But he then settled and got a grip of himself, fought through the sizzle.

Keep the bastards talking, he thought to himself.

'You chucked the acid at DS Blackstone, I presume,' he said. 'Scarring her for life, too.'

Hindle dinked his head. 'She got too close for comfort.'

Then Henry stared at Clarke. 'And you hit her on the head.'

'Needs must.'

'She was just unfortunate enough to stumble on to where we'd taken the girl,' Hindle admitted.

'And you,' Henry said to Clarke, 'sent the hounds off chasing an imaginary fox, didn't you?' remembering how Blackstone had told him Clarke said she'd spotted a van matching the description of the one in which the girl had been abducted on the other side of Blackpool. 'You never saw a van, did you?' He could hardly hide his revulsion for this woman. Not that he needed to. That time had long since passed. 'You sent the cops off in another direction and then you came to warn your . . . *brother.*'

Clarke shrugged. 'That's about right. I got to the Belmont just after Debbie, followed her in and gave her a whack just as David threw the acid at her. We could've killed her too,' she concluded. 'Just like we could've killed you.'

'On reflection, I suppose you wish you had,' Henry said.

'Something that's about to be rectified – in your case, anyway,' Hindle said grimly. 'Just like those two girls – and so many others – you're going to end up under the floorboards, wrapped in plastic with your face burned off by the acid, never to be found again.

'People,' Hindle said, hardly able to contain his mirth, 'will literally be dancing on your grave, Henry. This, y'see,' he said, pointing down at the floor and opening his arms in a wide gesture to indicate the room they were in, 'is going to be a ballroom, and this bit' – he pointed down again – 'will be the dancefloor, nice and springy, and your nose will be just inches below it, almost touching as people boogie the night away.'

Henry then realized where he was: Hindle's Builders' latest acquisition – a dilapidated old mansion called Treales Manor that had once been a country house hotel and fallen into disrepair, now with plans to be converted into a high-end wedding venue. Henry had read about it when he'd been surfing for information about the company. The latest boast by a cruelly twisted man.

'Boss, we got a problem.' Henry heard the voice of the man who'd been one of the two who'd bundled him into the Range Rover, the one who'd threatened to blow his head off. From where he lay in between the floor joists, though, he could not see him.

Hindle stood up and walked away. 'Problem being?'

'I couldn't stop him,' the man whined a bit pitifully.

'Stop who?'

'Cohen.'

'What's he done?'

'Took the guy's car for a spin. He couldn't resist it, wanted to really hammer it. I thought he'd be back by now . . .' His voice trailed off.

Henry shouted, 'If he damages my car, there'll be hell to pay.'

'How long has he been gone?' Hindle asked.

'Ten minutes, maybe.'

'Idiot . . . We need to find somewhere to bury it.' Henry heard Hindle emit a very pissed-off sigh.

Henry heard footsteps retreating, then Hindle reappeared over him.

'If he damages my car . . .' Henry began again.

'Gosh, you're a funny guy, Henry,' Hindle said as he squatted down again. He placed the acid bottle and pipette on the floor and took out an extra-large plastic food bag from his pocket and shook it out. It looked big enough to go over a small turkey or, Henry thought, *my head*. Hindle placed the bag carefully on the floor and picked up the bottle again, inserted the pipette into it and drew out a syringe-full of acid.

NINETEEN

Blackstone switched off her engine and lights and cruised the last fifty metres in neutral before stopping silently by the sign at the entrance to the driveway up to Treales Manor: *Hindle's Builders' latest acquisition*, it read. *THE wedding venue to be seen at – due for completion Spring 2021.* There were several computer-generated images of what the place might look like and under them was the Hindle's Builders logo which made her seethe.

The entrance to the manor was through a pair of stunning gateposts that looked two hundred years old and then along a sweeping gravel driveway bordered on either side by an eight-foot-high hedge.

She was on the phone to Rik Dean. 'I've got to go and look, boss.'

'No, wait . . . I'll be there with armed back-up in less than ten minutes.'

She screwed her nose up and ended the call abruptly, quietly opened her car door and got out, closing it just as quietly before going through the gateposts and walking quickly up the drive at a crouch, keeping to the dark shadow cast by the hedge and trees. After about a hundred metres, the driveway opened out to become a large, circular turning area at the front of the once magnificent Treales Manor, with a stone pond and a fountain in the centre; the pond was empty and the fountain was not spouting water.

Two vehicles were parked at the front entrance of the manor house: a black Range Rover and a fabulous-looking sports car. Blackstone didn't know the make, but it could have been a Ferrari or a Lamborghini, something of that ilk.

A man leaned on the Range Rover, smoking.

Blackstone scooped up a large stone in her right hand from the edge of the driveway. As she did, from somewhere inside she heard a scream. A man, screaming – Henry Christie.

Suddenly, she knew she was right. Waiting ten minutes for back-up was not an option.

Keeping the bulk of the Range Rover between herself and the smoking man, she made it unnoticed across the last twenty-odd metres of open ground; if he'd turned, it would have been all over, but she did it and dropped out of sight on the opposite side of the car and crept slowly around the rear of it for more cover, gripping the stone which was slightly too large in her palm for comfort. She could only just curl her fingers around it.

She heard Henry scream again. And as clichéd as it was, the noise was blood-curdling and terrifying.

'C'mon, gal, keep this together,' she told herself silently as she reached the back corner of the car, maybe only just over a metre from the man, whose smoking reeked like noxious gas.

He was lounging against the car. He took a deep drag on the cigarette, tipped his chin up and blew out a long, satisfying lungful of smoke – at which moment, Blackstone moved.

She spun around the corner of the car, pivoting as she brought her hand around in an arc and smashed him in the face with the stone. Stunned, he sagged sideways; Blackstone continued with the attack, and as the man fell, she slammed the stone on to the crown of his head and he pitched forward, face first into the gravel.

He didn't move.

In a parallel thought, she was already imagining her court appearance for the assault. In response, she thought, *Fuck them.*

That prospect did not deter her moving on towards another scream from inside the manor. She flew up the front steps and through the front door, pausing in the tiled vestibule, then ducking behind a screen as she heard footsteps approaching and a man shout, 'Boss says we need to bury the Audi when Cohen gets back with it,' presumably calling to the guy outside who, at best, could not hear him.

Blackstone backed tight against the wall just as this man walked past, calling, 'Boodie, you hear me?'

He stopped moving at the threshold of the door, having spotted his mate splayed out by the front wheels of the Range Rover.

'Shit.'

He must have sensed a movement and turned as Blackstone emerged from the shadow and pounded the brick into his face in a haymaker-like punch, the power coming from the combined twist of her waist and shoulders, which unleashed a mighty blow.

But the man reacted quickly, instinctively jerking his head back and the stone glanced off his jaw. Blackstone dropped it but, realizing she hadn't connected with force or accuracy, she blasted into the shocked man, using her momentum, pounding him with her fists repeatedly, using a power surge from her core until he went down and did not move.

Murder number two, she thought, gasping and standing astride him, wondering if her kung fu training had been useful or not there. She was pretty sure it was mostly anger combined with her survival instinct that kept her going, because she knew that if she had hesitated even slightly, he would have taken her.

But he didn't. And she was the one still standing.

She did not pause to admire her handiwork; she stepped across him into the reception foyer of the old manor, then into the long hallway from which she heard Henry scream again. At the far end was a door from which light shone.

One thing she knew was that there could be no hesitation as, even then, the thoughts of that time four years earlier flooded back and engulfed her – that moment when her life had changed, seemingly irrevocably. And perhaps this was the new moment she needed in order to save herself as well as Henry Christie.

Henry's screaming stopped.

Blackstone trod quietly along the uncarpeted hallway, aware that the floorboards could creak and give her presence away.

She paused at the door. Swallowed. Took an unsteady breath, steeled herself, then stepped across the threshold and looked into the room beyond and took it all in.

Julie Clarke standing with her arms folded and a smile on her face as a man, who Blackstone guessed was David Hindle, squatted over Henry Christie, who was lying trussed up in the space between two floor joists. Hindle held a plastic bag over Henry's head, in the process of suffocating him.

She saw Henry's face as he tried to breathe, but all he was doing was drawing the plastic into his mouth and over his nostrils, and she heard the noise he was making: a gagging, gurgling, desperate sound as he panicked, unable to fight against the process, other than to squirm and twist within the confines of his wrapping.

Clarke saw Blackstone at the door, but the detective was already hurtling across towards her.

Clarke seemed transfixed as Blackstone grabbed her, swept her feet from underneath her and dropped her hard, followed up by a debilitating punch to the side of her head. Blackstone then turned on Hindle, who dropped Henry back into the floor space with the plastic bag still on his head. He scooped up the bottle of acid from the floor and advanced on Blackstone threateningly.

'Glad you could make it,' he said dangerously.

'Yeah, well, there's more than me coming.'

Her eyes flicked between Hindle, the bottle in his hand, and Henry, who was drawing breaths that sounded like a chisel being sharpened.

'Nevertheless, I assume you want another face full of this?' Hindle held up the brown bottle and Blackstone's heart sank. 'Sulphuric acid – your friend.'

'Put it down,' she ordered him, 'and don't test me, because I will put you down.'

'Ha!' Hindle jerked the bottle threateningly towards her and some of the liquid flipped out.

Blackstone flinched back in a moment of terror.

Down to her side, she was aware Henry had stopped moving, that there was no longer the sound of that rasping breathing.

Her eyes turned back to Hindle, locking with his for a second. Then, in a blur, she covered the distance between them, fending away the bottle with her left forearm and kicking Hindle in the groin with her right foot – a driving, powerful, yet balletic blow that made him drop the acid – the bottle shattered – and sink down to his knees, emitting an unworldly howl of pain and cradling his balls with both hands as, Blackstone prayed, his testicles were driven a foot up into his lower intestine. She followed this up by spinning on her left foot and slamming the sole of her right into Hindle's face, sending him toppling backwards.

She instantly turned to Henry, kneeling down alongside him and grabbing the plastic bag between the fingertips of both hands and ripping it apart.

For one moment, she thought she was too late. There was no reaction, but then Henry inhaled with a huge, shuddering breath and almost choked as air surged back into his lungs.

She saw the acid burns on his shoulders and nipple and across his chest.

'Oh God, oh God,' he gasped, coughed and spluttered. 'I honestly thought that was it.'

She gave him a quirky smile and said, 'Well, old guy, it wasn't. Welcome to the acid-burn club. I'm the founding member.'

TWENTY

Henry Christie sat on the terrace of the Beach Hut Café (ironically named as it was nowhere near a beach) and waited for his second Americano to be delivered by the face-masked waitress. The café was actually next to the sea lock at Preston marina and the pyramid-like structure of the lock control tower was on the opposite side of the dock.

There was a pleasant, grassed area by the control tower on which an outdoor martial arts class was just winding up after an hour-long lesson, some of which Henry had observed. One of the participants was Blackstone, and Henry had focused on watching her as the class practised the kung fu moves in perfect synch with each other, like a mesmerizing, slow-motion ballet performance to begin with. The slow blocking of blows by the left and right forearms, the steps forward with the curl of the hip, the punching out, right and left fists twisting like projectiles travelling down a barrel, then the sideways move on the left foot to allow the right to kick out. All these moves practised over and over, building up intensity and speed until finally the class moved together like an advancing army, fast, precise and dangerous.

In the middle of one of the lines was Blackstone, easy to spot with her bright red spiked hair, totally focused on what she was doing, moving with grace, power and concentration. Henry was impressed.

Finally, the class ended and split up. Blackstone gave Henry a wave, grabbed her rucksack and jogged across the bridge to join him; he had ordered her a chilled water.

She sat at the table and smiled, breathing not heavily but healthily, he thought.

She ripped the top off the water bottle and guzzled half its contents, before gasping and wiping her mouth. Then she said, 'OK, old guy?'

Henry gave her a withering look and she held up her hand.

'OK, I'll stop calling you that, even though it is the truth . . .

well, y'know, in comparison to me and, obviously, your girlfriend.'

'Enough,' Henry stopped her, but not in an abrupt way.

'For today.' She winked mischievously and took another few glugs of the water. 'What did you think?' She pointed across the lock, meaning the class.

'You're a good little mover.'

Despite himself, Henry had noticed she was kitted out in boxing shorts and a tank top, exposing her bare arms and legs, whereas most of her classmates were wearing more traditional-looking martial arts outfits.

'It's a good focus,' she said seriously. 'It's a confidence booster, makes you feel in control, like you could take on the world. Better than drugs, or CBT come to that – at least for me. That said' – she grinned again – 'sometimes a stone in the hand is worth a kick in the nuts.'

Henry chuckled and said, 'Are we ready to roll?'

'Yeah – got a change of clothes in here,' she said, hoisting up her rucksack. 'Best bib and tucker, obviously, for court.'

Henry wasn't completely sure he liked the sound of that. He finished his coffee and they walked around to the front of the café where he'd parked up a cheap rental car provided by his insurance company. His Audi, having been pitched radiator-first into a ditch and lifted out with a crane, was a total write-off. He was parked next to Blackstone's Mini Cooper which was still awaiting repair work to its rear end.

'How's the chest – and the left nipple?' she asked him as she threw her bag into the Mini.

'Still sizzling . . . but all they're giving me is paracetamol, which takes a long time to take effect and wears off quickly,' he said, shifting uncomfortably as a little gust of pain wafted through him, making him clench his knuckles. He'd had a few dabs of acid and that was bad enough. Just a taster of what Blackstone had suffered.

She winked at him. 'Show me yours and I'll show you mine.'

'Like I said, I'd never get past those big knickers.'

They got into their respective cars and drove off, Henry in front, heading up to Preston with another busy day ahead.

*   *   *

As if the last three days hadn't been hectic enough.

Henry and Blackstone had – rightly this time – been kept away from interacting with the prisoners, but worked tirelessly behind the scenes while DCs Eddows and Cattle (who Henry thought were tremendous) went to work on Clarke, Hindle and the three henchmen, and slowly prised open a can from which other names began to wriggle into the light.

Once the sibling relationship between Clarke and Hindle was established beyond doubt, Clarke crumbled under pressure, admitting to having an incestuous relationship with her brother all their lives and, when she became a police officer, assisting him in identifying youngsters who could help him in his violent paedophilic lifestyle. This was coupled with a criminal enterprise that spanned decades, exploiting kids as thieves and drug mules, using his burgeoning building company as a front for much of it. The properties he was in the early stages of developing were where the youngsters identified by Clarke were abused . . . and, in some cases, buried.

Hindle was more difficult to deal with: broodingly silent, mostly offering no comment. Henry got frustrated watching him being interviewed, but knew he would probably have lost his rag with the man if he'd been allowed in the same room.

The other three were just heavies, interested in nothing but beating people up and making money, most of which they pissed down the drain or spent in the casinos in Blackpool, trying to impress women.

They were nothing. Hindle and Clarke were the main players and it was them the detectives concentrated on.

Finally, after a day of interviews and an extension to their period in custody authorized by Chief Superintendent Lee at Preston, Rik Dean decided it was time to go and look for bodies.

At Blackstone's insistence, the first floorboards to be pulled up were the ones in the room at the Park Lane Hotel, formerly the Belmont. The owner, Risdon, gave them permission, and Henry, Blackstone, a forensic and CSI crew, and a Support Unit team all dressed in forensic suits went into the room. The bed was moved, the carpet lifted, the floorboards exposed, then eased up one at a time, until a section between two floor joists was revealed and in it the bodies of Kelly Hampson and Ruby Weatherall, wrapped in shrouds of airtight plastic.

Blackstone looked down at the girls for a long, long time. Finally, she walked across to Henry, tugged him out of the room into the corridor, wrapped her arms tightly around him and cried softly into his chest.

'I want to kill those people,' she said as she drew away from him.

'So do I . . . *but* the thought of them separated, in different jails, for the rest of their lives gives me some sort of comfort. Not much, but some sort.'

She nodded.

When they went to look for Risdon, he was nowhere to be seen. They wanted to thank him and explain what was happening. They searched for him and eventually found him in the walk-in larder fridge at the back of the hotel kitchen.

It had been hastily done, clearly, and there was a scribbled note left on a worktop which Blackstone found before they found him. It said simply, *I never thought you would come back. I am so sorry. I am ashamed.*

Blackstone opened the larder door with trepidation to find Risdon hanging by his neck from a high shelf, and although Blackstone rushed to him, he was dead, beyond resuscitation.

After three days of questioning, Clarke and Hindle were put before the magistrates. They were charged with two counts of murder and also the attempted murder of Henry Christie. As Henry and Blackstone watched the two prisoners led away down to the holding cells before being whisked away to jail, they knew that this was only the beginning of a long, complex enquiry that would uncover many unpalatable things. Even now, Henry and Blackstone suspected there were many people in positions of power, or who had previously held such positions, who were running for cover. Both detectives were looking forward to knocking on a lot of doors behind which would be innocent-looking characters with very dirty secrets.

Blackstone said, 'I hope you've nothing else planned for the next six months, old guy.'

They never found Thomas James Benemy's body, and neither Clarke nor Hindle would tell them where he was buried. Nor did they disclose where *any* bodies were buried, which meant a long police operation visiting all the properties renovated by Hindle over the years, with police dogs trained to sniff out bodies and specialist X-ray equipment, plus good old-fashioned digging.

Henry managed to squeeze a couple of thousand pounds from the constabulary towards funeral expenses for Trish Benemy. She was cremated at Lytham Park Crematorium and her ashes interred in the grounds. Henry himself paid for a headstone. It read simply:

Patricia 'Trish' Benemy
1958–2020
Loving Mother to Thomas James Benemy